The Middle Ages Come to Life . . . to Bring Us Murder.

A Play of Isaac

"The player Joliffe appeared occasionally in Frazer's delightful series featuring . . . Dame Frevisse. Now he has his own story . . . In the course of the book, we learn a great deal about theatrical customs of the fifteenth century . . . In the hands of a lesser writer, it could seem preachy; for Frazer, it is another element in a rich tapestry."
—*Contra Costa (CA) Times*

"Careful research and a profusion of details, especially those dealing with staging a fifteenth-century miracle play, bring the sights, smells, and sounds of the era directly to the reader's senses. There's also a fine sense of history, all woven together in a medieval tapestry of rich colors. Looking over Ms. Frazer's impressive list of novels already to her credit, I can see a lot of pleasurable reading ahead. I especially look forward to meeting Joliffe and the players again."
—*Roundtable Reviews*

"The mystery, and the events surrounding it, are played out quite naturally through Joliffe's unquenchable curiosity. For lovers of mystery and lovers of history, this is a find; a mystery backed by solid research. I hope to see much more of this likable group in future volumes."
—*The Romance Reader's Connection*

"A terrific historical who-done-it that will please amateur sleuth and historical mystery fans."

c(

A Play of Dux Moraud

"Deftly-drawn characters acting in a stage of intricate and accurate details of medieval life."
—*Affaire de Coeur*

"Puzzling . . . The author is a much-respected authority on medieval times, in addition to a good storyteller."
—*Romantic Times BOOKclub*

"A meticulously researched, well written historical mystery that brings to life a bygone era. The workings of society [are] seen through the eyes of the players . . . Historical mystery fans will love this series." —*Midwest Book Review*

"Another wonderful entry in the author's long series of medieval mysteries . . . As always, the author provides a treasure trove of historical detail surrounding the everyday lives of the characters woven seamlessly into the narrative. In less assured hands, this detail might be intrusive; here, it simply adds to the ambiance . . . Each character is complex, possessing flaws and ambitions . . . [G]ood, solid mystery." —*The Romance Reader's Connection*

Praise for the Dame Frevisse Medieval Mystery Series By Two-Time Edgar® Award Nominee Margaret Frazer

"An exceptionally strong series . . . full of the richness of the fifteenth century, handled with the care it deserves."
—*Minneapolis Star Tribune*

The Novice's Tale

"Frazer uses her extensive knowledge of the period to create an unusual plot . . . appealing characters and crisp writing." —*Los Angeles Times continued . . .*

The Reeve's Tale

"A brilliantly realized vision of a typical medieval English village . . . Suspenseful from start to surprising conclusion . . . another gem." —*Publishers Weekly* (starred review)

The Squire's Tale

"Meticulous detail that speaks of trustworthy scholarship and a sympathetic imagination." —*The New York Times*

The Clerk's Tale

"As usual, Frazer vividly recreates the medieval world through meticulous historical detail [and] remarkable scholarship . . . History aficionados will delight and fans will rejoice that the devout yet human Dame Frevisse is back . . . a dramatic and surprising conclusion."

—*Publishers Weekly*

The Bastard's Tale

"Anyone who values high historical drama will feel amply rewarded . . . Of note is the poignant and amusing relationship between Joliffe and Dame Frevisse. History fans will relish every minute they spend with the characters in this powerfully created medieval world. Prose that at times verges on the poetic." —*Publishers Weekly*

The hunter's Tale

"Will please both Frevisse aficionados and historical mystery readers new to the series." —*Booklist*

The Widow's Tale

"Action-packed . . . a terrific protagonist."

—*Midwest Book Review*

A Play of
Knaves

Margaret Frazer

BERKLEY PRIME CRIME, NEW YORK

THE BERKLEY PUBLISHING GROUP
Published by the Penguin Group
Penguin Group (USA) Inc.
375 Hudson Street, New York, New York 10014, USA
Penguin Group (Canada), 90 Eglinton Avenue East, Suite 700, Toronto, Ontario M4P 2Y3, Canada
(a division of Pearson Penguin Canada Inc.)
Penguin Books Ltd., 80 Strand, London WC2R 0RL, England
Penguin Group Ireland, 25 St. Stephen's Green, Dublin 2, Ireland (a division of Penguin Books Ltd.)
Penguin Group (Australia), 250 Camberwell Road, Camberwell, Victoria 3124, Australia
(a division of Pearson Australia Group Pty. Ltd.)
Penguin Books India Pvt. Ltd., 11 Community Centre, Panchsheel Park, New Delhi—110 017, India
Penguin Group (NZ), Cnr. Airborne and Rosedale Roads, Albany, Auckland 1310, New Zealand
(a division of Pearson New Zealand Ltd.)
Penguin Books (South Africa) (Pty.) Ltd., 24 Sturdee Avenue, Rosebank, Johannesburg 2196,
South Africa

Penguin Books Ltd., Registered Offices: 80 Strand, London WC2R 0RL, England

This is a work of fiction. Names, characters, places, and incidents either are the product of the author's imagination or are used fictitiously, and any resemblance to actual persons, living or dead, business establishments, events, or locales is entirely coincidental. The publisher does not have any control over and does not assume any responsibility for author or third-party websites or their content.

A PLAY OF KNAVES

A Berkley Prime Crime Book / published by arrangement with the author

PRINTING HISTORY
Berkley Prime Crime mass-market edition / August 2006

Copyright © 2006 by Gail Frazer.
Cover art by Brigid Collins.
Cover design by Lesley Worrell.
The Edgar® name is a registered service mark of the Mystery Writers of America, Inc.

ISBN: 978-0-425-21111-3

BERKLEY® PRIME CRIME
Berkley Prime Crime Books are published by The Berkley Publishing Group,
a division of Penguin Group (USA) Inc.,
375 Hudson Street, New York, New York 10014.
The name BERKLEY PRIME CRIME and the BERKLEY PRIME CRIME design are trademarks belonging to Penguin Group (USA) Inc.

PRINTED IN THE UNITED STATES OF AMERICA

10 9 8 7 6 5 4 3 2

To the memory of George Wade,
for the summers of Shakespeare and Company
under the sky.

Chapter 1

The winter of this year of God's grace 1435 had been cold beyond the ordinary. A false flourish of warm days in March had brought hope, but the cold and rain had come back and held on until almost the end of Lent. Only finally, in the week before Palm Sunday, had something like spring begun to happen, and now as the players, their cart, and their horse trundled at footpace along the road's gentle lift and fall and curves, there were flowers in the wayside grass and under the hedgerows and everywhere a flirt and busyness of birds seemingly intent on making up for so many lost days of proper springtime.

"There's a lark," Piers said, pointing high. "A mark to me!"

"It's a woodlark," Joliffe returned. "That doesn't count. We're counting skylarks."

"We're counting larks!" Piers protested with all the outrage of his much-put-upon eleven years, and added, because he had a strong belief in conducting his campaigns on as many fronts as possible, "Besides, it *is* a skylark."

Joliffe, something like twice Piers' age and—as often pointed out by their companions—old enough to know better, returned, "Isn't."

"Is."

"Isn't."

"What *I'm* going to count," said Basset, the company's master, Piers' grandfather, and used to their ways, "is how many knots I'm going to rap on the tops of your heads if you don't stop it."

Piers, preferring diversion to defeat, darted sideways, stomped his foot on the wayside grass, and declared from the old proverb, "Five daisies underfoot means spring is here!"

Walking on the other side of their mare, Tisbe, whose part in all of it was to pull the cart and ignore them, Joliffe said, "That was only four."

"Five!" Piers said, skipping back onto the road. "And you couldn't see from there anyway."

"Five knots," Ellis growled behind the cart where he walked with Rose, Piers' mother. "On both your heads. With a big stick."

"I'll cut the stick," young Gil said helpfully.

Of the company, he was the only one not on his own feet. Having somewhat turned an ankle coming sideways off an unseen stone two days ago, he was riding on the cart's seat, his bandaged ankle propped up and idleness chewing at him, so he claimed. They were a company of six—seven if Tisbe the mare was counted, as Joliffe claimed she should be. Time had been it was a larger company and all too lately it had been a smaller one, with times hard and failure likely, until chance and good fortune had brought them to Lord Lovell's notice and then into his favor. They were Lord Lovell's players now, with the canvas tilt hooped over their cart painted in the red and yellow of his heraldic colors to proclaim it. Along with that, they could wear his badge and claim his protection should they need it.

In return, of course, he had claim on their skills and they had spent this just-past Holy Week performing plays seemly to the time for Lady Lovell, her children, and the household at his manor of Minster Lovell. Unhappily, Lord Lovell had not been there, gone on one of his sometimes ventures to France where the war was presently stumbling over the duke of Burgundy's unwillingness to continue as England's ally because, as Lady Lovell had said firmly and loudly in the great hall at one mid-day dinner, "Burgundy sees better profit to be had in joining with Charles, so-called king of France, than in keeping faith with all his oaths. For profit, the duke is willing to forget his father was murdered on so-called King Charles' order. So much for Burgundy's honor, for all that he proclaims it to the world."

For the players, the duke of Burgundy's honor was neither here nor there. More to their own point, Lady Lovell was as generous a patron as her husband, and through their stay at Minster Lovell they had been well-fed in the hall with the general household, well-housed in a clean barn in the outer manor yard, and at the end had been sent well-paid on their way with Lady Lovell's great thanks, given publicly in the great hall after their playing on Easter. At supper she had called Basset to the high table and given him a gift of coins, saying for the household to hear, "These you've well-earned. I've rarely been so moved and ready in heart and mind for Easter as by your plays this week. Myself and my household owe you much."

And well they did, Joliffe still thought. When Lady Lovell had sent them word a month ago that she wanted them at Minster Lovell for all the week before Easter, Basset had determined, "We should do something beyond the ordinary. What of a run of plays right through the week?

On Palm Sunday we can begin with Christ's coming into Jerusalem and carry on to the Resurrection on Easter Day."

Joliffe had started shaking his head against all that before Basset had finished saying it, had said, "No!" and if he had not been sitting down, would have been backing away. They had no plays like that already fitted to their small company, and because he was the one among them most skilled with words, he had known what was coming next.

But Basset had gone cheerfully on. "We have that rough-handed copy of the Coventry plays I bought off Jack Melton, what was it, eight years ago? It has all the plays of the Passion. You can rework them to our use, easy as anything."

"Rework them and have done in time for us to learn the lines once I've written them, let alone do all the rest of it in a month's time?" Joliffe had returned. "You've gone witless."

He had looked to Ellis and Rose for their good sense, but while Rose would have agreed with him, Ellis had already been seeing himself as Christ, the part he would surely have; and Piers and Gil had added their voices in favor, probably thinking of how many lesser parts there would be for them to share in. They had all joined in eager talk with Basset, leaving Joliffe and Rose shaking their heads hopelessly at one another.

And yet, against all likelihood, they had somehow succeeded. Joliffe, working madly—"And mad I must be to be trying this," he grumbled—had trimmed and reshaped the plays, keeping barely ahead of Basset rehearsing them, everyone learning their lines as they went, while Rose sewed her fingers sore readying their garb. She had even submitted, in their necessity, to taking parts, sometimes wearing a man's long robe and a false beard to be an Apostle and fill out a Crowd—with only six in their company, Crowds were difficult. And of course she was the Virgin, gowned in blue and veiled in white, weeping and wringing her hands at the Crucifixion on Good Friday and exclaiming with joy at the Resurrection on Easter Sunday.

She did stand firm, though, on never, ever having to say anything.

Despite the Church's muttering at the unseemly display, women were able to be players, but surprisingly few chose to be. Or not so surprisingly, Joliffe had thought more than once and especially on those days when the going was harder than ordinary because of weather or mishap, or a village was unwelcoming, or a town outright refused to let them play at all. On days like that he thought that women must be, on the whole, simply smarter than men. Not that Rose was a fool. Far from it. Her trouble was that as Thomas Basset's daughter, she had been born to the life, then had married herself to it, too, taking a player in her father's company for husband.

That husband was long gone. No one knew—nor anymore much cared—where he might be, but her father was still master of the company and here she and her son Piers still were, and Joliffe feared to think what the company would do if ever she left them. She managed their money and them with a steady hand, sewed and mended their players' garb and properties, made meals worth eating out of whatever food came their way, and for good measure nursed any of them who fell ill. She was even able to bring Ellis out of the dark humours that sometimes came on him. But when Joliffe had pleaded to write one speech for her as the Virgin Mary—"Just one. A short one"—she had answered, "No," in the voice with which none of the players, including her father, ever cared to argue, and he had let it go.

Instead he had added to young Gil's speeches, which had pleased Gil. Part of their company less than a year, he was already well able to hold his own in anything asked of him. Besides that, Minster Lovell was his home manor and it could be only to the good for him to have a chance to show well there among his own folk.

Own folk or not, Minster Lovell's priest had been stiff at first about having the playing scaffold set up in his churchyard. He had allowed it only because Lady Lovell ordered it, but as the week went on and each day they performed a different play not only for Lady Lovell and her children and household but for all the manor folk and—as word spread—to folk from neighboring manors and villages, and attendance at his Holy Week services and the offerings to his church grew, he had warmed wonderfully to the players. By the week's end, when they had triumphantly performed the Resurrection on Easter Sunday afternoon, he was so mellowed toward them that he had hoped aloud they would do it all again, come next year.

Joliffe's own unsaid thought was that they had succeeded so well only because they had gone so headlong and desperate at the whole business that ill fortune had not been able to catch up to them. They had, as it were, outdistanced it, and he would not care to wager on their chances of doing it again.

Nonetheless, after Lady Lovell's harsh words about the duke of Burgundy, he had cobbled together a play with a fat, waddling "Duke" declaiming his allegiance to "Lady Honor" but being led, with much comic business, astray and to the Devil by "Mistress Greed." The business was long on farce and short on piety, and the players had put it on in the great hall, with their speeches still raw and barely learned, the day after Easter. Everyone was ready to be done with solemnity by then, and the household had rocked with laughter, Lady Lovell so much enjoying it that she had had them do it again then and there, and afterward, there in the hall, given each of the men a silver coin in token of her pleasure.

With all of that behind them, they had been tired but

well-contented the next morning as they waited with Tisbe harnessed to the loaded cart in the manor's outer yard for Basset to return from formally asking Lady Lovell's leave for them to go; and when he did, he had patted his belt-hung leather purse and said, "There we are. Well-paid as well as well-fed by our good Lady Lovell's bounty. Gee-up, Tisbe. We're away!"

Piers had led them out of the yard playing a reed pipe held in one hand and rattling away with the other at the drum slung on his hip by a strap around his shoulders. They had passed through Minster Lovell village waving to folk who waved, smiling, back at them, and twice girls ran out into the road to give Gil quick kisses, so that it was in a general glow of good feeling they had left the village by the narrow bridge over the Windrush River and taken the steep climb of road up from the valley to the wide highway that could take them eastward toward Oxford or westward toward Cirencester, as they chose.

Until then they had thought their choosing was to go west and curve northward into a round of villages and town familiar from other years and meant to bring them back to Minster Lovell toward Michaelmas at the end of harvest. But that morning at the roads' meeting, Basset had signaled Joliffe to halt Tisbe and said to everyone, "Lady Lovell has asked a favor of us, that we go south from here instead of elsewhere. What do you say?"

He had cheerfully made it sound a choice, but Joliffe's own thought was that to choose other than what Lady Lovell asked of them would be stark foolishness.

He was saved from his urge to say that by Ellis demand-ing, "Why?"

Basset had surely known that question would come, and he answered promptly, "Because when Lady Lovell did her Lenten retreat at St. Mary's Abbey in Winchester, the lady abbess was worried over something that may be shaping to the bad at one of the abbey's manors in the White Horse Vale. The bailiff there has passed on word by way of the abbey's steward for that part of the abbey's lands that there are angers among her best folk there, but they won't talk openly enough about whatever is the trouble for him to be certain what it is and put a stop it."

"So Lady Lovell thought we could do . . . what?" Ellis asked. "What's her interest, anyway, in a worry delivered at third hand about people that have nothing to do with her?"

"I gathered it's a favor to the abbess," Basset said, patient with Ellis' impatience. "There's worry the trouble will boil up and it will all turn to lawyers and other costly business. What she's asked of us is that we go there, listen, look, hear what we can, and pass on to the bailiff anything we learn."

"Does this bailiff know we're coming?" Joliffe asked. "Or are we going to surprise him with our helpful interest?"

"Lady Lovell is going to send word of us to him by way of the abbess."

"It's daft," muttered Ellis. "What are we likely to learn in a night spent in a place we don't know at all?"

"We should be able to draw it out to three nights likely," Basset said. "There's a village and several manors all in the same parish. Enough to keep us there longer than a night, anyway."

"Where is it we're going?" Joliffe asked, since choice didn't seem part of it. "White Horse Vale is a long place." Named for an ancient figure of a galloping horse carved into a white chalk hillside above the vale, the valley ran broad and for miles between the Cotswold Hills to the north and the Berkshire Downs to the south.

"A village called Ashewell. We do know the place a little, if we remember it," Basset said. "We were there, what, six years ago it would be now. At one of the Scourings."

The Scourings were when the local folk turned out every

few years to clear the encroaching green turf from the Horse, to keep the chalk shining white, and although that in itself was no great draw, there was always a large fair held with it, with all manner of sports and other pastimes among and around the earthen banks of an ancient fortress on the hilltop above the Horse. Joliffe no longer remembered why the players had gone so far out of their usual ways to be there that year, but he remembered other things about it well enough and asked, "It's not a Scouring time now, is it?"

"It's not," Basset agreed. "There'll be just us, with everyone there surely ready to be diverted now Lent is finally done, same as any other way we might go instead. With all said and done, there are as many places to play to the southward as on the way we usually go. I doubt we'll lose by obliging Lady Lovell in this."

Or not lose so much as they might if they *dis*obliged her, Joliffe had thought.

Ellis, usually able to find something to grumble at, had simply shrugged and said, "Makes no odds to me. We'll be walking whichever way we go, so let's get on with it."

They had, taking the highway toward Cirencester only to the first crossroads and there turning southward, the newly risen sun throwing their morning shadows long to their right across the wayside grass and the world bright with spring all around them.

That had been three days ago. The weather had held fair, the travel easy along roads gently twisting through the Vale's mostly level miles, the villages where they stopped to play open-handed, and they were all in good humour now as they neared Ashewell. The flat fields here must have once been marsh; the road ran level between constant, reedy ditches sometimes fringed by pollarded alder and willow trees, but ahead were the smooth-flanked high downs, a great heave of land against the sky.

The White Horse was there but they were coming toward it at a slant, not able to see it from the road they were on. Their goal was marked by Ashewell church's gray-stoned square tower, seen long before they neared it. The village was built on the first lift of land at the foot of the downs, and when the road began to climb toward it, narrowing into a steep-sided lane so deep between hedge-topped banks that the church and even the downs were lost to sight, the players stopped to put on the bright red and yellow tabards with the Lovell badge of a hound that proclaimed them Lord Lovell's players. Then Joliffe set Tisbe to the climb, and the players matched their pace to her plod as she took the slope until the road gave a tight bend and suddenly they were at the beginning of the village's narrow main street, with houses close-clamped along both sides and ahead the church's tower again with its promise of a churchyard where they could set up to play if the street never widened enough to let them. Always supposing the priest was not one of those who held stiffly against allowing plays.

But come what may, it was lookers-on that were most needed or else there was no use to the players being there at all, and Tisbe, knowing the players' business as well as they did, paused, without need of Joliffe to tell her, for Rose to take her place at her head while the rest of them, even Gil, who was not much limping now, arrayed themselves into procession ahead of the cart with Piers in the lead, having fetched the small drum and his reed pipes from their hamper in the back of the cart. With the drum hung from his shoulder by its belt, he began to beat on it with one hand while playing the pipes with the other, and Tisbe, again not needing an order, started forward behind them as they all strode onward as if sure of their welcome and happier to be at Ashewell than anywhere else on earth. As Basset had told Joliffe in Joliffe's early days in the company,

"If you come skulking in like a dog that expects to be kicked, kicked is what you'll likely be. Show a lordly assurance of being welcomed and folk will believe you're worth welcoming."

Although not always true, it held more often than not, and as they went merrily along the street, doors opened and people looked out. As they reached the church, they found that where their lane crossed another beside the church there was enough widening of the streets along the churchyard for them to set up to play without troubling whoever was priest here, and Basset said, "We look to be in ever-better luck."

Even more to their luck, they could *not* set up just now because today must be the village's market day: half a dozen tables and a few canvas-sheltered booths crowded the street's widening, with among them a gathering of men and women and children who greeted the players with shouts and waves. Adding the villagers drawn from the houses by the drum and pipes gave a goodly crowd to whom Basset proclaimed that the company would, "by your good grace, perform a play, if there be none to say us nay!"

If there were any nays, they were lost among the many shouted "Ayes!" and Basset bowed as if in submission to their will and stepped aside with a wordless sweep of his arm to bring Ellis forward. What they had been playing most places since leaving Minster Lovell was Joliffe's rude play about the duke of Burgundy, it being quick and with no need to set up a particular playing space, and while Basset had proclaimed to the crowd, Joliffe, Ellis, and Gil had been behind the cart slipping out of their tabards and into the needed garb. Helped by Rose and Piers into wigs and loose gowns over their usual clothing, Gil became "Lady Honor" and Joliffe "Mistress Greed," while a red cloak, a pair of horns, and a swagger sufficed to turn Ellis into "the Devil," ready to come forward to take Basset's place and hold the crowd with a speech about the joys of seizing souls, giving Basset time to go behind the cart and put on a "rich" chain of office—oversized and gaudy, made of brass-dipped tin and false jewels—and the company's brass crown to become the Duke and ready at the end of the Devil's speech to come forward hand in hand with Lady Honor.

It was just as well the farce was brief, because as they finished to loud laughter and cheers at the Devil and Mistress Greed dragging the yelling, kicking Duke away to Hell behind the cart, leaving smiling Lady Honor curtsying to the crowd and Piers skipping out with bag in hand to collect whatever coins people might be pleased to give, a man came shoving through the crowd along the churchyard wall, demanding as he came, "What are you doing here? What's this pollution?"

Behind the cart Ellis and Joliffe let Basset go, knowing the sound of trouble when they heard it. Hurriedly stripping off the Duke's chain and crown, Basset handed them to Rose while Ellis took off the Devil's horns and cloak and tossed them into the cart, freeing him to go with Basset back around the cart to face the trouble.

Joliffe took longer to be rid of wig and gown but followed bare moments later, to find Basset and Ellis facing a stout, balding man in a priest's long black surcoat loudly railing at Basset for his blasphemous work. Basset seemed to have yet to get a word in edgewise, but having long experience at such trouble, he was standing with hands clasped and head respectfully cocked to one side, waiting for the priest to run down before attempting any answer. Behind the priest, none of the villagers were leaving, as willing to enjoy this new show as the last. Piers, intent on the most important part of everything, was still weaving among them, gathering coins, while Gil in Lady Honor's wig and gown still stood where he had been, giving the priest someone to point at while ranting, "There is only one of the blasphemies! A hitherto innocent boy lured and corrupted into playing at being a woman! Making mock of the Lord's creation! You!" He all but spat at Basset. "A man of your years, making sport . . ."

While the priest went on, Joliffe said in Gil's ear, "Go on and change. He can yell at me for a while."

Gil gasped out a breath he probably had not known he was holding and willingly retreated. Behind the priest, two men were now pushing to the front through the crowd. Tall and fair-haired, they were well-dressed in almost-matching, short, dark houppelandes split for riding, with tall, soft-leathered boots that told they had horses somewhere nearby. It was easy to tell they were not plain villagers even before the older of them said, "Father Hewgo. What's toward here?"

"Medcote," the priest said without need to look around. "These men, these servants of the Devil, these . . ."

"By your leave, sire," Basset inserted with firm respect. "We're the Lord Lovell's men, not the Devil's."

That stopped the priest, at least briefly. It was one thing to confront the Devil's servants, another to cross a lord whose power in the world might not be as great as the Devil's but was more immediate. And in that pause Medcote said at Basset with cold authority, "Have you proof of that?"

From the back of the crowd someone said, "That's my question to ask, not yours, Medcote."

Heads turned and the crowd shifted, making way for a dark-haired man somewhat less tall and more plainly dressed than Medcote in surcoat and low riding boots but fully as assured as he came into the open, followed by a boy of maybe fifteen or sixteen years who was enough like him surely to be his son or some other near relation.

"Then why haven't you asked it?" Medcote demanded at the man.

"Because I saw them come up the street wearing Lord Lovell's colors and badge on their tabards." His tone added, And aren't you a fool not to know that?

Medcote faced the newcomer, hooked his thumbs into his broad leather belt, and said with insulting challenge, "Well, I didn't."

"That doesn't change that it's my business, not yours, whether or not they play here in the village," the newcomer said, with an edge to the words that made them almost an affront.

The priest, his voice still ripe with indignation, declared, "It's *my* business more than anyone's, here in my own parish."

That was answered by a few scattered jeers from well back in the crowd. The priest ignored them, pointing again at Basset and insisting, "His kind make mock of the Lord's grace with their mincing and prancing and profaning. If you saw them arrive, then you saw that, Master Ashewell."

"I saw them making mock of the kind of men who betray honor and serve greed," the newcomer answered. "You were not here and did not see what they did at all and so are without grounds to judge."

Father Hewgo opened, closed, and opened his mouth soundlessly, looking for something to say but apparently offended past words. It was the man called Medcote who challenged, "Anyone can stitch a badge, Ashewell."

"True," Master Ashewell granted. "Therefore I shall ask, with something like due courtesy—" he turned to Basset "—have you something more to prove whose men you are?"

Basset bowed to him, saying with equal courtesy, "We do, sir," and held a hand out to the side, not needing to look around to know Rose was already there, ready to put into his hand the folded parchment that was their signed and

sealed license from Lord Lovell, assuring the world they
were in his service and under his protection. Taking it, Basset went forward and handed it to Master Ashewell, who
unfolded and read it, then said solemnly, "I find no fault
with this," and solemnly handed it back. The hint of laughter behind his solemnity was just enough to offend without
being enough to be challenged as he added to Father Hewgo
and Medcote, raising his voice enough to be heard by everyone, "On Lord Lovell's behalf I am more than ready to welcome these players here. Am even glad to do so." And to
Basset again, "Master Player, welcome to Ashewell parish,
both in Lord Lovell's name and in honor of your skill."

If he noted Father Hewgo was gone rooster-red—
choking on his own choleric gall, Joliffe hoped—Master
Ashewell gave no more sign of it than Basset did, bowing
to Master Ashewell again and answering in kind, "Good
sir, your ready welcome does both yourself and my Lord
Lovell honor. My thanks and that of all my company."

Copying his thanks, Joliffe and Ellis bowed and Rose
curtsied.

Master Ashewell bent his head in gracious return, but
Father Hewgo started, "I still protest that . . ."

"Protest to your heart's content," Master Ashewell said
sharply. "Just not to me. Maybe Medcote likes to hear you
gabble. I don't."

The priest turned toward Medcote in clear expectation of
his support, but Medcote said, as if having duly considered
it, "Since they indeed have Lord Lovell's approval *and*
Master Ashewell's, I think objection can hardly be made."

Father Hewgo's rooster-red deepened toward a dangerous purple and again—probably most unusually—words
failed him. Master Ashewell, with smooth pleasure at probably that as well as other things, said, "With that agreed on,
Master Basset, may I offer you and your company a place

to stay, with hope you'll perform for my family tonight at supper?"

Basset bowed to him. "It will be our pleasure. Thank you, sir."

"But there'll be no more of your profanity here in the village!" Father Hewgo said. "I forbid it!"

Master Ashewell looked about to make sharp answer to that, but Medcote cut in first and smoothly, "On that I've had a thought, Father Hewgo. Since Lord Lovell vouches for them and they're here, why not use them to the church's good?"

"To the church's good?" Father Hewgo made it sound as if he'd been asked to eat hot worms.

"A church ale, Father Hewgo," Medcote said smoothly.

The priest began what looked to be yet another protest, despite that a church ale was usually to a church's profit. Parishioners were expected to donate food and drink to be sold for the parish church's good, and although that donating was sometimes grudged by those who had to do it, folk were generally willing to make a holiday of the time, and Joliffe suspected that in the latter was where Father Hewgo's objection most deeply lay. He did not seem a man who favored jollity. Probably because people busy with jollity, pleasure, and joy were less biddable than people kept bowed under a heavy sense of their sins and the world's wickedness.

But Medcote cut over whatever protest the priest might have made, going on, "To raise money toward that east window you've been wanting."

Father Hewgo's look went from outrage to disconcerted willingness to listen. Medcote surely knew him well and how to deal with him, smiling while saying, "This Sunday coming would suit. That will give time for word to spread that, come Sunday after Mass, there'll be a play here in the churchyard and . . ."

Father Hewgo bristled into new protest. "In the church-yard? No. That's beyond all and into desecration."

With mellow respect, Basset said, "By your leave, sir, all last week and on Easter Sunday afternoon itself, we performed in Minster Lovell's churchyard by leave of my lord's priest, for Lady Lovell and the household and half the countryside around. By the time we left, people had been moved by piety to such gifts that there was talk of building a new aisle for the church."

That was more than Joliffe had heard, but he and Ellis both nodded their heads in agreement. Gil had rejoined them and nodded, too. After all, as Basset sometimes said, truth sometimes lay as much in what was possible as in what was. It was *possible* someone had talked of a new aisle to Minster Lovell church.

For now it was enough that Father Hewgo was paused; and into that pause Joliffe said, more as if thinking aloud than to anyone, "It's in my mind that Lady Lovell may have said that in her Lenten time at St. Mary's in Winchester, my lady abbess told how she'd a company perform there at Shrovetide. In the guest-yard, was it?"

Ellis took that up with, "Didn't she say there was enough made to buy a new gold-embroidered altar frontal?"

"Might have been," Joliffe agreed. Just as Lady Lovell might have said something about a Shrovetide play—but had not.

"There," said Medcote. "If such as Lady Lovell and my lady abbess find no fault . . ."

"Yes, yes," Father Hewgo snapped. "I see the point. Well then, yes, if it's to be to the good of the church, it may be an allowable thing."

Basset, knowing it was better settled now than later, said smoothly, "Our fee is a tenth of whatever good our work brings to the church."

The priest opened his mouth toward either protesting

that or else attempting to bargain it down, but before he could do either, the young man behind Medcote, silent until now, said, "I'll take word to Faringdon myself tomorrow. There's always some will come that far for a good ale, and the more the merrier." Somewhat mocking, he added, "Since it's for the church."

Several men among the lookers-on cheered and maybe jeered that, and Father Hewgo swung around and said at all the crowd, his voice raised to pulpit-strength, "But never think I'll not be giving heed to who comes only to the ale and not to Sunday Mass before it! Come to one and not the other and there'll be a price to pay!"

There were priests who could have made that into a jesting jibe with their authority's weight behind it nonetheless. Father Hewgo made it simply a threat, surveyed the crowd as if to be sure they understood it, then gave a curt nod of farewell more or less at Master Ashewell and Medcote and stalked away toward the church.

To no one in particular, Medcote said, "We've somewhat rumpled his tonsure, I think. I suppose I'd better go smooth it. By your leave, Master Ashewell."

There was something lightly mocking in the words and the way he bent his head to the other man in a courtesy that Master Ashewell answered with a curt nod.

"Master Nicholas," Medcote added to the boy behind Master Ashewell and seemed not to see the glare the boy gave him along with a barely jerked nod.

Medcote and the Ashewells might be united against the priest, but they were not friends with one another, that was clear. And as Medcote went away in the priest's wake, the youth with him—looking as if he had found the whole business vastly laughable—gave Master Ashewell a nod and, behind his back after going past him, a look down his nose at the boy Nicholas, who flushed red and looked furious but was too young and not nearly tall enough to look down his nose in return.

Joliffe did not know whether any of the other players saw that exchange, but he heard Basset let out his breath on a whoosh of relief that matched Joliffe's own, because when a village's priest kicked up hard against players, the players rarely came out the winner. Whatever was the sport among Father Hewgo, Master Ashewell, and Medcote, it had come out in the players' favor, and at a guess, they had now seen the men who were worrying the abbey's bailiff.

But Master Ashewell was coming toward them, and Basset, Ellis, Joliffe, and Gil all bowed to him, Basset saying, "Master Ashewell. Our thanks for being our champion in this."

"It was my pleasure. Father Hewgo is overbearing beyond his office and a hypocrite. I have too few chances to thwart him and welcome every one."

That was surely blunt enough, Joliffe thought, as Basset asked, "The church isn't in your gift, then? To shift the priest as you choose?"

"Unhappily, no, or he'd be long gone. I'm only reeve here for the nuns of St. Mary's Abbey in Winchester. The village and the gift of the church are both theirs."

"Oh," Basset said. "I had thought from your name . . ."

He trailed off the sentence, leaving an opening that Master Ashewell filled, saying easily, "No. I take my name from the village but I own what used to be the desmesne manor lands that were once part of it. Now, if you would care to come with us, I'll show you where you're welcome to stay." He stopped as if on a sudden thought, then said, "Do you know, I think no one asked if you wanted to stay long enough here to perform at a church ale come Sunday. Do you? Or are you bound for somewhere else and expected there?"

"We're always bound for somewhere else, sir," Basset said, "but rarely expected anywhere. We're more than pleased to linger here through Sunday."

Master Ashewell smiled. "Very good. My son and I will fetch our horses while you ready your cart and then we'll show you the way. There's a field I think will serve you well."

Basset and the others again thanked him with deep bows. Far more than once, Basset had said, "There's no such thing as showing too much respect to those who ease our way through life."

Especially considering how little ease there often was, Joliffe always silently added.

As the Ashewells left, Piers came from where he had been hovering well to the side, jiggling the bag that clinked and jinked very satisfactorily as he said, pleased with himself, "I think people were paying for both the shows they got. Ours and that priest's."

"And well they should," his grandfather said, taking the bag and weighing it in his hand. "Well done, Piers."

Rose was waiting behind the cart to give them their tabards, not needing to be told that, since they would be here for a time, her father would want to make as good a show leaving the village as coming in. Basset gave the bag of coins to her—she saw to their money as well as to so much else—before taking up his tabard while Joliffe, Ellis, Piers, and Gil were slipping their own over their heads, Ellis saying as he settled the weight of the cloth across his shoulders, "Do you have the feeling we just became a rope in a tug-of-war the priest and these men are having?"

Joliffe shrugged, partly in answer, partly to shift his own tabard into place, and said, "Thus far anyway the tugging has been to our good."

"That's probably what the rope says just before it breaks," Ellis growled.

"Ellis," Basset said, "you'd find something to complain of if God himself dropped gold coins in your lap."

Ellis paused, seeming actually to consider that, then said seriously, "You're right. I probably would."

Rose laughed at him and kissed him on his cheek.

Chapter 2

The Ashewells returned riding bay rouncys, horses meant more for service than show, but these two were of good quality. Not wasting words but with a smile and a nod, Master Ashewell led the players not back the way they had come but onward, to turn right at the cross-lanes and along the churchyard's end and out of the village, the downs now at their backs. Beyond the village's crowd of houses the lane did not deepen between steep banks like the other one had, but made a long, straight slope to the level land, the broad village fields spread away to either side beyond the ditches that kept them drained, with hedges and stands of trees here and there and, it soon proved, Master Ashewell's own manor not far from the village.

The place was not walled. The hall and its house, barns, stable, and sheds sat close and clean around an open yard beyond the far end of a wooden bridge across a ditch widened to make a reed-filled moat around it all. With freshly white-plastered walls and roofs golden with new reed-thatch, the clustered buildings shone with settled prosperity and welcome among the young-greened fields and pastures around them. But at the bridge's outer end Master Ashewell drew rein, said something to his son, lifted a hand to the players, and rode on across the bridge into the manor yard.

Left to wait for the players to come up, Nicholas dismounted, and when they reached him said to Basset, a little shy but smiling, "It's not much farther to where you're welcome to tent. My father hopes you'll pardon being left to me to show the way."

"We are as grateful to the son as to the father for all their courtesy and kindness," said Basset with a bow.

Nicholas acknowledged that with a slight bend of his head in return. "If you'll come this way, then," he said, turned, and leading his horse, fell into step beside Basset.

While they went on along the road, he made solemn talk about the weather and how long the players had been on the way from Minster Lovell. Basset answered him just as gravely, and when they had turned from the wider way into a side lane between hedges high enough to hide the fields beyond them, took his turn to ask whether Father Hewgo was so cross-grained about everything or only about players.

Forgetting to be grave, Nicholas exclaimed, "Him? He's cross-grained about everything." And added with scorn, "Besides, he's like glove to hand with the Medcotes."

That had not seemed true just now, Joliffe thought, while Basset prodded mildly, "You'd think he'd take better care to keep well with your father, him being the abbey's reeve here."

"You'd think so, yes," Nicholas said with a boy's readiness to talk to someone as ready to listen as Basset. "But when John Medcote got Brook's manor, the right to a quarter of the village came with it, and the right to half the village court, too. That gives him more sway in matters than he'd otherwise have." In obvious echo of his elders, he added, "He uses it ill, too. He's been buying up grazing rights for his sheep and then overcrowding the pasture-lands. So far Master Kyping hasn't been able to curb him."

"Master Kyping?" Basset asked.

"He's the abbey's bailiff for its lands in this half of the Vale. He answers to Master Carswell, the abbey's steward, but Master Carswell only comes at quarter-years, so mostly it's my father and Master Kyping who have to deal with the Medcotes."

"Ah," said Basset with flattering interest. They had stopped at a gateway into a field, probably where they were to be left, but before Nicholas could say anything in parting, Basset asked, "Medcote is new here, then?"

"He's from Wantage and doesn't belong here at all. The manor came to him by way of his wife after . . ." Nicholas suddenly fumbled, turned red, steadied himself, and said in a rapid mumble, ". . . after her cousin died and she inherited."

"While your family has been here far longer, having the village name and all," Basset said, pretending not to see that stumble.

"Yes," Nicholas agreed. But all his eager urge to talk was gone. He gestured through the open gateway, saying rapidly while gathering his reins and readying to mount, "This is Grescumb Field. There's a stream among the trees there, and you can take what wood you need for your fire." He swung into his saddle, finishing, "If you come to the house a little before sundown, you'll be in good time to perform at supper, my father says," and was turning his horse away even as Basset thanked him and gave assurance they would be there.

Basset stood and watched him ride back the way they had come. Joliffe, starting Tisbe into the tight turn through the gateway into the field, asked dryly, "You don't suppose we've learned what we came for, do you? That something about Medcote upsets Nicholas Ashewell?"

"I doubt that's a secret to anybody," Basset answered as dryly. "I'd say, though, that we've moved nicely into the center of the trouble this Master Kyping the bailiff is worried over."

"Ashewell has done well enough by us, anyway," Ellis said. "Look at this place."

Untilled and ungrazed, Grescumb Field was surely going to be hayed come high summer, but presently the grass' young green was scattered with cowslips' yellow flowers and the fire-red sparks of campion. The young-leaved hedges on three sides gave good privacy, while the fourth side was mostly thickly grown alders and willows except where a wide gap marked a ford across the stream there to the ploughed field beyond, hazed with the green of newly sprouting wheat, the hope of a harvest better than last year's.

With no need to talk out a choice, the players, Tisbe, and their cart headed for that gap, Piers flinging himself into half a dozen cartwheels and then running ahead to disappear down the shallow slope to the stream. By the time the rest of them reached the top of the slope, he was sitting on a stump beside the water, pulling off hosen, his shoes already cast aside. Intent on wading into the clear, shallow-running water, he did not look up as the cart creaked to a stop at the edge of the trees and the other players stood smiling down at him with the same smile Joliffe knew was on his own face. As traveling players, they had stayed in places ranging from ghastly to good enough to pleasing. Here was a very pleasing place, with grazing for Tisbe and water and wood close at hand, and they would have it not just for the one night but for probably four.

Joliffe clucked to Tisbe and turned her to draw the cart

aside from the ford a few yards but still sheltered near the trees. That brought him around and looking back toward the downs, unseen since the players had taken to the narrow lane into Ashewell village. From here, with the field open around him, the high, steep rise of hills was in clear view, their smooth-grassed flanks curving upward like a huge sea-swell to the sky. And high across one curved shoulder was the White Horse of the Vale, stretched in its eternal gallop just as Joliffe remembered it from six years ago, and he came to a stop in mid-stride, staring at it as he had stared then. At some time beyond the reach of men's memories, for a reason long forgotten, the hillslope's grassy turf had been cut away to lay bare the white chalk underneath in sweeping lines that were not so much a horse as the *sense* of a horse, more potent in its seeming than any plain-made horse shape could have been. There was the proud arch of a horse's neck, the long sweep of its back, the curves of its running legs, and the flare of its tail, all stretched across a hillside, immense and strange and beautiful.

Coming past Joliffe, Ellis made a quick, one-handed warding sign against evil toward the Horse, muttering, "I'd forgotten how fey that thing is. The way it takes your eye, whether you want to look at it or not, makes my skin crawl."

Turning to begin unharnessing Tisbe, Joliffe said, hiding irk under jest, "That's not the Horse making your skin crawl. It's lice. You've got them again. You're lousy."

Behind him, Rose said with pretended displeasure, "I'll thank you to take that back," knowing as well as he did that none of them had lice, not after the trouble she took with fleabane, tansy, rue, lousewort, and other herbs, both as ointments on them and, dried, among their hampers of garb and other clothing.

Joliffe gave her a quick half-bow. "I take it back on the same breath that I gave it, and beg your forgiveness, sweet lady. I did but speak in jest."

Too long among players for fair words to divert her, Rose said back at him, "You spoke to irk Ellis." But she smiled at him as she said it.

They each had their familiar duties when it came to settling anywhere, though Gil, to spare his ankle—better though it was—took Piers' usual task of gathering dry wood while Piers, already wet from his wading, went down to the stream with the water bucket. Basset and Ellis set up the tent they used on nights they had no other shelter, while Joliffe saw to unharnessing Tisbe and wiping her down, then hobbled her to let her graze as she would.

For her part, Rose dug a small firepit, setting the grassy turves aside, both for banking the fire when need be at night and to replace in the hole when time came that they moved on. Gil brought dry wood from among the trees and set to making the fire for her, while Piers, having returned with the water, brought the long-legged metal trivet for setting the cookpot over the fire, and then the cookpot itself. With the tent up, Basset and Ellis unloaded their bedding into it, while Joliffe fetched what Rose called the kitchen box, setting it near the firepit for her. Readying to begin their supper, she said, "We should have bought food while we were in the village. It will be oat pottage and yesterday's bread for tonight, I'm afraid. But maybe you'll be fed at the manor after you've played."

"We'll buy something tomorrow anyway," Basset said easily. "My thought is that, rather than sitting about for the two days until Sunday, we should do a wander through the nearest villages to let folk know we're here and to hear what we can hear. We'll buy what you want while we're about it."

Joliffe had brought from the cart and was dropping beside the fire the canvassed cushions they used for sitting, but Basset, somewhat troubled with arthritic joints, sat himself on the open back of the cart while saying, "We might even go back to Faringdon while we're about it."

"That fellow with Medcote said he'd go to Faringdon," Ellis pointed out, lifting the cooking pot onto the trivet for Rose now that the fire was burning well.

"He'll tell his friends," Basset said. "We'll tell everybody."

Joliffe sat down on one of the cushions, glad to get off his feet. Piers and Gil, their share of tasks done, were gone back to the trees where Gil, perched on a half-fallen willow limb, was giving Piers advice on what was a suitable sapling for a fishing pole.

Ellis poured some water into the pot to boil for the pottage, set down the bucket, and turned to Rose, who was just straightening from the kitchen box, the bag of oatmeal in her hands, her back to him. He put his hands on either side of her hips and pulled her back against him, bending his head to kiss her neck and say something in her ear too quietly for anyone else to hear.

Not that Joliffe could not make an easy guess at it by the look on Ellis' face and how he was pressing his body to hers, and he dropped his gaze to give them what passed for privacy among them all. There was love between Rose and Ellis, and desire for each other. The trouble lay with Rose's missing husband. However much she did not want him back, for all she knew he still lived, and if he did, then whatever pleasures of the body she and Ellis shared went beyond the sin of fornication to the far worse sin of adultery, and whenever she gave way to her need and Ellis', her shame afterward was deep and her penance never enough to ease her conscience. This year she had insisted that she and Ellis keep the Church's law against giving way to bodily lust of the loins through all the forty days of Lent.

Joliffe did not know how hard that abstinence had been for her, but Ellis, despite having accepted it, had not taken to it well; but Lent had ended at Easter and since then Ellis had been letting Rose know in small, hopeful ways that he was ready to be done with abstinence. Now he looked to be asking outright for what he wanted.

But Rose twisted free of his hands, shrugged away and aside from him, and said, "No."

"I meant tonight," Ellis said. "Not now."

Rose stopped still, paused, then said with her head bowed so she was speaking more to the top of the meal bag in her arms than to him, "We've held chaste this many weeks, Ellis. Please. This is our chance to be done with our lust once and for all. Please let's take it."

Joliffe could not keep from glancing at Ellis then, and if he had been cruel he would have laughed at Ellis' look of confused hurt, disbelief, and beginning anger. Instead, he became very busy with taking off one shoe as if there was a pebble in it that he had to find this instant and no other. Basset, too, had sudden need to be half-turned around, rustling at something in the cart behind him, saying somewhat loudly, "So, what should we play at Ashewell's tonight?"

Ellis drew back from Rose, snarled, "*King Cophetua and the Unwilling Maid*," and stalked away toward the stream.

Rose closed the kitchen box, set down the meal bag, and went on to readying their supper, keeping her back somewhat too carefully to Basset and Joliffe. And Basset, for only Joliffe to hear, said, "No, not that play tonight, I think."

"The *Robin and Marian*," Joliffe offered, because as Robin, Ellis would be able to fight, save his fair lady Marian, and kill the Evil Sheriff—pretend triumphs, to be sure, but maybe some comfort against his present complete defeat by Rose.

"Um," Basset agreed. "Is it your turn or Gil's to be Marian?"

"Gil's."

In their small company's lean years, before they became

Lord Lovell's players and Gil joined them, the women's parts in their plays had been mostly Joliffe's. That had been a worry as he came into his twenties and was no longer quite the stripling that he had been. He could still play them but it was good to have Gil take the younger ones most of the time. Besides, their company could now do plays with two women and that greatly increased how many plays they could do. But *Robin and Marian* only needed the one woman, and Joliffe had written in a Henchman for the Evil Sheriff, with him and Gil trading between Marian and Henchman, while Ellis was always Robin and Basset was always the Evil Sheriff. Except now Basset said, "So, do you think you could do the Sheriff tonight?"

Joliffe looked around and up at him with worry. "Why? Are your arthritics worse than you've let on?"

"I keep telling you they're not 'my' arthritics," Basset complained. "I would, given choice, keep no company with them at all."

"They're bad, then," Joliffe said.

"They're neither good nor bad at present. They just are, and my thought is why should I work harder than I have to? So, back to my question. Could you do the Sheriff tonight?"

"I can," Joliffe assured him. Besides that they had done almost all their plays so often they all knew each other's lines and movements almost faultlessly, he had already done the Evil Sheriff a few times before this. "You'll be the Henchman then?" With one line and little to do but be stabbed and die.

"I will." Basset heaved a satisfied sigh, rested both hands on his knees, and sat up straight. "I do like being master of a company and giving orders."

"You didn't order me. You asked," Joliffe pointed out.

"From a lord, an ask is as good as an order," Basset returned.

"I'm going to sleep," said Joliffe, and stretched himself out on the grass with his head on the cushion, and set himself to it.

He awoke to Gil grumbling at having to shave, Ellis scrubbing Piers behind the ears with water warmed beside the fire, and Rose getting out the bowls for serving the pottage.

"Good," she said at Joliffe as he sat up. "You can cut the bread for me."

When they had finished eating, the afternoon was far enough gone that it was time to go. Leaving Rose to watch the cart and Tisbe, the men and Piers set out on foot, with Ellis and Joliffe carrying the needed garb and gear in a hamper between them, usually a task Joliffe shared with Gil, but they were still sparing his ankle and it was no great trouble anyway; the manor was only a short and easy walk away.

As they neared it, Joliffe thought the half-timbered, white-plastered buildings curved around their yard, peaceful and warm in the westering sunlight, were like a cat curled and comfortable in a favorite sunny corner. It was an ordinary place belonging to an ordinary, prospering man, hardly differing from any number of other ordinary places the players had played in their time, but Joliffe had the sudden sense that this was a home, a place people had settled into and belonged and would belong to for a long time to come. If "home" had been a thing he had wanted for himself, he would not have gone the ways he had gone with his life, but for that one moment, as he and the others crossed the bridge over the reed-filled moat into the dusty yard, he felt the draw of pleasure there could be in such a thing as "home."

A small boy with a plume-tailed brown dog came running across the yard toward them from the doorway of the tall-roofed hall, saying excitedly as he reached them,

"You're the players! Father said I could watch for you! The last of supper has just gone in."

Basset bowed to him. "Then we've come at just the time we meant to, good sir."

The boy eyed their plain clothing with unhidden disappointment and asked, "Do you need to change your clothes?"

"We do, if it please your worship," Basset said. "A room or even the smallest corner will suffice, if in your great kindness you might let us use so much."

As he was supposed to, the boy giggled at all that, but behind him a man had come from the hall and was saying friendliwise as he crossed the yard, "The players. Welcome. Tom, go tell Master Ashewell they've come. I'll see to what they need."

"Dyer will see to you," Tom said happily and ran back toward the hall while Basset slightly bowed to the man and said, "We do need somewhere to change, sir."

"This way, if you will," Dyer returned as courteously and led them not into the hall or house but aside to the kitchen yard. Like many older places, the kitchen was built away from the house for better safety from fire. Here, with everything kept close together in the surround of the moat, the kitchen was not very far from the hall, nor was its yard very large; but the man took them to a door standing open into the house itself, into a small passageway between several heavy wooden doors standing open to several small rooms on either side and at its end a glimpse into the tall openness of the hall. Joliffe supposed the small rooms would be the butlery, pantry, and stores, where wine, bread, and other needs for meals were kept. Though probably usually locked for safekeeping, the doors were open now, this being mealtime, and the man showed them into the pantry with its wide board table along one wall still scattered with crumbs and crusts from bread cut for tonight's supper.

"Will this serve?" he asked.

"Very well. Thank you," Basset said.

"Supper is nearly done. Will you be ready soon?"

"Very soon," Basset assured him. "When we open the door, you'll know it's time to announce us."

The man nodded to that and began to withdraw, but Basset said, "One thing. What humour are folk in tonight?"

"Quite good," Dyer answered. "Gosyn is here—him and his wife and daughter. He's somewhat given to shouting, but all's well between him and Master Ashewell. If there's shouting, it will be about something else."

He went out, shutting the door, leaving Joliffe to wonder who this Gosyn was and what he might shout about. But Gil had begun to unlace his doublet as soon as they were in the room, and while he shrugged out of it, Joliffe pulled Marian's gown out of the hamper, ready to help him into it and lace it up the back since Rose was not here. There was not that much any of them had to do to be ready for *Robin and Marian*. Gil had painted his face for Marian before they left their camp, and for playing in so small a place as the hall, the rest of them had not bothered with their own faces, simply left them as they were. Piers, playing the Peasant Boy in his own everyday tunic, had put on a pair of his outgrown, well-patched hose at the camp and busied himself here with getting out the men's sword belts and swords while Basset put on the Henchman's loose surcoat over his own doublet and hosen and Ellis took off his walking-days brown doublet and put on Robin Hood's gallant one of green and gold. Even bought as it had been at third or fourth hand from a dealer in used clothing, it was far better than any outlaw would wear in the greenwood, but when Joliffe had long ago pointed that out, Basset had answered, "That's commonsense, yes, but folk live every day with commonsense and what-is. They won't pay us to show them more of the same. Robin gay in gold and green will get us more coin than Robin dull in brown and mud, so Robin gay in gold and green is what they'll get."

So Robin and Marian were both gay in gold and green and the Evil Sheriff—"On the chance someone may not otherwise be able to tell he's evil?" Joliffe had jibed—wore a black, padded surcoat studded with gray rivets as if maybe it was armored underneath, which it was not but nonetheless was heavy enough and too warm in today's warm weather to be comfortable. Having laced Gil into Marian's gown, Joliffe left Basset to help him with the long wig to go with it and turned to Ellis, who was garbed and sword-belted and holding up the Sheriff's black surcoat for Joliffe to slide into. That on, Joliffe buckled on the Sheriff's sword belt, settled the sword on his hip, and took the helmet Piers had ready for him. It was an unvisored man-at-arms helmet bought cheaply, not much dented, and open-faced so he could both see and his face be seen. Despite that, he settled it down on his head with a sigh. He hated the thing, but it was agreed among the other players that he was too fair-haired to be a villain, his protests that he had known fair-haired villains enough in his time being always ignored.

Basset finished with Gil, stepped back to look them all over, nodded that he was satisfied, and opened the small room's door to tell Dyer that they were ready. Dyer nodded and went the few yards more along the passageway and out into the hall where he announced in a firm and carrying voice, "My Lord Lovell's players!" and stepped aside, clearing the way for them to enter and begin.

Chapter 3

Neither the hall nor the household were large. Besides the cloth-covered table at the far end where Master Ashewell, another man who must be Gosyn, and two women sat, there were only two short trestle tables, one on either side of the hall, with several children along the outer side of one and several household folk at the other. More folk were hurriedly crowding in through the hall's door from the yard, elbowing each other into place along the near wall—kitchen-women and stablemen who didn't dine with the family but were welcomed to the hall for something like this, Joliffe guessed as he quickly assessed the place where they would play.

Although the hall's windows were few, narrow, and unglassed, their shutters were set open to the fair day, letting in the late afternoon sun to shine off the white-plastered walls and fill the hall with light. This time of year there was no fire on the open hearth in the hall's middle to frond smoke up to the high rafters under the thatched roof, and the rushes scattered across the floor looked to

be fresh and clean, not treacherous underfoot, so that Joliffe swaggered out boldly, hand on sword hilt, laying
claim by his outward arrogance to all the space between
the tables for the players' own by declaring loudly,
"Robin Hood, that false outlaw, dare not come forth, lest
my sword I draw, for cowards all these outlaws be that
hide away in the greenwood free!"

The play went well, too familiar to them to be a trouble
now that Gil was past sometimes stumbling on his long
skirts. Willing though Gil had been to learn everything he
could of the players' craft, skirts and "playing the lady" had
come hardest to him, but he no longer went crimson about it
and could even do a credible curtsy when need be. Ellis of
course enjoyed playing the hero, and Robin's sword-clashing
with the Evil Sheriff brought encouraging shouts from the
lookers-on. The Henchman died with suitable agony and
then so did Joliffe's Sheriff; and to table-pounding and clapping, Robin and Marian and the Boy took their bows. Then
the Evil Sheriff and his Henchman came back to life, with Joliffe pulling Basset to his feet with a flourish that covered
Basset's stiff knees, and the both of them took their own
bows to very satisfactory hissing. The hand-clapping went on
as Basset, Ellis, Joliffe, and Gil made a bowing retreat from
the hall, leaving Piers behind, beginning to juggle five
leather-wrapped and brightly dyed balls he had pulled from
the front of his tunic. He would follow that with the tumbling
and somersaulting he had learned from his mother, filling the
time it took Joliffe to strip off helmet, sword, and surcoat and
rejoin him, bringing juggling balls of his own.

Joliffe's juggling being notably worse than only poor, he
always played the fool to Piers' skill, which pleased Piers as
well as the lookers-on; and then Basset came out, followed
by Ellis, followed by Gil, all in their usual clothing, with
Basset making great show of being head of the company,
shooing Piers and Joliffe briskly aside and stepping forward

to address "my good, assembled gentlemen and ladies all."
While he made a word-flourishing speech, Ellis and Joliffe
made to strike dignified poses behind him but ended up
shoving and sniping rude comments at each other while
Piers climbed onto a table, and from there onto Gil's shoulders, and started to juggle again, so that finally Basset broke
off his speech, turned on them all with a roar, and chased
them from the hall with threats and much arm-waving,
leaving laughter, table-beating, and clapping behind them.

They came back in for quick bows and disappeared
again, this time for good. Dyer, who had seen them in, followed them out, still laughing, telling them as they collected
their hamper, "Mistress Ashewell says I'm to see you to the
kitchen for food and drink."

Basset thanked him and they followed him out into the
kitchen yard where he left them to sit on the wooden
benches either side of the kitchen doorway while he went
in. The players looked back and forth at each other, grinning at how well the playing had gone, then stood up as
two women and a half-grown girl came hurrying around
from the hall's front door and across the kitchen yard. Suddenly flustered to see the players there, the girl and the
older of the women ducked their heads and went into the
kitchen, but the younger woman stopped, eyeing them all
but mostly Ellis. She was well-curved, with enough of her
there for a man to get his hands on, and curls of butter-
yellow hair creeping out from under the edge of her head-
cloth. Smiling mostly at Ellis, she said, "You gave fine
sport. I've not enjoyed myself so much since Shrovetide."

Ellis, suddenly holding himself less like Ellis and more
like Robin Hood, smiled in return and thanked her, and Joliffe knew trouble was coming.

Dyer came out of the kitchen and said, "Titha," with the
worn patience of someone who had had to give the same
order too many times.

Titha gave him no look, just wrinkled her nose at Ellis and went away into the kitchen with a come-hither sway of her hips.

Giving her no more heed than she gave him, Dyer said to Basset, "Nan will bring your food in just a moment," and left them, going back toward the hall.

They all sat down again and Joliffe, looking at Ellis, said, "Don't."

Ellis made a wordless, unfriendly sound at him.

Basset said, "Leave it, Joliffe," and then they all stood up again as the woman who must be Nan came from the kitchen with a laden tray. Basset offered to take it from her but she shook her head, saying, "Nay then, I'll just set it down on the bench end here. Sit yourselves."

There were cups of ale and wooden bowls of gravy-brown pottage with meat in it—likely lamb at this time of year—and some thick slices of bread. Joliffe was immediately most interested in the food as Nan handed the bowls around, but Basset took the chance to ask, keeping his voice light, to make the question less than it might otherwise have seemed, "So, what can you tell us of Master Ashewell, who's being so lordly good to us? How does he come to be the abbey's reeve rather than lord of the manor himself, since he and the village bear the same name?"

As lightly, plainly telling no secrets, Nan answered, "Ah, that's because he's village himself and no lord at all. His father was just plain Tod Thatcher hereabouts. But old Tod bought his boy's freedom from the abbey and young Lionel took himself off to France as one of the duke of Bedford's men-at-arms and made his fortune in the war there."

"Did he?" Basset said admiringly. "There's been many tried that who didn't succeed."

"Well, he did, right enough." Nan sounded as proud as if she had done it herself. "They say he got the ransom of some French lord's younger son or some such thing. Came home, bought his wife's and their Nicholas' freedom—Nicholas was just a little, little boy then—and would have bought old Tod's, too, but Tod told him there were better uses for his money. Sensible man, was old Tod. So Master Ashewell bought this part of the manor from the abbey when my lady the abbess was in need of money for taxes because of the French war, and he changed his name and is a gentleman now, with his last three children all born free."

"And old Tod?" Basset asked.

The woman beamed on him. "Died three winters ago in a soft bed in his own room right there across the yard, with his family all beside him."

The players were all eating by then, with Basset slowed from more questions by mouthfuls of stew, but Nan was in no hurry to leave them, and stood watching them eat as if men enjoying their food was a pleasure to her, and Joliffe took the chance to say, "Master Ashewell doesn't seem to go on well with the priest here. Father . . . ?"

He stopped on a question, as if he could not remember the priest's name.

"Father Hewwwwgo," Nan obliged, mockingly rude and not at Joliffe. "There's not many around here get on well with that pull-faced priest. John Medcote maybe comes closest to it, but then, well, that's him for you, isn't it?"

Joliffe did not know if that was John Medcote or not, but while he tried to find a way to ask more that way, Basset asked, "Who else was at table with Master Ashewell tonight? His wife, surely, but there was another couple, too."

"That's the Gosyns. Walter and Geretruda. The Ashewells and they have all known each other since forever."

"Did Master Gosyn make his fortune in the French war, too?" Joliffe asked.

"No. He kept to home and took up his father's holding. Nor he's not 'Master' Gosyn, just plain Walter Gosyn, though there's those say he's done well enough adding lands to what he had that he has money enough to buy himself and his wife and their girl all free if he wanted to. There's some say, too, that the abbess will soon make him do it whether he wants it or not, because then he'd have to lease his land from her, and his rents would likely bring her more than his villein service does." Nan smiled widely. "There's been some going-round with my lady abbess' bailiff and steward over that, I've heard."

The players all grinned back at her around mouthfuls of stew and bread or over the rims of cups; there was always a backhanded comfort for those holding no land at all to hear the troubles of those who did.

In the yard in front of the hall a busyness of people leaving the hall had started while they talked, and Nan said now, "That will be the Gosyns leaving to be home while there's still light. It's but a mile but that Geretruda doesn't walk so fast now she's been ailing." The sun, just touching the horizon, would go from sight fast now, but the afterlight would linger long in the clear sky. Nan, watching who was in the yard, chuckled. "The walk will do Gosyn, good, though. He's fattening up a bit with his easy living, he is."

Joliffe had had no chance for a clear look at anyone in the hall and so took the one he had now as the Gosyns and Ashewells briefly stood in talk in the yard. As Nan had said, Gosyn was a stout-set man, but the woman leaning on his arm was thin as if she was indeed ailing. She was laughing, though, at something being said between Gosyn and Master Ashewell, and as they all began to stroll toward the bridge she looked as if she held to her husband more from affection than need. Nicholas and several other children of various heights were grouped around Master and Mistress Ashewell, while a girl much about Nicholas' age went with the Gosyns as they left, all of them waving to the

Ashewells as they crossed the bridge, and the Ashewells waving back.

With that much friendliness between the families, and a son and daughter on either side of much the same age, Joliffe was willing to guess that Lionel Ashewell and Walter Gosyn were thinking of a marriage there.

That surely couldn't be where the trouble was rooted that had the abbess' bailiff worried.

Could it?

Joliffe would have led Nan's talk that way, but two serving men came from the hall's kitchenward door, and Nan said, as she began to take the players' empty bowls and cups and stack them on the tray, "Here comes the rest of what's yours," and Joliffe saw the men were each carrying a wooden platter stacked with the bread-made trenchers that had served in place of plates for most of those dining in the hall. Such trenchers soaked up the meal's gravies and sauces and made good eating in their turn. In towns they were often given to the poor and beggars who would wait at house-doors to have them. Here in the country if there were no poor to hand they could go to fatten pigs. Or, this time, to fatten players, and Joliffe for his own part had no complaint about that at all.

Taking the tray, Nan said, "I'll see to it being wrapped up properly for you to carry away," and followed the men into the kitchen.

"No money?" Ellis complained, too low for anyone beyond themselves to hear.

"We're eating well. Content thy soul in patience," Joliffe suggested.

"I'll content you," Ellis said back.

"Food for the stomach will serve as well as coins for the purse just now," Basset said peaceably.

"Food and good talk," Joliffe added.

"You and your talk," Ellis muttered; but Titha came out with the trenchers bundled in a waxed cloth, and he straightened back into being Robin Hood, standing up to take the bundle from her.

The rest of them stood up, too, and it was to Basset that she said, "Nan says she'll not mind having the cloth back."

"Then she most assuredly will, though I must needs crawl on my knees to do so," Basset said with a bow.

Titha laughed at him, but her smile went back to Ellis, and when the rest of them started toward the gateway, he lingered in talk with her. He did not overtake them until they were over the bridge, when not even Joliffe said anything at him about it even though they all knew what that lingering probably meant. They all lived too much together not to know each other's ways, and although there were men who could deny or curb their needs, Ellis was not among them. For him a willing woman was a woman he was willing to have. He would have been otherwise if Rose had been more fully his, Joliffe thought; but Rose was not, and things being as they were, neither Joliffe nor any of them were surprised that when they were about to turn into the lane that let toward their camp, Ellis thrust the bundle of trenchers at Joliffe and said, "Take these. I'm going to tarry here a while."

Twilight's shadows were already thick here between the hedges, hiding their faces. It was by Ellis' taut voice that Joliffe knew he was being dared to say something, anything, in answer. So he did not, just took the bundle and turned away. The others were equally silent, nor could Ellis have seen their faces any better than they saw his: it had to be from their silence and the way they turned from him that he felt their reproof. Or maybe the reproof inside himself was enough. Either way, he said angrily, "It's my business. You can just leave me to go about it."

Not looking around, Joliffe said, "We are leaving you,

Ellis. See? We're walking away. So it must not be *us* you're angry at."

Briefly and clearly, Ellis wished him to go to hell.

Joliffe waved backward over his shoulder at him and kept going.

By the time they turned from the lane into Grescumb Field, most of the last light was drained from the sky, the twilight deepened enough into dark that the red leap of small flames in the firepit was welcoming. But as they neared it, Rose came from beyond the cart and in the flickering light Joliffe saw the small, quick shift of her head as she sought for Ellis and did not find him. She said nothing about that, though; instead held out an arm for Piers to come to her and asked, "How went it?"

"We played well and were well-received," Basset said, his hands out to the fire's warmth. With the sun gone, April's too-usual night chill was quickly asserting itself.

Pressed against his mother's side, held close by her arm around his shoulders, Piers declared, "They did well enough, but I was great!"

Quellingly, Joliffe said, "You were no worse than usual," and held up the bundle. "Here are the bread trenchers from supper. A kitchen-tribute to our skill."

"They'll be our breakfast," Rose said. "Put them in the kitchen box, will you?" While Joliffe did, she added to Piers, "Bed for you now. Nor will it hurt you either, Gil, to be off your ankle."

Gil at least was past the age to be told his bedtime, but both he and Piers went so readily that Joliffe suspected they were looking on it as escape, as if maybe afraid Ellis' guilt would somehow rub off on them and they wanted to be away before they suffered for it.

Joliffe was half-minded to escape, too, but that would leave only Basset, and after putting the bundle of trenchers in the kitchen box, he hunched down on his heels beside the fire next to Basset, who was still standing with his hands out to the warmth. Joliffe put his hands toward it, too, watching the flames rather than looking up at Rose standing on the fire's other side, her arms now wrapped around herself. The silence among them might have been comfortable but it was not, only better than Rose asking in a small, tight voice when all had been quiet in the tent for a while, "Where's Ellis?"

Joliffe very carefully went on looking at the fire. He had conscience enough not to desert Basset but left it to him to say, after a fatal pause, "He stayed behind. He needed to—" Knowing whatever he said was going to be painful or a lie, he paused, then settled for feeble and said, "—to talk with someone."

"With a woman," Rose said bitterly. "Nor is it talking they're doing."

Joliffe knew as well as Basset did that she had not needed to ask where Ellis was. She'd known. What she had needed was to say that aloud, even if saying it did not lessen the pain. That the pain was familiar did nothing to lessen it either, and Basset, in useless urge to ease her hurt, said a little desperately, "You know him. You know how it is. You know . . ."

"I know why he does it," she snapped, maybe as angry at her hurt as she was at Ellis, Joliffe thought. "What I don't understand is why he *has* to. You never do. Why must he?"

Basset held off his answer for a long moment before finally saying carefully, "Rose, I had your mother's love and whole heart, and she had mine. After that, to have less isn't bearable. If I could find the same—no, there'll never be the same, but if I found something like to it—that would be different. But to settle for less . . . no."

"Then tell me, why is Ellis able to make do with less?" Rose demanded.

Basset hesitated again. Seeming to be looking only at the fire, Joliffe was watching them both, sorry for their mutual pain, unable to help. And finally Basset answered gently, "Rose, it's different with every man, surely, but I think with Ellis it comes down to he's able to make do with less because he's never had a whole heart and a full love given to him."

"I can't give him more than I do!" Rose cried softly, mindful of Piers and Gil too nearby in the tent but angry with her pain. "I shouldn't give him even what I do. We shouldn't even have what we have! But I do love him. With my whole heart I love him. But I can't . . . we shouldn't . . ." She broke off, choking on tears she did not mean to shed.

Quickly, trying for comfort, Basset said, "I know. Ellis knows. It's just that sometimes . . . sometimes knowing isn't enough."

"No," Rose agreed sharply and suddenly her tears seemed gone a deadly distance away. "Sometimes knowing is *not* enough. Not for me any more than for Ellis. Which might be something he'd better start to think on if he doesn't want to lose me altogether. Now you'd both do well to go to bed. No, I'll see to the fire," she added at Joliffe as he moved to bank it for the night. "Just go."

Willing to escape, Joliffe stood up quickly and started away with Basset, then turned back and said with attempted lightness, "If it helps, Rose, just think that it's a lack of wits with Ellis rather than a lack of love."

From where she was laying turf onto the coals, Rose snapped back at him, "You've no place to talk. You do as much as he does when you have the chance, meaning you must lack wits, too."

"Ah, there's a difference," Joliffe returned. "I have no one woman all my own to love the way he does, do I?"

"True," Rose granted tartly. She lifted her head, her face mostly in shadow but with enough upward cast of low red light from the dying fire for him to see her bitter smile. "God in his mercy has spared some poor woman *that* misery."

Joliffe clutched a hand over his heart as if she had given him a hard blow there, said lightly, "Well struck, my lady. Well struck," and ducked to safety in the tent.

Chapter 4

The morning was cool, with mist writhed thickly along the stream and thinly across the meadow, so that both the fire—roused from its banked coals into flames again—and the hearty breakfast of last night's trenchers were welcome. More welcome than Ellis was, that was sure.

He had come back sometime in the night. His settling into his blankets had disturbed Joliffe's sleep only a little, and if anyone else awoke, they had said no more to him than Joliffe did. The trouble was that this morning there was still no one speaking to him. It wasn't anger on the men's part, merely wariness. None of them wanted to find himself between Ellis and whatever anger Rose had stored against him.

That Ellis brought a defiant strut to the morning did not help. Nor did Joliffe by saying aside to Basset, just loud enough for both Ellis and Gil to hear, "Being cock of the walk doesn't keep the cockerel out of the stew pot when the time comes."

That earned him a glare from both Ellis and Basset,

while Gil had to turn laughter into a choking cough that brought him a sharp look from Rose as if maybe considering him for a dose of hot honey water. But she kept to her stiff silence as she saw to her morning work with no look at all—so far as Joliffe saw—at Ellis, who in his turn seemed in no hurry to have her "see" him.

They all knew she could keep in that silence for hours, and if everyone was fortunate, she would, for her own sake as well as Ellis', Joliffe thought, because better cold silence than hot words that could not be taken back when the anger was gone.

It was while they were gathered about the fire, taking turns at toasting their shares of the trenchers and passing around the leather bottle of ale, that Ellis broke under the strain of her silence and said somewhat too loudly and too near defiantly, "I learned a few things last night."

Hard though it was, Joliffe held back from saying, She must have been good; I thought you knew it all.

Ellis, oblivious, went on, "I found out there's bad blood between the Ashewells and the Medcotes. Bad blood as in murder."

That got him looked at by everyone save Rose, who went on tending to the trencher presently toasting as if he had said nothing at all.

A little lessened by that, Ellis said, "Or a chance-death anyway. Not outright murder, like. Young Nicholas Ashewell killed the cousin of Medcote's wife a few years back, when he was nine years old or thereabouts."

"When Nicholas was nine years old?" Basset asked. "That's young to have been killing someone."

"Seems he was out birding with a small crossbow, bird-shooting along the stream here, the way boys do. This cousin happened by, just riding the bounds of his land that meet up with Ashewell's not far off, and took a birding-bolt just under one collarbone."

"That was a killing wound?" Joliffe said. "From a birding-bolt?"

"He didn't die right off. Seems he must have been bleeding inwardly, though. He died of a sudden a few days later, just when it was thought he was on the mend."

"It would have been manslaughter more than murder," Basset said. "And Nicholas was over-young to be tried, yes? He must have got his pardon," it being usual for a child who killed someone to be arrested but afterward to have the king's pardon, being below the years of discretion when a person could be held to account for their acts. Unless deliberate malice could be proven, of course.

"He was pardoned surely and no trouble about it," Ellis said. "He ran for help as soon as he saw what he'd done. No one thought there was intent about it. Hasn't made for friendlihood between the Ashewells and Medcotes, though." Ellis gave a short snort. "Should have, you'd think. It was by way of the cousin dying that Medcote's wife inherited the manor here, being the nearest heir. Before then, Medcote kept a butchering place in Wantage. Had no land at all. Now he holds a manor. Not that he and his much liked. There's those that still call him Butcher John behind his back."

This was the kind of talk that could help in finding out the things for which Lady Lovell had sent them here, and Basset prompted, "He's not liked?"

"Not him or his wife or their son or their daughter," Ellis said, pleased with himself. "Medcote takes a high hand with everything, and like we've heard, he and that priest tend to work as one in most things, with Father Hewgo no better liked than he is, from what Titha says. She says all that makes it odd that . . ." Realizing he should have named no names, he stopped short, too late, as Rose snapped the long-handled toasting fork toward him, flipping the trencher at him so that he had to catch it or be hit in the chest. He did catch it but had to juggle it, hot and greasy, from hand to hand, protesting while he did, "Hai! What's that for?"

That was another stupid thing to say, Joliffe thought, but fortunately for Ellis, Rose did not trouble to answer as Basset hurriedly asked, "Makes it odd what?"

With the bread now in one hand, Ellis left off sucking the sore, greasy fingers of his other one to say sullenly, "That maybe Medcote wants to marry his daughter to Nicholas Ashewell, and Master Ashewell is maybe thinking to do it."

From what he had seen yesterday, Joliffe would not have thought there was that kind of liking between the men, but it was Basset who said doubtfully, "That's several 'maybes' there."

Ellis shrugged. "Ashewell's been heard saying something about it to his wife, and she's been downcast of late, and Nicholas, too, as if maybe he's been told and doesn't like it either."

"It's servant-talk then, this maybe-marriage?" Basset asked, not disparaging it for that. Servant-talk was often the surest way for the players to learn what was likely to sit well in a household they were to play for and, as importantly, what might *not* sit well.

"Servant-talk," Ellis agreed, "and not meant for them or anyone to know, seems like. That's the feel I had from . . ." Far too late he saw the peril in what he had been about to say and shifted to, ". . . it," with a wary sideways look at Rose.

Rose, still giving him no look at all, left the fire, picked up the water bucket, and walked away toward the stream, eloquently leaving them all behind her in a shared silence of guilt.

Which wasn't fair, Joliffe wanted to protest—*he* hadn't done anything. But likely at this moment just being men was enough to damn them all in Rose's eyes.

"Go help your mother," Basset said to Piers.

Throwing a baleful look at Ellis, Piers scrambled to his

feet and went, making clear on whose side he was, and it wasn't Ellis'.

For his part, Ellis looked ready to take refuge in sullenness, probably beginning to feel as wronged as Rose did. In hope of heading that off, Joliffe said to Basset, "You think this could be the trouble the bailiff hasn't been able to put his finger on?"

"I'd guess it's likely," Basset granted. "It's something to keep our ears out for, anyway."

"If the Ashewells don't like the thought," Gil said, "why can't Master Ashewell just say no to the offer and there's an end?"

"A good question," Joliffe said.

"If I was asked," said Basset, "I'd have thought a marriage between young Nicholas and that Gosyn's girl more likely, what with the families looking so friendly together yesterday."

"That's what Titha said, too," Ellis said. "Seems that's what most people have thought. More than that, a marriage to Medcote's girl would do Ashewell's friendship with Gosyn no good. Gosyn is on the outs with Medcote over sheep-grazing rights hereabouts. Medcote got the lease Gosyn has had for years. Out-bid for it to the abbey's steward and took it right out from under Gosyn. So there's bad blood there."

"You must not have been much use to Titha if she did all this talking," Joliffe said.

Ellis bristled. "I was use enough. It was between whiles of it that we talked."

"Oh, 'whiles of it,'" Joliffe baited. "What time was it you crawled to your bed, anyway?"

"Leave off, Joliffe," Basset said, too used to them both to rise even to irk about it. "Ellis, what else did she have to tell?"

"What more do you want?" Ellis protested. "There's an

old murder between the Ashewells and Medcotes. Medcote maybe wants a marriage that maybe Ashewell doesn't. Gosyn and Ashewell are friendly. Gosyn and Medcote aren't. That's something more than anyone else of you has gathered."

"What about the priest?" Basset asked. "How does he figure into it all?"

"Not as a peacemaker, I'll warrant," said Joliffe.

"You don't much talk of priests at a time like Titha and I were having," Ellis said. Boasted. "There was only what she said about him and Medcote, and that we knew already. So. Is all that enough to satisfy this bailiff that we've done as Lady Lovell asked? Will it clear us of the business, do you think?"

Basset sat staring at the fire, rubbing the knuckles of one hand while answering slowly, "That Gosyn is angry over losing the grazing rights can't be a secret to anyone. The marriage business, though, that's something, since it seems Ashewell and Medcote are trying to keep it to themselves. That could well be what the bailiff was hearing rumbles of. Yes, Ellis, you may have done our duty for us. If we chance to hear more while we're here, well and good. If we don't, what you've brought us should serve well enough to go on with. Well done."

"Which is what I trust Titha said to him, too," Joliffe said.

"Leave off with her," Ellis snapped.

Basset clapped his hands down on his knees and went on briskly, "But we're still here for three more days and have yet to decide what we'll do for the church ale."

"Something short, sweet, and easy," Ellis said.

"I don't know," Basset said thoughtfully. "I'm still thinking on it."

Uneasy at what Basset might be thinking, Joliffe said,

"Whatever we do, we'll probably have little thanks from Father Hewwwwgo for it."

Ellis snapped, "Leave off with the 'Hewwwgo,' too, will you?"

"That was probably the other thing Titha said," Joliffe grinned, and added in a shrill girl's voice, " 'Leave off, Ellis.' "

Ellis looked around for something to throw.

Not waiting for him to find it, Joliffe went to see how Tisbe did.

If Basset had not already planned for them to do more than be about camp all day, he would probably have come up with the thought now, as much to have Ellis away from Rose for the day as any other reason. As it was, he shortly announced that he and Ellis, Joliffe, and Piers should be on their way to Faringdon, to play at places along the way and there to draw folk to Sunday's church ale. "The more there, the merrier," he said.

"The more there, the larger our share of the take at the day's end," said Ellis.

Gil started to protest, "Why can't I . . ."

Basset stopped him with, "No, Gil. You're not coming. Your ankle can do with that much more mending since there's chance for it, and the cart and all shouldn't be left to only Rose the day long. We'll only be doing our lighter street work anyway. The juggling and suchlike, to draw people's heed and laughter and leave them wanting more, so they'll come on Sunday."

Given no choice, Gil watched, disgruntled, while Ellis, Joliffe, and Piers changed into their bright, parti-colored playing garb and Basset put on his Lovell tabard, and set out, with Rose waving good-bye to at least Basset, Joliffe, and Piers. As soon as Ellis raised his hand with the others to wave back, she dropped her own hand and turned away.

Aside from that, it was a fine spring day. The mist was already gone, the morning sky lightly fretted with white clouds, the sun just clearing the tops of the hedgerows that seemed more green and open-leaved than they had yesterday. The thumb-sized daisies were thicker than ever in the wayside grasses, white stitchwort and red campion were blooming, and plovers were sweeping and calling over the ploughed fields. There was a warm heaviness to the fitful wind that made Joliffe suspect there would be rain before the day was done, but weather was something about which—like so much in life—he could do nothing except enjoy it, endure it, or ignore it. The rain would come or it would not, and meanwhile he had the pleasure of the kind of day when he remembered why he had left behind the other possibilities his life had held—of settled work and certain livelihood, of daily roof and walls and meals—for the one he had instead and presently would have changed for no other.

Mind you, if the weather turned back to cold and wet and the tent leaked tonight and his feet began to hurt, he would surely feel differently, but he was not such a fool as to let that knowing spoil the moment as it was.

At one place and another along the way to Faringdon, Ellis and Piers did brief juggling, Joliffe sang short and usually bawdy songs while playing on his lute, and Basset announced the church ale and promised a play. A few times Joliffe caught a grumble about "that priest and his money-getting ways," but the promise of a play seemed to outweigh any dislike of Father Hewgo. The miles went easily and they reached Faringdon on its hill a little past noontide, when people were just starting back to work from their dinners or else to the afternoon's shopping and either way were ready to stop a while and be entertained.

This far from Ashewell and no longer in its parish, Joliffe heard only welcoming cheers and nothing about Father Hewgo when Basset declared their business, nor were people

behindhand in dropping coins in the bag Piers offered them.
As usual he made use of his wide blue eyes and fair curls to
charm women into pity for his plight as a poor little boy
a-wander in the world in need of care and mothering. That
seemed always good for extra coins, but Joliffe was already
seeing a few years ahead to when the trouble Ellis now gave
them would be nothing to the havoc Piers was likely to
cause when he could do more than look winsomely at
women.

From many other times, the players knew that, gaudily
dressed as they were, sitting down in a tavern or anywhere
else to eat and drink rarely went well, and they waited
while Basset shed his tabard and went to buy the bread and
other things Rose had asked him to fetch back, then went
all together, following their noses, into a side street off the
marketplace to a bakeshop where they bought meat pasties
both to eat as they headed back to camp and for supper.

Leaving the bakeshop, they went on along the street,
knowing it would take them back to the road out of town. In
the lead, Basset shifted aside to make way for a woman going the other way, leading a small boy-child by the hand, a
market basket on her other arm. She was dressed in the good
brown gown and white wimple and veil of a tradesman's re-
spectable wife, and the players, following Basset's lead,
stepped aside, all of them bending their heads to her in re-
spectful, wordless greeting. Slowed by the child dragging at
her hand while staring at the strange-garbed men, she bent
her own head in return while briefly but not boldly looking
at them, too. Only as her gaze passed across Joliffe, coming
behind the others, did her eyes widen and her steps falter.

Joliffe's steps more than faltered.

With memory sweeping through him of a warm Sep-
tember night and the scent of wild thyme on a hillside, he
stopped where he was and said, before he could think to do
otherwise, "Mary?"

She stopped, too, smiling so warmly that her memory of that night must be as sweet as his own. "Joliffe. You remember."

Both gallant and truthful, he said, "A memory as sweet as that one will keep me company to my dying day."

But the next moment his mind caught up to the fact there was a boy-child staring up at him from her side, and sweet memory was overlaid by a desperate attempt to judge how old the boy was.

His thoughts' rush must have shown on his face because Mary laughed her lovely laugh—he had remembered her laugh was lovely—and said, "This is James." She paused, her look teasing Joliffe, before she added, "He'll be four years old come St. Bartholomew's. I've been happily wed to a good man these five years."

And it had been six years since the players had last been this way, Joliffe remembered and tried not to let his relief show, but she laughed at him again and this time he laughed with her. Moonlight and her lovely laughter and her generous loving. That's what he remembered of Mary.

Basset, Ellis, and Piers had kept walking and there was no one else near. Quickly, while there was chance, Joliffe asked, "All's well with you?"

"Very well. And with you?"

He made a small, flourished gesture. "As you see," he said lightly. "Much the same."

But it was into his eyes she went on looking and said gently, still smiling, "I see."

And then there was nothing else to say between them that mattered or would make different what was.

He said, "We're Lord Lovell's players now."

And she said, "You'll pass our shop farther along the street here. A cordwainer's on the left." Her child tugged at her hand, impatient to be going, and she gave way to him with one last smile at Joliffe, and went her way.

And Joliffe went his and did not look back and doubted she did either.

No promises had ever been asked, made, or expected between them the little while they had had together. There had been need on both sides, then pleasure, then parting. What they had given between them had been given unburdened by afterward-demands for more on either side, so that what had been between them had stayed whole, a moment complete and enough in itself.

At least that was how it had been for him, and now he thought it had been that way for her, too.

He lengthened his stride, overtaking Basset, Ellis, and Piers just as they passed a prosperous-looking cordwainer's shop where various well-made shoes and gloves and purses were laid out on the shopboard for display. Joliffe looked but caught no glimpse of its owner, and that was probably just as well, he thought as he kept on going.

Tired from the morning's work, the players did little but walk on their way back to camp. Piers sometimes plucked a daisy from the wayside to chew the sharp-tasting stems, but for the rest of them walking was enough, until almost back to Grescumb Field, when Piers ran ahead to tell his mother and Gil the others were coming; and, with him away, Ellis said suddenly and aggrieved, "Rose still loves me or she'd not care so much what I do," sounding as if it were something he had been thinking on and had to say out.

"She still loves you so much," Joliffe said back, "that she'll likely grieve when you're dead because she's stuck a knife into you the way she did that bread this morning."

"Let's just hope she does it here," Basset said, "with nobody to see it happen and good places to bury your body among the trees afterward."

Ellis had probably hoped for better than that from them and started to say something in answer, but they were at the gateway and neither Basset nor Joliffe paused to give him chance. He had to close his mouth and follow them word-less into the field, where Rose and Gil were seated on cush-ions on the ground near the cart, Rose with sewing on her lap, Gil with one of the script-rolls of a play. Piers was sit-ting cross-legged on the ground in front of them both, telling how the day had gone. Joliffe, likewise ready to sit, made for one of the other cushions, while Rose put aside her sewing and stood up, lightly touching the top of Piers' head on her way to see what Basset had brought back. Piers went on talking at Gil. Joliffe dropped down and closed his eyes with a satisfied sigh at being off his feet. Basset, hand-ing the food over to Rose, was started telling her what they'd brought back but broke off mid-word, paused, then asked in an altogether different way, "Rose, what is it? What's hap-pened?"

Joliffe opened his eyes. Saw Ellis spin around from where he had been leaning into the back of the cart for something and Gil start getting slowly to his feet. Saw, too, the look that Gil and Rose traded with each other before Rose answered her father with, "Medcote and his son were here while you were gone. They want you to play for their household tonight. I said you would. He's told me the way to there from here."

There was nothing in that to be angry about but there was anger in her words. And fear. Joliffe heard it, and that was maybe what Basset had seen in her face, because he said, sounding angry himself now, "That isn't all. What else happened?"

Another look passed between Rose and Gil. Had they meant to tell whatever it was? Joliffe wondered. But it was too late to keep their secret, and with anger as plain as Rose's, Gil started, "It was Medcote. He was . . ."

"No!" Rose ordered at him. "It's mine to tell." She faced her father squarely and said, "After I told him you'd gladly play for his household tonight, he turned over-bold.

Gil was gone to the stream for water, so Medcote thought I was alone. He asked if I ever 'played.' He said that, traveling with so many men, I must surely know all manner of 'play.' He told me he'd like to see my 'play,' and that if I were generous to him, he'd be generous to me. In more ways than one, he said. And his son sat there on his horse looking ready to laugh and take his turn if it came."

Ellis started toward her with a furious oath, adding, "If either of them laid a hand on you . . ."

Rose turned on him with a fury to match his own. "What business is it of yours if anyone did?" Ellis stopped as short as if she had hit him, and she turned back to her father, saying, still fierce, "It went no further. It might have. I don't know. But Gil came back and they rode away."

Gil, standing with clenched fists, said, "I should have . . ."

"You should have done just what you did," Rose said. "Nothing. There was nothing for you to do. They left." She added to Basset, "I'm sorry. I meant to keep it to myself, not make trouble about it. But . . ." She faltered and the fierceness went out of her. "I was frightened," she said softly; and Basset held out his arms and she went into them.

For a long moment they held to each other, both of them needing assurance that she was safe. Ellis looked at them for a helpless moment, then turned and stalked away toward the stream, out of sight among the trees. Joliffe realized his own hands were as tightly clenched as Gil's and carefully unfolded them before just as carefully asking, "So, do we play for the Medcotes anyway?"

On a little choked laugh, Rose stepped back from Basset's hold. He did not fully let her go, held to one of her arms to keep her near him, and asked, "Should we, Rose? Or should we stay right away and be-damn them?"

Rose lifted her chin. Dry-eyed and firm, she said,

"There's never a time not to play if someone wants it and is willing to pay."

"Don't go saying my own words back to me," Basset complained, trying to make light of it.

Rose smiled. "You've no one to blame but yourself if I do. No, I won't have more made of it than I already have, and it's been foolish of me to make so much. Of course you'll play for them tonight. It's not our place to feud with our betters."

" 'Betters,' " Gil muttered. "Not nearly."

Joliffe wondered if there had been more that Gil had seen and Rose was not telling, but aloud he only said lightly, "What if we do *Susanna and the Elders*? That would suit." The biblical story of a woman refusing her favors to two men who then accused her of unchastity, wanting her dead but earning their own deaths instead.

"Joliffe!" Rose protested, while Basset said dryly, "We'll give them *Robin and Marian*, just like we did the Ashewells. Then no one can claim we gave one family a better play than we gave the other, and we'll not be sucked into whatever contentions there are between them."

Besides that, thought Joliffe, there would be particular pleasure in making, in front of Medcote, the Evil Sheriff "pay with his life" for laying hands on Marian.

Chapter 5

With thought that they would be paid at least with supper for their work, the players ate lightly before setting off to walk the mile or so to Medcote's manor. Because Medcote had told Rose the way, they were spared the need to go by way of the village to ask it, meaning they were spared, too, the risk of encountering Father Hewgo—no small matter to Joliffe's mind. The only part that probably none of them liked was leaving Rose behind alone. It was no one's place but Basset's to say so, though. Or else Rose's. Joliffe pretended not to see Basset in close talk with her not long before they left, but Ellis watched openly and scowled fiercely when Rose shook her head against whatever Basset was saying.

Ellis knew better than to say anything for her to hear, but he was still scowling when they left her, and as soon as they were far enough along the lane, going opposite the way to the Ashewells, he demanded angrily of Basset, "Should we be leaving her there?"

More calmly than Joliffe suspicioned he felt, Basset said,

"As Rose said when I asked her, someone should stay with the cart and Tisbe and all, and who is there but her to do it?"

Ellis growled something unclearly under his breath.

"She also said she would keep the iron skillet to hand while we were gone," Basset added. "Besides, Medcote will be right where we are."

"And if he isn't," Joliffe said, "we'll be back to Rose so fast the dust won't have settled behind us before we're there."

Ellis growled again, plainly not satisfied, then said, "Medcote *and* his son. I didn't like the look of either of them."

"Yes," Joliffe said thoughtfully. "The son was the better looking of the two, wasn't he? And younger. He might not have the trouble his father did . . ."

He sidestepped well beyond Ellis' reach even before Ellis started to clout at his head. Basset, with much the same sharp impatience he would have used at Piers, said, "Stop it. The both of you. And you more than Ellis, Joliffe."

Joliffe hung his head in pretended penance and scuffed his feet along the road like Piers in a sulk. That brought the grins he had wanted from at least Gil and Piers, but Ellis muttered something fortunately not clearly heard and stalked onward, saying nothing else the rest of their way.

Where the lane crossed another, wider lane between fields, they turned left, toward the Downs, the lane soon beginning to rise with the first lift of the valley toward hills. Sight of the White Horse came and went between hedges until the land briefly leveled below its hill and they came to the wide highroad that ran east to west along the valley's length and beyond, set between the Vale and the steep rise of the Downs. Joliffe's guess was that, although the Horse was ages old, the road must have been there even longer, with the Horse made to be seen by travelers passing by.

Going left where the lane met the road would have

taken them into Ashewell village from another side than they had come yesterday, but they turned right and soon came to a gateway that, if they had been told rightly, must be Medcote's. A man slouched against one gatepost watching them approach straightened and stepped into their way as they neared him, asking, "You're the players?"

For all the welcome he put in that, he might have been asking if they were the dung cart.

Basset, too used to the many ways players could be greeted, smiled, swept off his hat, and bowed lower than the man surely deserved. "We are, good sir, and ask your leave to enter."

The man frowned. By his good doublet, he was more than merely a servant here but apparently was as unused to receiving courtesy as giving it. "Come in then," he said and walked off toward the hall at one end of the yard beyond the gate, saying over his shoulder as he went, "They're somewhat overheated in the hall tonight. Whatever you're going to play, it had best be good."

"We're Lord Lovell's players," Basset said, weighting the words enough to make them both a sufficient answer and reminder that courtesy for courtesy was therefore called for. As he had said often enough to the company, even in the straitened years before becoming Lord Lovell's men, "No one is going to value us at our own worth unless we let them understand we have some worth."

In one of his black humours Ellis had challenged, "Even if we have none?" And Basset had fixed a mocking gaze on him and answered back, "We're going to be looked down on steeply enough by most folk without we make it worse by believing them. We can at least *seem* to have worth. If we *seem* it well enough, they'll believe it and then we *will* have worth." Then he had grinned and added, "If nothing else, there's small use in letting them get away with counting us less than need be if we can fool them to otherwise."

And now they were Lord Lovell's men and so had their lord's worth to uphold as well as their own, and Basset lengthened his stride to fall into step beside the man as they crossed the yard, rather than letting him lead them all like a shepherd with a flock of idiot sheep. A little less friendly, beginning to go lofty on the man, he asked, "And you, sir, are . . . ?"

That seemed to take the fellow by surprise. He hesitated, looking as if he were about to settle for merely glowering, then gave way and admitted, "Lynche. I'm steward here."

And if the rest of the household was as down-faced and unfriendly, playing for them would have all the pleasure of pulling one's own teeth, Joliffe thought.

From an even greater height of dignity than before, Basset said, "Before we play, we need somewhere to put on our garb and somewhere to leave our goods safely."

The man eyed him sideways with a look that suggested they were getting no such things if he could help it. Basset eyed him right back.

Joliffe, for his part, was eyeing what he could see of Medcote's manor. It was older than Ashewell's and somewhat larger, its house and its hall of middle size and built of gray stone with blue slate roofs. The rest of the buildings around the yard were of timber and wattle and plastered daub, with here and there a need of new plastering and the thatch gone gray with age, but all and all a place not so much ill-kept as simply old and maybe beginning to sink under the heavy weight of its own years.

Lynche's heaviness was weighing, too, Joliffe thought. The man had brought them, grudgingly, to a little square yard cramped between the end of the hall and the kitchen building with a penticed walkway between the two. Already deeply in shadow between the buildings, it was an

unwelcoming place, meant for passage and nothing else. A
youth, who by his looks was near kin to the steward, was
just passing from the hall toward the kitchen, carrying a
large, covered platter. Lynche asked him, "They're nigh to
finished, then?"

The youth scowled at the players while answering,
"They are. Just the custard tart and fruit left."

With a nod at the yard, Lynche said at Basset, "You'd
best be quick about it, then."

"Here," Basset said flatly, stating, not questioning.

"Here," Lynche agreed.

"And our hamper while we play?"

"You'll have to take it in with you, won't you?"

The man's stare challenged Basset to protest that. Basset gave him a grim little smile in agreement. "If you'll
leave us, we'll make ready."

The youth went on to the kitchen, and Lynche paced
away to stand next to the side door to the hall, making it
plain he meant to go no farther, as if there might be something in the bare little yard for the players to steal.

Refusing to show themselves in the least bothered, they
set to changing, but as they gathered around the hamper for
Piers to hand out their garb to each of them, Basset said
low-voiced to Joliffe, "You have him?"

"I have him," Joliffe answered.

Piers smothered a small laugh.

Ellis, more grim by the moment, said, "Just the play,
nothing else, right?"

"Just the play," Basset said. "Besides all else, I'm thinking we'll be fortunate to be tossed a farthing when we're
done. Not if it's master-like-man here."

"Supper isn't likely either, is it?" Gil said regretfully.

No one bothered to agree, all of them being too sure he
was right. He had been with them long enough now to

know the feel of a place and judge how welcome or unwelcome they were going to be. Not that this place was that hard to read, with Lynche glowering at them from the doorway.

Willing to oblige him by being finished and gone as soon as might be, they wasted no time in changing. That done, Basset and Ellis picked up the hamper and Basset nodded to Joliffe. Joliffe nodded back, swung around, and led them in small procession toward the steward. He eyed them with no more favor than he had before, turned away, and led them inside without a word.

The hall was much like Ashewell's for size but altogether a darker place, with smaller windows and the thickness of the stone walls lessening the setting sunlight. Candles were already lit and set along the table at the hall's far end, but the tables that ranged down both sides were in gray shadows. It was only by good luck that where the players would play in the hall's middle was still in a final shaft of sunlight. It would be gone before they finished, but that was beyond their help and all the more reason to make quick work of everything, Joliffe thought as he followed the steward a few yards into the hall, stopped, and took his arrogant stand as the Sheriff. Behind him, Gil and Piers would be taking their stands, too, and Basset and Ellis be setting down the hamper against the wall beside the doorway before joining them.

Not needing to see what they were doing, Joliffe looked up the hall's length instead, to the two men and two women behind the high table. John Medcote and his son, Hal, with the older woman likely Medcote's wife, the younger probably Hal's, since she was wimpled and veiled like the older woman, showing she was married. He wondered where this daughter meant for Nicholas Ashewell was, but had no time to look for her elsewhere in the hall because the steward, as grudgingly as if every word were costing him money, was declaring for everyone there to hear, "The players."

His unpleasant duty done, he stalked to the aside. Joliffe strode forward to where he had been, and there were small snorts of laughter among the household at the tables along either side. At the high table, Hal laughed aloud and the younger woman put a quick hand over her mouth to smother her own laughter. Medcote cast them a frowning look, not seeing the jest, but Joliffe was satisfied. Enough of the lookers-on had caught his unerring match of the steward's stiff-legged, self-satisfied stride that for the next few days there would be laughter behind the man's back every time someone saw him.

It was a small revenge, but a small revenge was better than none. Joliffe only wished he could do as much for Medcote.

Then he had no time for thought of anything but surviving the play, because as soon as Ellis began his first speech to Gil, Joliffe knew they were in trouble. Ellis always and rightly played Robin boldly and fought the Evil Sheriff fiercely. Tonight, though, he was fierce from the beginning. That was warning he was forgetting to be Robin, was staying Ellis, and was still furious at the Medcotes. Forewarned, Joliffe was still almost not ready enough when the fight between Robin and the Evil Sheriff came, and Ellis came at him with a fury just short of uncontrolled. Every stroke and guard and move of the fight was planned, meant to be the same every time they played it, and Ellis did at least keep to the pattern, but his sword-blows were delivered with a force that had Joliffe really defending against them. He was worried, too, for Basset and Gil when Robin spun around and thrust for the kill to save Marian from the Sheriff's Henchman. Done wrongly, there could be injury, but Joliffe had no time to know how it went as Ellis spun back on him to finish their fight. He was merely grateful the "killing blow" went under his arm as it should and he could cry out, stagger, fall down, and be done with it.

His death was met with cheers and the last speeches between Ellis and Marian were followed by welcome table-pounding and hand-clapping from the lookers-on. Basset and Joliffe rose from the dead to take their bows with Ellis, Gil, and Piers, before they all went out together, "Robin" and "Marian" hand in hand, Basset and Joliffe picking up the hamper, Piers coming last, throwing himself into a series of backward somersaults and ending with walking out of the hall on his hands, feet in the air, to more clapping.

Lynche did not follow them out, probably supposing that now they knew which corner of the yard was "theirs" and he need waste no more time on them. That left Basset free to turn on Ellis as soon as they were into the yard and alone and say furiously, "What were you doing in there? You carried on as if you'd never been in a set-fight before. It's none of us you're angry at!"

Determinedly busy ridding himself of Robin's garb and looking at none of them, Ellis muttered, "It was seeing them. The Medcotes. Sitting there. After what they tried."

"That should have made no difference to your playing, and you well know it!" Basset poked him in the upper arm with a stiff forefinger. "Whatever we're—any of us—feeling or thinking about our own lives, it stops when once we start to play. Once we start to play, the play is where you are and nowhere else until it's over. You do *not* take out on us what you want to take out on someone else. Now tell Joliffe you're sorry."

Joliffe readily supposed that Ellis would rather have been beaten with a stick—a large stick—than apologize, but Basset had not offered him that choice, and grudgingly, still not looking at anyone, Ellis muttered, "I'm sorry, Joliffe."

Joliffe, knowing now was not the time to make any scoffs, muttered back that it had ended well so no matter.

"Heads up," said Gil in quiet warning from the far side

of the hamper where he was folding their garb and putting it away.

Joliffe looked aside to where the two women who had been at the high table were just coming from the hall into the yard. Seeing them more closely, he shifted his guess about them. Though the younger was the taller by half a head and more sturdily built, there was enough the same in their sharp-boned faces for them to be mother and daughter; and indeed the older woman said as the players straightened from their low bows, "I'm Anela Medcote. This is my daughter, Eleanor. We've come with our thanks and payment for your playing."

She held out her hand toward Basset, who stepped quickly toward her to take the several coins she gave him, bowing to her again and saying, "It's worth the more, coming from your fair hand."

Anela Medcote gave him a sharp look. Her daughter said with equal sharpness but a hint of laughter under the words, "Certainly better than having it from Lynche's hand." She had been looking among the players and now said at Joliffe, "You must have been the Sheriff. I'd be well away from here before someone tells Lynche you mocked him."

"Mocked him, my lady?" Joliffe said, raising his eyebrows in innocence and surprise. "Whoever might think that surely mistakes."

"They surely don't," Hal said with smiling ease, coming into the yard behind his mother and sister. "It was plain as anything."

The players bowed to him, but as soon as they were done, Ellis turned away and became busy rearranging garb and properties in the hamper. For his own part, Joliffe smiled back at Hal and said, "Then I must only hope that no one tells him."

"Hal probably already has," Eleanor said. "Haven't you, Hal?"

"I may have mentioned it on my way to protect my mother and widowed sister from the scandal of being with strange men unattended."

Eleanor looked both pointedly and scornfully around at the open yard, hardly the place for making scandal, with servants starting to pass back to the kitchen with the supper's dishes, while her mother said impatiently, "Oh, Hal, don't be a fool. Your father sent me to pay them and you know it."

"But here's my young and sadly widowed sister," Hal said. "Ready to have her head turned by such rascals, poor innocent that she is."

He reached out and tweaked her cheek as she tried to duck away and had to settle for slapping his hand aside, hopefully hard enough to hurt, as she snapped, "My late, unlamented husband was sufficient to put me off men a while, thank you." She was her brother's height and not a dainty woman and did not bother to hide that she was angry. As well she should be, Joliffe thought, seeing the red mark on her cheek where Hal had twisted it.

"Eleanor," her mother said, not in surprise but in warning. At such open talk or against provoking her brother further? Joliffe wondered.

Over his mother's warning Hal said, still goading, "You chose him, Eleanor. He was your choice."

"I chose him instead of another beating from Father," she snapped back.

"That's *enough*," Anela Medcote ordered, whip-sharp and stone-hard, silencing them both long enough for her to turn to the players and say somewhat more stiffly than before, "Again, our thanks. I look forward to Sunday."

They all bowed to her again, including Ellis, who had given up on the hamper to watch the quarrel, and Basset said, "It's been our pleasure to serve you."

Anela Medcote nodded her gracious belief of that and

left them, taking hold of Hal's arm as she passed him to draw him away with her and gathering Eleanor with a look to follow them. Eleanor did, saying just loudly enough— and still angrily—that Joliffe heard her as well as her mother must have, "I should have taken the beating."

Ellis slammed shut the lid of the hamper, Piers and Gil leaped to fasten the straps that closed it, and Basset said, "Let's get out of here."

Chapter 6

They left the Medcotes' manor yard with more haste than grace. Not until they were well away along the highroad, almost to the turning to the downward lane, did Joliffe offer, "Would you say there's a family that doesn't like each other?"

"Or anybody else," Basset said.

"What were we paid?" Ellis asked.

"Four pence."

Ellis grunted, seemingly irked at not being able to disparage that. As such things went, that was a good wage for what they'd done. "So we've no complaint against the wife anyway."

Joliffe, gone elsewhere with his thoughts, asked, "Do you suppose that's the daughter Medcote wants to marry to young Nicholas?"

The others all gave him startled looks, but only Gil protested aloud, "No!" before Basset granted, "No one's talked as if there's more than one Medcote daughter. She must be it."

"She'll eat that boy alive," Ellis said.

"I liked her," Piers said stoutly.

"You would," Ellis said at him.

They had reached the turning to the lane. Joliffe stopped and said, "You go on. I'll catch you up later."

Ellis, carrying the hamper with Gil, nodded and kept going, taking Gil with him. Piers did not pause either, but Basset did, asking quietly, "Where will you be?"

Joliffe beckoned with his head toward the steep rise of the Downs. "Up there for a while."

The players were all used to Joliffe's sometime-need to be away and by himself. Basset gave him a nod and followed the others away, and Joliffe went on along the high-road until he found what he vaguely remembered should be there—a cart-track cut deep into the white chalk flank of the hillslope, leading upward between bramble-grown banks that had been covered with blackberries in the autumn he had last been here. He had picked and eaten them by the hand-fuls and their remembered sweetness was in his mouth now, though this was spring and the brambles were bare of anything but young green leaves.

It was good when memory brought back the sweetness there was in life and not just the sorrows.

The sun that had been almost set when they left Med-cote's manor was fully gone now and its yellow afterglow was draining down the sky. The light would last long enough to see Basset and the others back to the field, but the deep-worn trackway was already into thick twilight and Joliffe sure of his footing only because the white chalk showed pale in the shadows. He supposed that, like the White Horse and the highroad, this track must be ages old. It had probably been the way up to the wide circle of earthworks on the very crest of the hill above the Horse that were sup-posed to have been a Saxon fortress, though some said it was even older, had been made against the Romans, or that the Romans had made it against the Saxons. However it was, the track itself was surely old, to be worn as deep as it was into the hillside by cart-wheels and men's feet.

Joliffe always took odd companionship in the thought of all the others who had come along a way before him, and even in the thought of all the others who would come the same way after him. Even when alone in his going, as now, he was aware of them—of all those who had been and all those who would be on this way and all the other ways he had been over the years. A flow of folk going far back into times uncertain and forgotten and far forward beyond any years that he would see. A long wander and stream of people, and himself among them.

He wondered what happened to roads where no one came anymore. Did they grow sad with emptiness? Or did they sink into rest and relief at being no longer needed, no longer burdened with humankind's necessities?

The trackway forked, giving choice of going forward, on and up and over the crest of the Downs, or else by a lesser way out onto the open hillslope. Joliffe took the lesser way, climbing upward out of the trackway and passing through a stand of wind-bent trees to come to a stop at their outer edge to catch his breath and look ahead along the long, curving flank of the hill now bare before him. Full night had come. If any last band of sunset light remained, it was out of sight beyond the trees behind him. Here was only the soft blue darkness of a clear night under early starlight, with a slice of moon hanging above a far shoulder of the Downs. On his left the slope dropped steeply away into the velvet darkness of the Vale where, here and there, a pinpoint of light showed where a lantern hung or someone was late about their business. Here there was only the star-touched darkness, and he walked out onto the soft turf of the hillside. The short, sheep-cropped grass was smooth and springy underfoot and ahead of him was the White Horse, shining almost silver in the moonlight, stretched along its outward curve of hill.

Joliffe's thought was to go there, to sit on the green turf between its outstretched forelegs and the proud arch of its neck. Where he had sat with Mary through the end of that warm autumn afternoon six years ago.

The Scouring had been done that morning, the encroaching turf cleared back for another few years and the rest of the day given wholly over to the fair that went with it. From the hilltop the shouts and laughter and cheers from the races, greased pole climbing, wrestling, knife-throwing, and whatever other sports and contests there were, the happy raised voices among the booths selling food and nonsense, the cries and songs of those come to entertain among the crowd had come and gone as the warm wind went fitfully this way, then that. People, strayed from there, had been wandering over the hillside, many of them to the Horse, around the Horse, away from the Horse, as adrift and easily purposeless as the wind, but he and Mary had had their small part of the hillside to themselves.

They had both known what they wanted from each other. From the time she had brushed against him in the crowd on the hilltop and smiled at him and he had spoken to her, he had known she wanted what he did, but before they came to that, they had sat together there on the hillslope and talked. He did not remember how they had come to do that or much of what they'd said. They'd probably talked about the warm autumn and the good harvest. Maybe of where he and the players had lately come from and where they were likely going. Just talk, with no promises asked or given by either of them. She was a widow. He had learned that much about her. And her name, and that she was comely, young, and willing. That was all he had truly known of her, and except for what she had seen of him in the several plays the players had done that day, she had known no more of him either—his name and that he, too, was willing.

To say the least, he had been willing and all the more willing when he had understood that she was asking for nothing from him except a present pleasure, wanted no more from him than what they would have in this small while between them. Blessed St. Mary Magdalene, he had been young then. Gil's age maybe. Young enough, anyway, to think the body's momentary pleasure was all there was to having a woman. He had not even understood that when he had a woman, she likewise had him—that when the thrust and clutch were done, more was shared than only semen and sweat. However brief the meeting of their bodies, some piece of self was shared, too, a piece of self not to be reclaimed afterward.

But he had not known that then, and they had sat talking, had touched a little—her foot slipping sideways to touch his foot; his fingers briefly intertwining with hers on the grass—until the shadows had begun to lie long across the slope, and folk who were not going to go on sporting on the hilltop into the night by torchlight or did not have their camp there on the hilltop had begun to drift toward the trackway and downward to homes or wherever else they were going. The time was come and Joliffe had stood up, held down his hand for her to take and drawn her to her feet. Not into his arms. Not yet. Instead, she had kept hold on his hand and led him away from the Horse and the trackway, over the shoulder of hill and along the hillside's curve and down into a fold of the slope hidden from sight from above and both sides. The only view was outward, across the Vale far away below them and beginning to be lost in the shadows that were already deep in this small, hidden place.

There, finally, she had turned to him and they had drawn

together. Their first kiss had been careful, each holding back a little from the other. After it they had each drawn back a step, and Mary had begun unpinning her veil from the proper widow's wimple that circled her face. Joliffe had held her by the waist until veil and wimple were both off, baring her throat. Then he bent and kissed her neck. She had gasped softly, stiffening and shuddering with pleasure, and he drew back again, to take off the close-fitted cap still covering her hair, dropping it aside where she had already cast her veil and wimple, while she fumbled then at whatever pins held her hair until it came free and fell about her shoulders. And they had drawn together again in another kiss that was less careful than the first had been and then not careful at all as their bodies' needs rose, overwhelming all other thoughts.

The night had been warm, the thyme-scented grass soft under their nakedness, and when the dew had finally gathered and the late night began to chill, there had been his cloak to cover them both while they took pleasure in giving pleasure to each other. They had made love more than once that night, their delight with each other enough for that. And once their bodies' first lust was slaked it had been delight rather than only raw desire. They had said little by way of words, their bodies saying almost all that needed to be said between them. There had been laughter, though. Joliffe remembered Mary's laughter as soft as the starlight by which he'd watched her face as they pleasured each other and as rich as the first dawn color in the east that told them it was time they parted.

And yet there was never once question that this one night was all there would be between them. He never learned what her need had been beyond the plain one of the body, but he'd known even then that there was more want than wantonness in her use of him, as he prayed to God there had been in his use of her.

God help him, he had been so very young, but even then he had known there was a difference between bodily lust and true loving. He had had something of both before then, enough to know how much better the latter was—and how much harder it was to come by. What he and Mary had between them that one night had felt like love, and they had taken as much comfort from it as they did pleasure.

And tonight, sitting on the long flank of the Downs under starlight and a young moon, with his arms around his updrawn knees and only his thoughts and the White Horse for company, he was glad for the gladness he had seen in Mary today—not only her gladness in her life as it now was but gladness at seeing him. It was good to know that what they had shared had stayed good for both of them.

He laid his face on his knees and hunched deeper into his cloak. The day's rightful weariness was catching up to him, but his mind had taken hold on that "enough," and he turned the word over in his mind. Why had that one sweet night been "enough" between him and Mary? Why had brief loving always been "enough" for him with any woman? He did not know. Knew it served other men well enough, but had found that whenever he was careless enough to let himself think on it, there was a hollowness of longing in his own heart that made him suspect it was not enough for him. Knew, too, there was no help for that because he was not about to leave the life he was living and what woman would be fool enough to join him in it?

he awoke when the sky was just beginning to lighten toward dawn, before there was any color to the world. The night had not gone so cold as it might have, and the turf where he was lying had stayed dry under him, but his cloak was heavy with dew, and as he moved and made to rise, he remembered why sleeping in the open was a poor idea—unless there were compensations. Besides that he was stiff and somewhat chilled, he was hungry, too, and while he rose with a groan to his feet, he took what comfort he could in knowing that the walk back to camp would ease the stiffness and the chill, and that breakfast would be waiting for him. And as he returned to the trackway and headed down, he found he was thinking not of Mary and a night six years gone but of yesterday at Medcote's manor.

It had been more than the steward's unfriendliness and knowing what had passed between Medcote and Rose in the afternoon that had made the whole business uncomfortable. Looking back at it, what made him least comfortable was what had passed among Hal and his sister and mother. There had been layers of anger there, and not new ones but an old warfare of grievances well-honed by use, of old bitternesses uneased by any forgiveness. That had been the poison in the whole air of the place, from the moment the steward greeted them at the gateway.

Or maybe he was so hungry he was making fantasies out of his dislike of Medcote and of things that were not there at all. What should matter was that Anela Medcote had paid them none so ill, and if the trouble suspected by the abbey's bailiff lay in Medcote wanting a marriage that Ashewell did not want between his son and Medcote's widowed daughter, then the players could do their play tomorrow at the church ale, tell the bailiff what they'd learned, since surely he would be there, and the morning after that be away, free and clear. Even Ellis should hardly be able to find complaint in that.

But why would talk of a marriage be kept secret? It was easy enough to see why Medcote would want his daughter married so well. It was easy, too, to see why Ashewell would want better for his son. But why such secrecy about it that even servants had hardly heard the talk?

That, Joliffe told himself firmly, was the bailiff's business to find out.

Meanwhile, there was today coming light around him. Yesterday's possibility of rain had faded. He hoped if there was rain to come, it came today and not tomorrow; but he had learned long since that hope was what you had while you got on with what actually was, and presently what was was dawn sweetly around him, with birdsong in the hedgerows and, by the time he turned through the gateway into their field, daylight had fully come and the world around him was rich with the greens of spring.

Rose was tending a pot hung over the firepit. Piers was laboring up from the stream with a bucket, Ellis was leaning into the cart for something, and Basset and Gil were sitting beside the fire, with Gil's hurt foot propped up on a low basket.

Everyone greeted Joliffe easily, Rose looking up from stirring whatever was in the pot to nod to him, her look lingering as if she were trying to judge how he was. Pretending she was not, he nodded at Gil's foot and asked, "It's giving trouble?"

"Only some," Gil answered.

"It was the way he yelped when he first stood up this morning gave him away," said Basset.

"It's better," Gil insisted. "The ointment Rose gave me to rub on it has helped. It was just the walk to Medcote's and back it didn't like."

Joliffe sat down on his heels beside the fire, out of Rose's way. The gray, bubbling mass of oatmeal pottage in the pot was no more appealing than ever, but Joliffe's stomach growled with appreciation at the thought of food.

Ellis sauntered to join them, jibing at Joliffe as he came, "She must have been worth it, to keep you out all night. Or was it just the ale was so good you had to sleep it off under a tavern bench?"

"The ale was good and she was better," Joliffe jibed back.

"So was her friend, come to that. But sleep? I didn't get much of that."

Ellis glared at him. Gil stared. Basset cleared his throat and became very busy with rubbing his hands together toward the fire. Piers, hanging the bucket from the cart, had not heard. Joliffe, pretending not to see any of them, caught instead Rose's look at him. He had jibed at Ellis without thinking of her, and was disconcerted there was no anger in her look but instead a bitter-edged almost-laugh that told him she didn't believe him any more than Basset did.

More disconcertingly, when she had spooned the pottage into their wooden bowls, she not only added currants from their carefully kept supply and drizzled honey over each bowl, but he saw she had given him somewhat more currants and honey than she had to anyone else. She not only did not believe his tale, she was offering him the kind of comfort she gave to Piers when he was hurt or more-than-usually disappointed of something, and Joliffe decided he did not want to think about why just now and gave himself over to his hunger, taking full pleasure in breaking his fast.

Afterward, when everyone but Gil had finished and gone away from the fire, he offered to take the bowls and spoons and pots to the stream to wash. "After oatmeal, it's hot water they'll need," Rose said, smiling at him. "If you'll take the pot to the stream, fill it, and bring it back to set over the fire again, that will be enough. Especially since I think Basset means to work all of you most of the day today, to ready for tomorrow."

Joliffe showed mock horror at the thought. She laughed at him and handed over the pot.

At the stream, with the pot filled, he knelt to wash his face, feeling his beard along his jawline, glad he would not have to shave until tomorrow, and telling himself he had had plenty of sleep and was ready for the day, whatever Basset had in mind. As he came out of the woods, a lark was rising from the field's far end, taking its wondrous song with it into the sky. He paused to listen and watch as it soared high and hovered small with distance against the sky, its song still flowing, until suddenly it broke into its steep fall to earth again, to disappear into silence and the tall grass again.

In the stillness after it, Joliffe became aware of the pot's weight at the end of his arm and went on, carrying not only the pot but the thought of how the lark's flight was like so much of life. No matter to what heights of joy and beauty a man might go, in the end there was, always and inevitably, the return to earth. Still, he added to balance that somewhat heavy thought, it was surely better to live, however briefly, in joy and beauty than never to have them at all.

And, he added cheeringly, to live in a constant exaltation like the lark's would surely be wearying.

He wondered if he was sickening for something, the way his mind was throwing thoughts around. Ellis would probably say he was just sickening, and that run of his thought had him smiling as he set the filled pot over the fire and said to Rose, "Thanks for the goodly breakfast. You've a fine hand with currants and honey."

"And you've a fine tongue in your head," she said back. "Best you go put it to work instead of flattery." But she met his smile with her own, understanding his thanks without his having said them.

She had warned truly, though, that Basset meant to work them today. With breakfast and all else seen to and done, he gathered them all to him and said, calm as if it were nothing, "Now, about tomorrow's play. I've thought we could made good use of some of what we did at Minster Lovell."

That brought united groans from all the players, not just Joliffe, even before Ellis asked, "What do you mean by 'some of what we did'?"

With all the blandness of knowing how unwelcomed his

words were going to be, Basset said, "I've thought we could start with *Christ Against the Money-changers* and go right through to the *Resurrection*, but leaving out the *Crucifixion*, it being so hard to do, and . . ."

"Leaving it out?" Joliffe said with sudden suspicion. "And do what in place of it?"

"Why, have you write a speech to bridge the gap," Basset said brightly.

"By tomorrow?" Joliffe protested.

"Before tomorrow. To give whoever has it . . ."

"Not me," Ellis muttered.

". . . time to learn it."

"I'll do it!" Piers offered readily.

Too readily. His grandfather fixed him with a look and said, "I think whatever Joliffe writes will need more weight than you can give it."

"Fledgling," Ellis said, leaning sideways to give Piers a shoulder-to-shoulder shove. Piers shoved back, then remembered he was still angry at Ellis for his mother's sake, and moved to the other side of Gil.

Ignoring all of that, Basset went on, "So, Joliffe will write us a speech to begin it all. Then we'll do *Christ Against the Money-changers*, *Judas' Betrayal*, *Last Supper*, not the *Crucifixion*, not the *Harrowing of Hell*, then the *Resurrection*, and we're done. That's none so bad, is it?"

A general chorus of "Yes!" answered him. Basset beamed on them as if they had shouted approval and said, "There now. This will be to the good for us all. You don't want all that to slip out of mind through not being used. If nothing else, think of what a hit in the eye it will be for Father Hewgo. Holiness from us instead of profanation. So, to work! We'll do a light run through it, then give Joliffe time to write what speeches we'll need, and do it again."

"Mad," Ellis muttered. "Utterly mad." But he was getting to his feet with the rest of them. They had survived so long as a company because Basset's instinct was sure for what to play in whatever place they found themselves—and because, however much they grumbled, his company trusted him. Besides that, in this particular matter he was right: It would be to the good to keep these new plays fixed in their minds.

But what a pity it was, Joliffe thought with an inward grin, that no matter what noble-minded plays he did and wrote, he never seemed to grow more noble-minded in himself and above such petty desires as giving Father Hewgo a hit in the eye.

Chapter 7

Rough-running their lines while moving somewhat at speed through the plays to find out how much they remembered and how much they had forgotten in the week and less since they had performed them, they were as far as the *Last Supper* when Joliffe said, low-voiced, "Don't anyone look, but we're being watched from the woods."

Without looking, Basset said, "Three of them. Ashewell's younglings, I think. One of them is Tom that we met. They came while you were Judasing with the high priests."

"Shall I run them off?" Gil offered.

"It's their field more than ours," Basset said easily. "Their woods and stream, too, come to that. No, let them stay. There's no harm in it."

Aware of them now, Joliffe found himself lifting both his voice and the pace of his playing for the sake of the children. Not that it mattered that he did. The other players were doing the same, as unable as he was to resist any audience, however small. Despite the slips and pauses and startings again that came with rehearsing plays gone slightly out of mind, they had soon finished resurrecting Christ and, taking a rest before beginning again, were gathered to the water bucket for a drink, when Ellis said, "Heads up. We've more visitors."

Nicholas Ashewell and Gosyn's girl, seen briefly at the Ashewells' the other night, were walking through the gateway. Joliffe caught a sudden small flurry of branches from the edge of the trees, making him guess their watchers there were retreating, and he wondered where they were supposed to be instead of here as Basset went to meet Nicholas and the girl, bowing to them and welcoming them, bringing them onward to the fire where the other players likewise bowed and Rose smoothed her apron and curtsied.

The girl looked about the camp with interest. Nicholas, trying to be less openly curious, gave Basset a stoppered leather bottle, saying, "It's cider. My mother thought you'd like it."

"Your mother is a kind and thoughtful lady. Please give her our thanks," Basset answered.

"She also asks if you've seen Nicholas' younger brother and sisters," the girl said.

"Until a few moments ago, they were secretly watching us from the woods," Basset said. Nicholas immediately looked that way, and Basset added, "But I somewhat think they've gone now."

"They sport along the stream like otters," the girl laughed. "Never fear, Nicholas. They'll come home wet and dirty and in time for dinner."

With a frown weighted heavily with duty rather than any anger, Nicholas said, "It makes for trouble when they come home wet and dirty."

"But not trouble for you," the girl reminded him kindly. "Let be."

He smiled at her a little shamefacedly, as if she often had to remind him of that, and Rose said, "If it please you and you care to join us, there's spice cake just done."

Nicholas seemed about to refuse, but the girl said happily, "That would be welcome. Thank you." And after a bare moment's pause Nicholas echoed her thanks but added, "We shouldn't stay long, Claire."

"There's not all that much hurry." Claire sat down on her spread skirts beside the fire, looked around at them all, and said, "I saw you at the Ashewells' hall the other night. We all greatly enjoyed your play."

Basset gave her a small bow and said, smiling, "It's our pleasure that you were pleased."

They were all still standing because Nicholas still was. Claire reached up, took hold of his hand, and pulled. He hesitated, then sat down. Freed, the players all sat, too, circling the fire, except for Rose, who stood cutting squares of spice cake in the cast iron pan she had just pulled from the ashes. Putting the pieces onto a wooden cutting board, she held them out to Claire with a smile. The girl smiled back and, thanking her, took one. Nicholas took his with matching thanks and an uncertain smile, as if not sure that smiling was safe. He wasn't unfriendly, Joliffe thought, watching him. He was merely unsure. But how unsure did you have to be to doubt that smiling was safe?

Of course the possibility of being married into the Medcote family could well be enough to make any man—let alone young Nicholas—feel unsure, Joliffe thought. But did Nicholas know what was being talked of between his parents and Medcote, or had they kept it secret from him, if not from their servants?

The spice cake was warm, tasting as rich as it smelled, and Claire said to Rose, "This is wonderfully good." Then said to Basset, "My father says you played for the Medcotes yesterday."

Nicholas had begun to ease a little but now stiffened again, his gaze jerking from face to face while Basset answered easily, "That we did. Medcote and his son stopped by our camp yesterday to ask us to it."

Looking around the field as if for damage they might have done, Nicholas demanded angrily, "They were here?"

Seeming not to hear the anger, Basset said, still easily, "Briefly."

"You went to their place and played for them," Nicholas said, not quite accusingly.

Basset shrugged. "We had no reason not to. I doubt, though, we pleased them much. They seem to be a prickly family."

Claire laughed. "My father says they make a hedgehog look smooth."

"At least a hedgehog curls up and leaves people alone," Nicholas said bitterly. "*They* never do. They're more like hawks. They clutch what they want and never let go."

That was somehow thrown at Claire, who said back at him as if challenged about something, "Not me. I'm not going to marry Hal Medcote, no matter what he wants."

"You're safe enough," Nicholas returned sharply. "Medcote doesn't want you married to Hal."

Joliffe, knowing he should not, asked at Nicholas, "What about you to his daughter?"

Both Nicholas and Claire turned startled looks at him before Nicholas burst out, "How have you heard that?" And answered his own question fiercely. "They were talking of it there last night, I suppose. Gloating."

Paying no heed to the dark looks Ellis, Basset, and even Rose were giving him, Joliffe said, "It was servants' talk. You know how they are."

That deepened Ellis' frown at him, but Nicholas accepted he meant Medcote's servants and shrugged angrily as Joliffe pushed further, saying, "But surely it won't come to you marrying her if you don't want to."

Instead of Nicholas, Claire answered, "That's the trouble! Medcote claims that because Francis Brook died that . . ."

"Claire!" Nicholas exclaimed.

Claire clapped her free hand over her mouth and said through it, "Oh, Nicholas, I'm sorry."

Nicholas stood up, threw what was left of his cake into the fire, and said even more bitterly, "It's all right. They've surely heard of it."

Scrambling to her feet, too, Claire said, "But it doesn't matter. You didn't do it."

"I did. I killed him, and nothing is going to change that and now I'm going to have to marry Eleanor Medcote to make up for it."

He turned harshly away and started for the gateway. Behind him Claire said hurriedly to everyone, and low so that maybe Nicholas did not hear her, "I'm sorry. He was only nine when it happened. It was only ill-chance but he . . ." She faltered, made a helpless gesture.

By then the players were all on their feet, too, Basset saying, "We understand."

Claire started to turn to follow Nicholas, but Joliffe said after her, "Surely Father Hewgo could help him. Could find him a way to ease his conscience?"

Claire turned around, walking backward and still away while answering, angry and scornful together, "Father Hewgo? He only makes everything worse whenever he's asked for help. He's a horrible man." Then with belated courtesy she said with a smile to Rose, "The cake was very good. Thank you," before she turned again, gathered her skirts, and ran to catch up to Nicholas, already disappeared into the lane.

In the players' momentary silence after she was gone, a green woodpecker's yelping laugh broke out in the woods along the stream. Then Piers faced his mother and said accusingly, "You gave away our cake!"

"Not much of it," Rose said evenly. She smiled at her father. "I thought you'd want the chance to ask or hear things from them."

"As ever," Joliffe said to her, "you're as wise as you are fair."

"And you're as ever rattling off your mouth like that rat-a-tat woodpecker," Ellis snapped at him.

"Which is better than what some people rattle off," Rose shot back at him.

Ellis' mouth shut with a snap as Gil and Piers found somewhere else to look and Basset said hurriedly, "Can we all have another piece of your wondrous cake?"

Making her point that it was only Ellis who had her anger, Rose smiled—albeit a somewhat tightened smile—on the rest of them and cut pieces for each of them, even Ellis, who took his with his eyes down and muttered thanks.

While they ate, Basset passed around the leather bottle of cider that young Nicholas had brought. The cider being good, too, they went on passing it when they had finished their second shares of cake. It was a contented moment, all of them sitting at ease together, not bothering with talk. In the quiet Joliffe could hear the burble of the stream away in the woods and the tear of grass as Tisbe grazed, and far too soon Basset stretched and readied to rise, saying, "Back to work with us."

Less ready to be up and about again, Joliffe said with a nod toward the gateway, "It doesn't make sense what the boy said. However guilty Nicholas may still feel, why would Ashewell be thinking to marry his son to Eleanor Medcote to 'make up' for a death the boy was too young to be blamed for? Just because Medcote may say it doesn't

mean Ashewell has to go along with it. There must be more
to it than we've learned."

"But not more that we *have* to learn," Basset said. "This
is enough to give the bailiff."

"But why wasn't the abbey's bailiff able to learn as
much as we have?" Joliffe wondered.

"For all we know, he may know all this and there's something more, something worse, that we've not found out any
more than he has," Basset said. "Or else, not being as lowly
as we are, he doesn't have free talk with servants and children careless with their betters' secrets. Nor are you putting
me off working the plays again. Up with you."

"Joliffe hasn't written what we need yet," Gil pointed out.

Basset shook his head. "I'm getting too old for all this,"
he muttered. "I'd forgotten." He brightened. "Still, he can
write while the rest of us work our words together. We're
not so steady on them as I'd like. An hour, say?" he said at
Joliffe.

"An hour?" Joliffe protested. "For all you want done?
An hour?"

Choosing to take that as agreement rather than protest,
Basset said, "Good. We'll leave you to it then." And to the
rest of them, "Come on. We'll set up the frame and curtain
before we start."

"We'll only have to take them down again to take to the
church," Ellis protested.

"So it goes," Basset agreed cheerily.

To the single wooden bar held up by two pairs of
slanted legs and hung with a curtain that had sufficed them
for years in their travels, Basset had lately added a second
frame that could be put up behind the first and then two
wood rods fastened between their ends to make a square
space enclosed by more curtains that gave the players
somewhere to retire out of sight to change their garb and
their person when need be in a play. Held together with

wooden pegs, the whole thing was easily put up and easily taken down by either several or all of them working together. Joliffe left them to it, collected his writing box with its paper, pens, and ink from the cart, and went off to the far end of the pasture where a stump at the woods' edge made a good place to sit well away from the others.

For all his protests, the needed speeches came readily— one to cover Christ's coming to Jerusalem and set up what was to come, another to cover the gap left by leaving out Good Friday's play of Christ's trial and torments, his crucifixion, and the bringing of his body down from the cross. Basset was right to forgo that one, difficult with too many changes of characters and garb except for Ellis as Christ.

Finished, knowing it was not his best work but sure it would suffice, Joliffe heard the others arguing over some piece of business in the garden at Gethsemane and decided against rejoining them just yet. With paper, pens, and ink closed into their box again, he gave way to the gentle blandishment of the midday sun's warmth and stretched himself out on the grass on the far side of the stump, his head cushioned on a grassy lump, his hands folded on his chest. He had slept little and poorly last night, was shortly drowsing, and awoke to find Rose smiling down at him.

"That," he said accusingly, "is how you smile at Piers when he's asleep."

"And for the same reason," Rose returned. "You both look so sweetly innocent when you're asleep."

"And we're quiet, too," Joliffe said, sitting up.

"That more than anything," Rose agreed. "Father wants to know if you're sleeping for inspiration or resting from your labors."

"Resting from my labors." Joliffe got up and picked up his writing box. "They're ready for another go-through?"

"Father is, anyway."

"That's what matters."

The other players had snatched a rest while Rose fetched Joliffe. They were eating spice cake again and drinking cider, and Joliffe quickly took his share before all was gone, handing the fresh-made speeches to Basset while saying around a mouthful of cake, "You've not said who'll have these, so I kept them short on the chance it was going to be me."

"You could have made them longer. I'm giving them to Gil," Basset said.

"Ha!" Ellis said, giving Gil a friendly shove on the shoulder. "You're the victim of choice this time!"

Gil, grinning, reached for the paper. He was like the rest of them: however much they griped and groaned, they were all usually happier with more lines than less. And while Joliffe had indeed kept the speeches short, he had expected Gil to be Basset's choice and written them richly because Gil, for all he was not yet a year in the company, was skilled beyond the usual at the work, taking to Basset's training much like the proverbial duck to water. Besides that, he learned with an ease to be envied and would have the lines to heart by tomorrow with no trouble.

For now, though, he took his place in front of the forward curtain and read the opening speech aloud from the page, finishing with a low bow and a wide sweep of an imagined hat to the imagined audience before disappearing around one end of the curtain as the other players came out from around its other end to begin *Christ Against the Money-changers*.

The play was difficult because it needed not only Christ but money-changers for him to attack, and at least the Jews' High Priest to be offended by it all and, if not all the Apostles, at least Judas to be horrified. With Ellis playing Christ, Basset as the High Priest, and Joliffe as Judas, it was left to Gil—crossing quickly behind the curtain to come out on the heels of the others—and Piers, and perforce Rose to be everyone else. They were not troubling with garb today, but tomorrow Rose would have to submit, reluctantly and only because of necessity, to being a money-changer, wearing a false beard and a man's long robe.

They made their way through all the plays more smoothly than they had earlier, finding that the new speeches eased and evened the pace, and at the end Basset said, "That went well enough. We've remembered what we're doing. Gil, are you going to be all right with learning what you need to by tomorrow?"

"No trouble at all," Gil said. "It's good, clear verse." He grinned. "For once."

Still grinning, he ducked aside from the clout that Joliffe aimed vaguely at his head.

"As ever, I'm damned with faint praises," Joliffe whined, and Ellis countered, "Don't complain. Usually we just damn you and forget the praises."

"Well, I'm satisfied with it all," Basset said. "Does anyone want to run through it again, or shall we let it rest until tomorrow and leave Gil to get on with learning his words?"

The vote was entirely in favor of rest for everyone but Gil, who went away contentedly to find a quiet place in the woods to work. Piers, stripped to shirt and braies, headed for the stream to play. Basset settled on cushions piled beside the cart where the sun was falling most warmly, "To consider the inside of my eyelids," he said, folding his hands across his middle and closing his eyes. Rose was stirring the pot of good-smelling stew that hung over the fire, and Ellis was making himself useful by bringing wood from the small stack under the cart to pile beside the firepit. Joliffe gathered what he needed to curry Tisbe, a soothing pastime for both of them, and started away to where she was grazing. Behind him, he heard Ellis say something, low-voiced, to Rose. If Rose answered aloud, Joliffe did not hear her; but when he reached Tisbe and looked back, Ellis was nowhere in sight and Rose was alone by the fire, still stirring the pot with a spoon in one hand while wiping her eyes with her apron with the other, despite the smoke was drifting away from her.

With a sigh for both of them, Joliffe set to brushing Tisbe, saying softly in her ear while he did, "In a lot of ways, it's none so bad being a horse, you know."

She nickered down her long nose at him, telling him—he supposed—that he said true but that an occasional feed-bag of oats would not come amiss.

Chapter 8

The players ended the day by loading almost everything into their cart again, excepting what they needed for sleep and eating, and that—except for the tent—they would load in the morning. They expected to spend tomorrow night in the field, but through the day none of them would be here and as Basset was wont to say, "Take care now and maybe lose less later."

That done and the sun trailing sunset colors down the clear western sky as blue shadows spread and deepened outward across the pasture from trees and hedgerows, they gathered around the fire and to their supper of Rose's good stew and yesterday's bread. For all that they had not been on the road today, they had worked and worded enough that they were satisfactorily tired and there was little talk among them. Even Rose's anger at Ellis seemed to be wearing out, Joliffe thought. Forgiveness might be a while in coming, but the worst edge to her anger was gone.

Joliffe's worry was that with each forgiveness given, a little more of Rose's love wore off. That what she gave was becoming not so much forgiveness as a slow wearing out of caring about what Ellis did or didn't do.

What Ellis should maybe begin to fear was not her anger but the day her love was too worn away for her to care about him enough to bother with anger anymore.

Where he sat a little way from the fire, Joliffe watched the White Horse on its hill slowly disappear into the gathering dusk as the sun slid away and was gone; he wondered if it was more painful for love to once have been and slowly die or worse for love never to have been at all. He didn't know. He had never loved in a way where losing mattered. Nor did he know whether that said good or ill about him, that he had never loved that way.

What he more deeply wondered was whether he ever would. And then, to the side, as it were, he wondered if there had ever been love between Medcote and his wife— or any love in that family at all. There had been nothing of it to be seen yesterday, surely.

Some late-awake bird called sleepily in the woods. The last light was gone and all the world's colors with it, save for the twilight's blue and the few, small, yellow-red-orange flames flickering to their end in the firepit. Ellis tossed the bits of a stick he had been breaking and breaking again into the fire, stood up, and said, "Bed for me, I think."

Having no quarrel with thought of his own blankets and a good night's sleep, Joliffe was already rising as Basset said, "Bed for all of us." Adding as he began to labor to his feet, "Tomorrow will start early and last long."

Basset was surely right about the starting early. The grass was still heavily wet with dew and the eastern sky flushed with sunrise colors but no sun yet as Joliffe fetched Tisbe to the cart. The others were helping Rose pack away their cooking things and bedding. The tent they would risk leaving, but the rest went easily into accustomed places in the cart.

Tisbe went less easily. Apparently offended at having her rest and grazing interrupted, she tossed her head and jerked at the halter rope and only went unwillingly between the cart shafts. "You've gone spoiled," Joliffe told her. "A week of easy living at Minster Lovell, a few soft days on the road, another rest here, and you think you should be a lady-at-ease ever after."

Tisbe tossed her head again in seeming agreement with him.

He laughed at her. "How if I promise you a feed-bag of oats to keep you company today while we work? Will that resign your ladyship to pulling the cart as far as the village and back again today?"

She butted her head against his shoulder. He laughed at her again and set to harnessing her.

From the rear of the cart Ellis called, "Just don't tell her we'll be on the road again tomorrow."

"You didn't hear that, my lovely girl," Joliffe told her.

If she did, she preferred to be gracious about it and accept the inevitable. Or maybe she shared Joliffe's opinion that sufficient unto the day was the evil thereof. Tomorrow's evil could wait until tomorrow to be complained of; today there was promise of oats.

They were early enough into Ashewell village that Father Hewgo was still saying the day's first Mass and only the very first of the stalls that would sell ale and food through the day were being set up along the outside of the churchyard wall at the cross-lanes.

"Good," said Basset. "We won't have to quarrel with Father Hewgo about where we put ourselves. We'll just do it and have it done before he comes out."

Having brought Tisbe and the cart out of everyone's way into the narrow lane along the north side of the churchyard

and close to the church's west door, they unloaded the frame
for their playing place and lifted it over the little stile that led
into the yard from that side. As usual with churchyards, there
were fewer graves on the north side. Basset easily chose a
level space not far from the church's west door for them to set
up, and fitting the wooden frames together was too familiar a
task to be a problem. The tapping into place of the wooden
pegs would likely be heard inside the church, but Basset said,
"Ah, well, Father Hewgo is going to be displeased with us no
matter what we do. Better we're done before he can demand
we move. Strike, Ellis, and the devil take the hindmost!"

There were, after all, few pegs, and they were meant to
fit loosely to make easy the taking apart of the frames, so
that hardly two taps were needed to set each one, but as the
first folk began to drift from the church at the Mass' end,
Father Hewgo, still in full priestly garb, came shoving out
past them, red-faced with ire. Basset, who had been waiting
for it, said, "Come, Joliffe. The rest of you, keep on." And
muttered as he and Joliffe went to meet the priest, "Try for
angelic, right?"

"Even heavenly butter won't melt in my mouth," Joliffe
assured him, all calm and sweetness.

Basset humphed in the back of his throat at that, but
they had played this business often enough before now to
know the way of it. Meeting Father Hewgo not far outside
the church door, with all around them the full flood of villagers leaving the church slowing to watch, Basset and Joliffe both bowed low and Basset said with cheerful certainty
of his welcome, "Thank you, Father, for this chance to
serve the church and you."

Father Hewgo pointed at Ellis driving home the last of
the needed pegs with perhaps unnecessarily loud thumps.
"That . . ." he began.

"We've come early, sir," Joliffe said, "to be sure we'd
not be late and disappoint you."

"This unholiness," Father Hewgo started again. "This . . ."

Seeming not to hear him, Basset continued on serenely, "We mean to do the plays we did for Lady Lovell this Easter past. From our Lord confronting the money-changers in the Temple through his resurrection and mankind's salvation. Four plays in all, and all as Lady Lovell herself saw them."

Joliffe, beaming with delight, nodded in fulsome assurance of that, echoing, "Four plays and Lady Lovell said she'd never seen better."

"But making your noise in the churchyard while I did the Mass! You're . . ."

". . . sorry," Basset finished for him. "Indeed we are. But we know that God sees our need and will bless you for your kindness to us."

It was not working. Instead of being herded the way they wanted him to go, Father Hewgo was only going darker red with anger. But behind him, from among the villagers, a man bulking large enough to be the village blacksmith said roughly, "Give over, priest. We want some sport, not more of your quarreling."

Father Hewgo turned on the man with hardly bated ire, but fool though he might be, he knew trouble brewing when it bubbled in his face. And hearing the general mutter and murmur and seeing the nodding of agreement among the villagers, he shifted like a blustering wind, changing direction without losing force to say angrily at Basset, "Have it your own way then." And at the villagers, "It's your souls I'm trying here to save . . ."

From well back in the crowd someone muttered anonymously, "Our purses to empty, you mean."

". . . and if you'll not have it, then go to the devil by whatever path these servants of hell will lead you!"

He threw a glare at Basset and Joliffe, who both quickly

bowed, but it was to his back as he pushed away from them, straight into the crowd who drew hurriedly out of his way, giving him clear passage back to the church, where he slammed the heavy wooden door hard shut behind him with a thud louder than any Ellis had made. The blacksmith gave a sharp nod at the door, as if satisfied to have him gone. Another man spat toward the church and was promptly hit in the arm by his wife, who hissed a warning at him to go with it. If no one else was quite so open in their dislike, Joliffe saw a few hands making quick, forked-fingered gestures at the door as if to ward off evil. Father Hewgo might still have his authority as a priest over his flock, but he looked to have lost their respect long before now.

The blacksmith turned back to Basset and Joliffe with a grin. "There now. That's him seen to. If he means well, he hides it better than most men I've known. It's been a while since any players came this way. We don't want him to fright you off."

"No fear of that," said Basset. "But we're thankful to be spared the fight. You have our thanks."

"Is there any help you fellows need that we can give?"

"None at all, except you come and enjoy our play."

There were general wide smiles and head-noddings of agreement to that from everyone. Then from across the churchyard someone called, "Ale's out!" and people started to shift that way, with Basset declaring after them as they went, "We begin at noon!"

"Til noon, then!" came back cheerfully from more than one among the villagers.

With enough time they need make no haste, the players finished with hanging the curtains—rough-felted gray wool that packed flat and wore well—and shifting what they would need from the cart to out of sight behind the curtains. There was nothing much for lookers-on to see, almost everything being in hampers, but children of all sizes hung about to watch it all, and a few women, too, as much to keep watch on the children as anything.

Because of that, Basset quietly set Piers to stay with the cart to discourage curiosity, and Piers, always ready to sit while others worked, took to the task merrily. While the rest of the players made sure all was where they wanted it behind the curtains, they could hear him beyond the churchyard wall making bright, willing talk with anyone who came near.

To the other side of the churchyard there was growing merriment as folk got into the way of holidaying. That the price of the ale they bought was destined for the church didn't lessen the pleasure of drinking it, and more than ale was being sold, too. The stomach-rousing smell of cooking meat came wafting along with the talk and laughter, and Joliffe began to be hungry again.

He was not alone. Ellis likewise sniffed the air with interest and asked, "Bassett, we're done here, aren't we?"

"We are," Basset agreed. "But whatever is roasting won't be ready yet."

"No, but there'll be something else to be had in the meantime," Gil said hopefully.

"But no more than one—that's *one*—cup of ale until we've finished our work for the day," Basset said. "Understood?"

Knowing what unpleasantness Basset would wreak on anyone who showed up drunk and unable to perform well, they all nodded agreement.

"I'll keep watch here, then," said Basset; and Rose said, "I'll take first watch with the cart. Gil, will you keep an eye on Piers?"

Being newest to the company and closest to Piers in age, Gil was too often saddled with keeping an eye on Piers, and for pity of that Joliffe said, "I'll take Piers this time."

Gil thanked him with a smile of ready gratitude.

"Then in an hour's time you'll all be here again," Basset

said, "to ready and then do our street-work. There's a dial on the church and we've the sun with us today, so don't anyone try to pretend they don't know when to come back. Right?"

"Right," they all chorused, and Ellis and Gil took off while Joliffe went with Rose to the cart to collect Piers, who protested he wasn't a baby that needed keeping.

"No," his mother said back. "When you were a baby, you'd stay where you were put, you and your yammering. Now you and your yammering move around and make altogether more bother than you're sometimes worth."

From Rose that was unusually harsh and, startled, Piers closed his mouth instead of saying more and went away with Joliffe in unaccustomed silence. Only when they were well away from the cart did he say angrily, "If Ellis doesn't stop making her unhappy, I'm going to put briars in his bed every night."

Since the practical rather than the moral was always the stronger way to take with Piers, Joliffe pointed out, "He'll tuck them down your neck afterward if you do." And added, because threats worked well, too, with Piers, "And I'll help him."

Piers growled.

"And I'd better not find anything in my bed either," Joliffe said for good measure.

They were out of the churchyard now and into the street among the crowd and the stalls set up for selling whatever was hoped would part holidaying folk from their coins. Piers, good at knowing when to give up one cause for another, exclaimed, "Look!" and darted away to a stall selling, among other things, bright sticks of sugar candy.

Joliffe followed without haste. Sugar was costly, not something the players commonly bought. Piers would take his time over choosing among the gaudy yellow- and red- and green-colored sticks. For his part, Joliffe had more interest in watching people. Far more stalls and merchant

tables were here than were likely from only Ashewell village. Judging by that and the steadily growing crowd, word
of the church ale must have spread even farther than
hoped, and maybe Father Hewgo would bring himself to
be pleased with the whole business and forgive the players
being alive, Joliffe thought.

He was just turning back to see if Piers had made up his
mind yet when a sudden snarl of voices not far away along
the street drew his look to where someone had made use of
spring having finally come to weave head wreaths of
young-leaved withies and a few flowers, now laid out in
pretty array on a table. Claire Gosyn was standing there,
choosing among the wreaths, while beside her her mother
had a hand held out to give a coin to the wreath-seller. But
Claire, her mother, and the wreath-seller, as well as a good
many other people, were head-turned toward Claire's father saying with voice-raised anger at a slung-jawed man a
few yards away, "What I'm telling you is to keep away
from there and anywhere else that's mine. You've no rights
along that stream or with those woods and I'm telling you,
like I've told you before, to keep off!"

"We've had rights to that wood time out of mind," the
man snarled back at him.

"There's those that do and those that don't, and you're
one of those that don't. And even if you were, you're not
careful what you take or how, and I'm telling you to keep
off and away from it!"

"You're a grip-fisted cur, Walter Gosyn, and there's
those that . . ."

Gosyn's wife, the coin dropped on the table, moved toward both men, saying firmly, "Now you leave off that talk,
Wat Offington. You know better than that, or if you don't,
your wife does anyway."

Given the size of Wat's anger, Joliffe expected Wat would
stretch it to her, but instead he made a quick duck of his head

her way and said, "I'll be first to say you were good to my Bartrice when that rheum settled to her chest, Geretruda. She'd have my ears and all if I denied it. It's not with you but with your husband's grabbing ways I've got quarrel."

"I've never taken what wasn't mine!" Gosyn declared hotly. "There's not a man can say otherwise except he lies!"

"You've had luck!" Wat flung back at him, his wrath right back where it had been. "That's what you've had, and you've no pity for those of us who don't!"

"I don't have pity for those too slothful to make their 'luck' by hard work the way I have and then come stealing from me to make up for it!"

They would be at blows in another moment or two, Joliffe thought and readied to draw Piers away because, once started, something like that always spread. But Geretruda Gosyn, for all she was a little, bony woman who hardly rose to either man's shoulder, put herself between them with a hand on her husband's arm, murmuring something to him and then to Wat that Joliffe could not hear. Whatever it was, neither man was ready to come to blows across her. They each even took an unwilling step away from one another just before Master Ashewell and another man came shoving toward them from among from the gathering gawkers.

Both Ashewell and the newcomer seemed to know more about the quarrel than what Joliffe had heard. Smiling and easy, Ashewell went to Gosyn, saying, "What-hey, Walter. Can't let work go even on holiday?" The other man went toward Wat Offington, who held up his hands shoulder-high and took another step backward, claiming, "T'wasn't me who started the jawing here, Master Kyping. Anybody can tell you t'wasn't me."

Despite Master Kyping being younger than the other three men, he clearly had some manner of authority here. But rather than throwing his weight ahead of him, he said as easily as Ashewell and on half a laugh, "If it wasn't you started it, it was only because Gosyn got his words in first by a thumb's breadth. Look you, both of you, I know what you're on about and it's a matter for the manor court, not the middle of the marketplace on a Sunday, right?"

Both Gosyn and Wat acknowledged that with grudging shrugs and half-nods. Geretruda still had a hand on her husband's arm and Ashewell was standing near him. Now Master Kyping clapped a hand on Wat's shoulder as if he, at least, was with Wat in this, and that was sharp of him, Joliffe thought. Someone like Wat, once he began to feel "everybody was against him," would only be the worse to deal with. As it was, Kyping looked to be siding with him, giving Wat the chance to draw off without loss of face, and to Wat's credit he took the chance. "Right," he said, starting to turn to leave. "Manor court then. Right."

Behind him Gosyn growled. "Just see you keep away from what isn't yours in the meanwhile."

"Walter!" Geretruda said at him sharply as Wat started to swing angrily back toward him.

But Master Kyping had his hand on Wat's shoulder again and his other hand raised at Gosyn, one finger up in warning as he said as sharply as Geretruda, "Gosyn! Let it go! Or the first business at the manor court will be a fine on you."

Ashewell, an arm firmly around Gosyn's shoulders now, said cheerily, "Come on. All this can wait. You haven't done your part in ale-festing yet."

Gosyn let himself be turned away, grumbling, between his wife and friend while Master Kyping saw Wat away the other way, talking with him friendliwise as they went. The gawkers went back to their other pleasures, and Joliffe looked to see what Piers was doing, only to find that the Gosyns seemed to be destined for quarrels today.

Claire had stayed beside the wreath-maker's table, sensibly out of the way, but in the brief while of the quarrel and its end, Hal Medcote and his sister, Eleanor, had joined her there. And while Eleanor was standing aside with a look that made Joliffe think she would rather not be there, Hal was far too close to Claire; had her backed against the table, unable to slip sideways away from him as he held a wreath above her head with both hands while leaning toward her in what could have been a lover's way if they had not been in so public a place and Claire had not been staring up at him with angry dislike and maybe fear. And in unthinking answer to that, Joliffe took a step toward them, only to have Ellis, come from somewhere, clamp a hand on his near arm, saying, "Don't even think it. Back off away."

He was right. Among the many things of which players had to be wary was becoming part of quarrels none of their business among people with no reason to take their side and all too likely to turn on them instead of on each other. As Basset was wont to say, "What's ours is ours and what's theirs is theirs and we're best to keep them well apart."

So Joliffe did not pull free of Ellis' hold, which was just as well, as Nicholas Ashewell came shoving past Eleanor to grab Hal by the arm and jerk him around and away from Claire, saying too loudly, "Leave her alone!"

Even if he had remembered that a soft word was supposed to turn aside wrath, Joliffe thought it would probably not have sufficed here, given how readily Hal's momentary surprise leapt into sharp-edged delight at Nicholas' challenge. With a sharp jerk he freed himself, gave a shove at Nicholas' shoulder that pushed him back a step, and said, "Keep your hands to yourself, bird-shot boy."

Nicholas flushed hot-red. Claire said, "Don't!" at both of them, and Eleanor moved toward her brother, saying, "Hal, let be."

Ignoring them both, Hal said at Nicholas, "Where's your birding-bow, boy? Don't tell me you'll take someone on without it." He put out his hand to shove at Nicholas again, with Nicholas' hand already on the hilt of the dagger hung from his belt and no doubt in Joliffe's mind that Hal was hoping he would draw it, because Hal could surely have his own dagger out as quickly as Nicholas could have his, and then . . .

Ellis was firmly drawing Joliffe further back, and Joliffe let him. Gosyn was now shoving his way toward the wreath-maker's table with black wrath on his face and Master Ashewell and Geretruda in his wake with no likelihood they would be able to stop him. Not that Master Ashewell looked like stopping Gosyn was what he had in mind. Instead he looked as angry for his son's sake as Gosyn was for his daughter's. But somehow Master Kyping was quicker than any of them, away from Wat Offington and to Hal and Nicholas before the others reached them, drawing Eleanor aside with one hand while blocking Gosyn's and Ashewell's way and saying with laughter at both Hal and Nicholas, "If you overset Jenet's stall in your quarreling, you'll find yourself not only paying for all her wreaths but having to wear them yourselves for the rest of the day, I promise you. And a pretty pair you'll surely make."

That startled Nicholas and Hal into looking away from each other and to him, and he went laughingly on, "So go your ways and save us all a deal of trouble." He caught up a wreath from the table. "Claire, these flowers suit your fair hair the best. May I?" Setting the wreath on her head himself with one hand while leaning to hand a coin to Jenet behind the table, he put himself between Hal and Nicholas so that they drew back from one another without he seemed to force them to it, saying to them on his next breath, as he pointed one way along the street, "Hal, there's the way I think you should go. And Nicholas"—pointing the other way—"I think there's your way."

It was all done too briskly to give anyone time to turn their quarrel on him, and now he drew Claire away to her father and mother before turning to clamp a firm friendly hand on Hal's shoulder, saying, "Come to it, why don't I go with you? I've heard Jack Twyne has some of the best ale here and he's the way you're going. Eleanor, as always, it is my pleasure to see you," he added with a smooth bow of his head to her but not pausing as he had Hal away.

From the smile quirked on Hal's face, Joliffe guessed he full well knew he was being baited away, but he went anyway. Behind them, Eleanor Medcote said to Nicholas and his father, sounding angry and embarrassed together—or angry *because* she was embarrassed—"I'm sorry." And to Nicholas more than to his father, "For it all."

Master Ashewell did not look as if he thought her "sorry" was worth much, but Nicholas ducked his head in awkward acceptance of it and stammered out, "I am, too. It wasn't any fault of yours."

"Or yours," Eleanor said, trying an uncertain smile at him that he did not return. He only ducked his head in another awkward bow before she gave way to Master Ashewell's glare and left them. She was a comely enough woman in her way, but woman she was, while Nicholas was still in that uncertain place between being boy and being man, done with one but only beginning to be the other. Aside from what her father wanted, did she want to be married to a boy, or did she feel more as Nicholas clearly did? And what of Hal? For a very certainty Hal had not looked like someone who wanted Nicholas part of his family.

But if this Master Kyping was the Master Kyping who was bailiff here, that would be good, because he looked to be someone who would take what they had to tell him and make best use of it.

Of more immediate matter, though, Ellis asked with sudden suspicion, "Where's Piers? Have you lost him?"

Chapter 9

For a wonder, Piers was where Joliffe had left him. If he had turned from the table at all, he was turned back, too held by the bright promise of the sugar sticks to bother much with lesser matters. With him safely seen, Ellis nodded to Joliffe and went whatever way he had been going, leaving Joliffe to rejoin Piers, who had finally made his choice. Holding a green sugar stick, he looked up at Joliffe hopefully, but Joliffe, reading the look a-right, said, "You have money. Buy your own."

Piers grimaced at him and turned back to the seller, digging his other hand into his belt-pouch.

Joliffe reached past him, chose a red stick and a yellow one, paid for them over Piers' shoulder, and when Piers turned away from the table, handed the yellow one to him, saying, "But I'll buy you one, too."

Piers grabbed it, remembered to say, "Thank you!" and with a sugar stick in either hand, licking at them turn and turnabout, started away to see what else there was to see, rightly supposing Joliffe would follow him.

There wasn't much else. It was a goodly gathering for the place and the short warning of it there had been, but used as Joliffe and Piers were to fairs and markets in larger towns, this was not much. When the shadow on the sundial carved high up on the south side of the church's tower showed it was time to go back to the cart, Piers made no trouble about it, darting ahead of Joliffe and through the churchyard gateway just ahead of a woman coming out, leading a child by the hand. Mary and her small son, James.

Joliffe stepped aside with a slight bow, out of her way, ready to pretend they did not know each other, expecting she would pretend the same, but she paused and asked, with a look after Piers, "Yours?"

"God forbid!" Joliffe said with such real horror that she laughed at him. He laughed, too, and added, "His mother is daughter to our master player. We all take turns keeping him from driving her mad."

"Ah." Mary nodded with a mother's understanding. "I know well how that goes." Her own son had seen the sugar sticks and was pulling at her hand toward them and, smiling, she said, "I have to go."

Smiling back at her, Joliffe agreed, "Indeed. So must I."

And they did, going yet again their separate ways, with a warm shared night on a thyme-scented flank of the downs far and ever farther away.

Gil caught up to him as he crossed the churchyard. Basset was still on guard at their playing place, but Ellis and Piers were already at the cart, where Rose had all their red and yellow Lovell tabards ready and was helping Piers into his. While the rest of them slipped their own on, she handed Piers the pipes and tabor, handed the short trumpet to Joliffe when he was ready, and left Ellis to get out the bright-dyed, leather-covered juggling balls for himself.

Joliffe never ceased to wonder at how much displeasure could be shown in the simple act of *not* doing something.

Ready themselves, they took Basset's tabard to him, and while putting it on, he told them, "I can't see there's need to make much of a show of announcing we're here and what we're going to do. We'll just go up the street here, announce ourselves at the crossroads, then proceed back through the churchyard to here. Gil, you'll stay here to hold back the curious throngs as they gather. Ellis, Joliffe, Piers, ready?"

They chorused that they were.

"Then let's away."

Piers led, dancing a merry-footed jig while playing the pipes and rattling on the tabor. People moved willingly out of his way, smiling and laughing. Ellis came behind him, fountaining the colored balls as he walked, followed by Basset, who strode along with head up and shoulders back, looking lord of them all and bending his head graciously from side to side, apparently unknowing of Joliffe capering and generally playing the fool behind him, doing everything with the trumpet except playing it, including using it for outright rude gestures at Basset's back, to loud laughter and some glad shouts.

Basset had bought the trumpet—second- or third-hand and somewhat battered—last winter. Because Joliffe was good at neither juggling nor tumbling for their street work and his lute was not always suitable, Basset had set him the task of learning to play the thing. His first blatting attempts to do so had been unappreciated, although Ellis had said, hands over his ears, "Still, he can't talk while he does it. There's something to be thankful for."

Joliffe had blown a particularly loud blatt at him, and Basset had said, "Why don't you go to the far corner of the next field and work at it, Joliffe?"

All in all, he had spent a good deal of time in far corners of fields for a while, until now, despite there being no likelihood of any town hiring him to play with their waits, he was no longer an offense to everyone's ears *all* of the time.

But more than playing on it could be done with a trumpet, and just now, as they made procession up the lane with folk watching and laughing, Basset began to look back at him suspiciously. Whenever he did, he saw Joliffe striding in a solemn copy of him that turned to mockery as soon as Basset turned away, bringing more laughter from the lookers-on and more suspicious looks from Basset. Following Piers, they circled the widening of the lanes that was Ashewell village's marketplace, and people gathered to see them better, until finally Piers marched into the center of the place and gave a final great beating of his tabor, at the end of which Basset suddenly spun around and caught Joliffe being particularly rude with the trumpet. Joliffe froze. Basset roared, faked a clout up the side of Joliffe's head, and violently gestured for him to play the thing. Joliffe, trying to recover dignity he had not had, flourished the trumpet, made a show of working his mouth to ready it, made to play, paused to spit, made to play, paused to ready his mouth again, and Basset, forgetting all dignity, booted his backside. Joliffe staggered forward with a startled blatt from the trumpet, bringing more laughter from the crowd so that he drew himself up with offended, tattered dignity and got out three notes of a fairly credible fanfare before Basset pushed the trumpet down with one hand, flung out his other hand widely to the crowd, and declared, "We come, good folk, to play for you!"

Their crowd was with them, roused and ready, but now Basset had to bring them around to readiness not for more foolery but for the plays they would actually see today. Joliffe, finally standing quietly with the other players, watched the watching faces change, led by Basset with practiced skill and a carefully readied speech from their present eagerness toward a different eagerness as they understood it was their Lord's life they were going to see, with Basset finishing, "And now, good folk, by your fair leave we go to ready for our play, that you may see and bend your knee before our Savior's victory."

At that, Joliffe raised the trumpet and played a quite sufficient flourish that Piers answered with a marching beat on the tabor that saw them forward—the crowd opening before them—to the churchyard gate and through it and across the churchyard to the playing place, leaving the crowd jostling through the gateway behind them.

Out of sight behind their curtains, the players hurriedly dumped juggling balls, tabor, pipes, and trumpet into a waiting hamper, stripped off their hats and outer clothing and dumped them out of the way into the hamper, too. Rose—already garbed and bearded—was standing ready to help Ellis into Christ's loose white robe and longhaired wig while the others helped each other into their garb, with Basset setting Judas' red hair firmly over Joliffe's own fair hair for him. That done, Basset looked around at them all and asked, "Ready?"

"Ready," they answered.

"How many?" he asked at Piers, who was peeking around one end of the fore-curtain.

"A couple score or so," Piers answered.

That was a goodly number when playing so small a place as Ashewell. Basset nodded, satisfied. He looked at Gil. "Ready?"

"Ready," Gil said firmly.

"Then go," Basset said, and Gil went out, around one side of the fore-curtain into full view of all the lookers-on, and with the speech Joliffe had written yesterday began the players' headlong run forward through the four plays.

The speech, telling of Christ's coming to Jerusalem "that fatal week when evil sought God's good for to destroy," went well, Joliffe thought, and then it was his own time to go out,

around the other end of the curtain from where Gil was retreating, to be Judas at the beginning of *Christ Against the
Money-changers*, deep in frowning worry that Christ was become "too bold at challenging both lords and priests, bringing trouble down on all our heads."

That brought the rest of the players bursting and hurrying out in a fuss and flurry of words and movements and
properties, because, besides Christ, the play had to have
the money-changers for him to attack, their table to overset, a scale and some bags of coins to be thrown down, a
whip to use against them, at least the Jews' High Priest
Cayphas to be offended, and if not all the Apostles, at least
Judas to be horrified. With Ellis playing Christ, Joliffe as
Judas, Basset as Cayphas, and Gil, Piers, and Rose as everyone else, they covered their lack of numbers by all of them
keeping in constant motion, giving their speeches in a rush
of accusations, angers, and outrage.

Joliffe knew their audience was with them when Christ
declared at the money-changers, "You knaves! You thieves
and rascals! Defaming the Lord God's honor as you do!
Making his house into a den of thieves and taking what is
not yours to take, like shepherds never shearing but butchering every sheep!" and among the lookers-on heads turned
and some people pointed at Father Hewgo standing at his
church door, glaring, his arms tightly folded across his chest,
well apart from it all but making sure his disapproval lowered over everything. Joliffe had not written the lines at him
but might as well have because his parishioners surely saw a
match; there was even scattered laughter that would do nothing to soften him toward the players.

With no help for that, they swept on without faltering
their lines or business, finished the play, and swept away
behind the curtains, taking with them the money-changers'
table—a hamper with a yellow cloth laid over it—the bags

of pebbles that served for coins, and the battered hanging scales, clearing the playing place for the simpler business of Judas betraying Christ to two Jewish priests.

While Joliffe, Basset, and Gil played that, the rest of the players readied for the *Last Supper* behind the curtains, throwing a white cloth over two hampers set end to end to make a table and hurriedly putting a goblet and a plate with bread on it. Joliffe, Basset, and Gil finished their scheming and went not behind the fore-curtain but away to either side and around and out of sight at the back, while Piers slowly drew aside the fore-curtain to show Christ standing (to save the trouble of stools the players did not have) alone behind the table, head bowed in deep thought over the bread and goblet. Still very slowly, Piers fastened the curtain out of the way, then went reverently to stand at one end of the table, a very short apostle.

Meanwhile, behind the rear curtain, Basset and Gil had stripped off their priestly garb with Rose and Joliffe's help, to become apostles. There being nothing the players could do about being too few to be the twelve apostles, they ignored the problem. By the time Piers was going to his place beside the table, they were ready, and the four of them, with Rose still in her wig and beard, went out with stately slowness to stand to either side of Ellis as Christ, who raised his hands to bless the bread and wine.

As he did, Joliffe skulked away from the table, going to loosen the curtain and then draw it closed, shutting the other players from sight before he turned to the audience and began to complain again of the trouble Christ was bringing down on them, carrying on the way he was. Judas' whining this time was meant to ease the taut quiet the *Last Supper* had brought over the audience and Joliffe succeeded, getting the laughter he wanted, everyone knowing how wrong Judas was about almost everything he was saying. But when Cayphas and the other Jewish priest, carrying a lantern to show it was now night, came out to him, a sharp quiet came over the lookers-on. And when the High Priest handed over the bag with its thirty pieces of silver as payment for betraying Christ, and Judas bowed and cringed to them in thanks, there were outright cries of anger and hissing from the audience.

Basset and Gil left, and Joliffe turned on the crowd, telling them scornfully that they were fools not to know money in the hand was worth more than a madman's promises of Heaven. That was met with catcallings and more hissing, and he shook his fist at them all, then skulked out of sight around one side of the curtain, clutching the bag of pebbles to his chest.

Immediately Piers drew the curtain aside again, this time keeping out of sight as best he could. The "table" was gone, and one of hampers with one of the players' gray ground cloths heaped over it was become the Garden of Gethsemane, with Ellis kneeling there. His prayer and pleading and final acceptance of his fate had the audience silent, tautly listening, so that when Gil—now the Apostle Peter—burst in on him, crying warning that, "Soldiers are come! My lord, now flee!" and Basset, Rose, and Piers—as soldiers now, in different garb—rushed in behind him, the startlement was complete.

Peter cut off a soldier's ear and Christ healed it, was bound and shoved and dragged from sight afterward, and Judas, at the back through all of that and finally left alone, came forward to say worriedly, "I fear, I fear I have done ill beyond all that I did mean. What doom shall come my heart mistells. I fear what the morrow shall bring. My death perhaps, as mankind's bane." He then went miserably away, followed by more hisses.

Now Gil went out alone again, this time to tell of Christ's torments and death, of Judas hanging himself, and of the

Crucifixion, with all the ugliness Joliffe had been able to put into it, and ending with Piers drawing the curtain aside again, this time to show Rose now gowned in blue as the Virgin Mary and seated on a cloth-covered hamper with dead Christ in her arms, the crown of thorns on his head, blood streaked down his face, and his nearly naked body showing the bleeding wounds in his side and hands and feet. Among the audience, that brought gasps and signings of the cross and some women to tears before Gil drew the curtain closed again and—to the slow, unseen beating of the tabor by Piers at the back—told of Christ's burial and the Harrowing of Hell.

That gave time for everyone else to ready for the Resurrection, so that when Gil pulled the curtain back again, there were Joliffe—with a long, loose gown thrown on over his other garb and Judas' red wig replaced by a woman's headkerchief—and Basset and Rose, likewise gowned and headkerchiefed as the Three Marys coming to the Tomb where Piers, with strapped-on wings, was the Angel standing on the gray cloth–covered hamper, now the tomb chest, to tell them in his clear, young voice that Christ was risen. With exclaims and tears, the Marys turned away, coming forward so they were in front of the curtain as Gil closed it. Joliffe and Basset spoke wondering words to each other and embraced Rose, the unspeaking Virgin. Then Gil opened the curtain one last time and there was Ellis standing where Piers had been, again in Christ's white robe, holding his hands out in blessing to the Marys and the audience while, out of sight, Gil and Piers sang a "Gloria." The Three Marys and not a few of the crowd fell to their knees. Then the Marys rose and moved forward so Gil could close the curtain behind them while he and Piers sang the end of the "Gloria." And when the curtain was closed and they fell silent together, Basset silently counted to three with nods of his head, for Piers on the fourth nod to start a triumphant drumming on his tabor, telling the play was done.

If they hadn't already known, the cheers, cries, and clapping that burst out then would have told them how very well their playing had gone, and Ellis dropped down to sit on the hamper with a grateful, weary *oof* of breath. It would be unseemly for Christ and his mother to take bows, so he and Rose did not join the others as they went out, for Gil and Piers to bow and Basset and Joliffe to curtsy acknowledgment to everyone. Only when they had retreated again behind the curtain was it all finally, fully finished for them, Basset beaming while he and Joliffe pulled off their headkerchiefs, Gil and Piers doing a small, quick-stepping dance of triumph.

Rose hurriedly took off the Virgin Mary's gown, her own gown underneath it so that she was free to see to everyone else as they began to strip, too, listening to the dispersing crowd's glad talk beyond the curtains around them. Most times the players would have had to be out there gathering coins, but since they were to have their share from whatever the whole ale-fest brought in, they were spared that effort just now, and Joliffe wondered if he was the only one tired enough to be grateful for that, until Ellis said wearily while changing Christ's robe for his own doublet, "So now that we've proved we can do these plays all at once, can we never do it again?"

"I make no promises," Basset said. That brought general groans all around him, but there was much smiling to go with it, because they *had* done it and the sense of triumph was more heady than a strong draught of good wine would have been just then.

In their own clothing again, they all helped Rose fold their garb and pack the hampers. At camp she would determine what would need cleaning and what would not, but for now it was enough to load it into the cart. That left the curtains and frame to be taken down, and while Ellis got out the mallet to knock loose the wooden pegs, Basset said to Rose, "We can see to this among us. Why don't you take this chance to see what there is to see here?"

"And bring back something to eat because you're all beginning to starve?" she said.

"That, too," said Joliffe. He caught one of her hands and kissed it. "Because food will nourish all the better if brought to us by your fair self."

She made a short sound between laughter and disgust and said, holding out a hand to Piers, "Come with me, out of the way here. You can help carry whatever I buy."

Ever preferring food to work, Piers went with her readily. Ellis, Joliffe noted, had kept his back to Rose the whole time, nor had she looked at him.

They were just finished loading the wood and curtains into the cart when Rose and Piers came back with two meat pies and a leather bottle of ale. Sitting in a row along the grassy edge of the lane, their backs against the churchyard wall, they ate and drank in what Joliffe thought was comfortable quiet until Basset said, "Rose, what's the trouble?"

She snapped at him, "Nothing."

"Except you're crying," her father said gently.

Everyone's head whipped around to look at her. Rose never cried. But large, shining tears were sliding down her cheeks, with more spilling over from her eyes even as she said, "No, I'm not," and wiped fiercely at them.

They were all stopped eating, staring at her, not knowing what to do. Rose was sometimes angry, sometimes impatient, often tired—and well she had right to be, given the life they led and what she had to put up with from all of them—but she didn't *cry*. And very gently Basset said, "What's happened? Have we done something?"

Trying to dry her eyes with a corner of her veil, she said, "It isn't anything," but the words came out on a sob.

Ellis, handing his piece of pie to Gil, got up from where he was sitting as far from her as he could. Somewhat uncertainly, he came and knelt in front of her, put his hands on her shoulders, and said tenderly, "It's no good saying it's not anything. It's something. Please, Rose. Tell us what."

"He came up behind me," she said on a sob. "Medcote. He . . ."

Covering her face with both hands, she began to sob openly. The rest of them looked at Piers, who was staring wide-eyed at his mother. To their unspoken question he shook his head, protesting, "I didn't see it."

With more control than Joliffe would have thought in him, Ellis said, still gently, "Please, Rose. Tell me. What did he do?"

With a broken gasp and sob, Rose dropped her hands into her lap, clutching them together to steady herself while she answered, looking down at them rather than at Ellis, "He touched me. Where he had no business touching me. And held on to my skirt when I tried to move away and whispered in my ear where he'd wait for me tonight. Because he knew I wanted him, he said. Because I was too good to waste . . . to waste on . . ."

Her hands flew to her face again, and Ellis, despite having turned dark red with anger and his mouth set into a hard line, drew her carefully forward into his arms, and she let him, burying her face against his shoulder, sobbing helplessly.

Her father stood up. "We're away from here tomorrow," he said grimly. "And we'll be well rid of the place, I think." He brushed his gown where he had been sitting on it. "It's time we went to see about our pay from Father Hewgo. Joliffe, you'll come with me. The rest of you start back to the camp. We'll catch you up when we've finished with the priest."

"Medcote . . ." Ellis started.

"If fortune favors us, we'll never lay eyes on him again," Basset said.

"If fortune favors him," Ellis returned, "*I'll* never lay eyes on him again."

Chapter 10

On the whole, most priests and churchwardens for whom the players had worked over the years had dealt fairly with them. From those who did not, Basset had learned enough to deal with their kind when he met them, and from what Joliffe had seen of Father Hewgo, he suspected Basset's dealing skills would be needed here, however clear the agreement had been three days ago. Their best hope was for fair-dealing churchwardens who would stand firm against whatever Father Hewgo tried to do. But he and Basset weren't even to the church door when Basset said, "Trouble."

It was not their trouble, though. Midway between the churchyard gate and the church door, Medcote and a man Joliffe had not seen before were confronting each other. And whoever the man was, he had had more to drink than was good for him, and was as angry as he was drunk, swaying forward and poking a forefinger into Medcote's chest, declaring loudly, "You cheated me! You know it! Everybody knows it!"

Medcote shoved his hand away. "I know you're a drunken fool, Jack Hammond. You can't hold your ale any better than you hold your land. What's done and over is over and done. Give up your whining."

Whining was hardly what Hammond was doing. His shouting was drawing more lookers-on than only Basset and Joliffe, and he declared loudly, maybe deliberately for all of them to hear, "Nothing's done! You're a cheat and a liar! Nothing's not even by half done!"

"I hope Hammond flattens him," Basset said, low-voiced and turning away.

"And stomps on him for a while afterward," said Joliffe, following, leaving the men to whatever their quarrel came to.

The heavy door into the church's nave was standing open. Joliffe shut it behind him, closing the arguing voices outside. Farther up the nave Master Ashewell looked around from where he was standing with Father Hewgo and Walter Gosyn and said, "Thank you."

Basset bowed. "Our pleasure."

"You've come about your payment," Master Ashewell said, "and are in good time. We'll do the counting out as soon as Master Kyping and Medcote come."

"You're all churchwardens together?" Basset asked.

Two churchwardens was a more usual number but four was not unheard of, and that Medcote and Master Ashewell were wardens here was to the good, Joliffe thought. They knew what had been agreed between the players and priest.

"Master Kyping isn't one of us," Master Ashewell said. "He's bailiff here for the abbey and merely going to watch the counting out."

"To see we don't come to blows about it," Gosyn said, and he was not jesting.

Joliffe wondered whose benighted choice had made Ashewell, Medcote, and Gosyn churchwardens together?

Behind him, the outer door he had just closed was shoved

open, and John Medcote stalked in, followed by Master Kyping.

"It didn't come to a fight then?" Gosyn called.

"Hammond hasn't the guts for a fight," Medcote snapped.

"Not this time," Master Kyping said smoothly over him. "A quiet word in the ear and a heavy hand on the shoulder can do wonders."

"Especially the heavy hand," Master Ashewell said, smiling.

"Shall we get on with it?" Father Hewgo demanded.

He was rubbing his hands together like a merchant expecting good profit, and Joliffe was braced for the unpleasantness that shortly came in the sacristy where they all went to count out the coins on a table. Master Kyping had brought the take from the ale-fest itself: the fees that folk had paid to set out their goods for sale and all the profit from the sale of the ale itself. Mostly, the coins were farthings and half-pennies, but when all were counted, they made a goodly sum, even before Master Kyping said easily, "Now, Father Hewgo, where's what you collected after the play? You put the pouch in your undergown's pocket, I think?" The bailiff put out a hand and patted the priest's side and said, smiling, "Yes, there it is."

As the proverb went, if looks could kill, Master Kyping would have been a dead man from Father Hewgo's glare just then, but he went on smiling, his hand held out for the pouch. Father Hewgo fumbled it from beneath his outer robe and tossed it ungraciously onto the table. Master Kyping, as if he did not see the priest's ire, loosened the wide mouth of the purse and poured out a very pleasant amount of coins.

Withdrawn into disdainful dignity, Father Hewgo said down his nose, "I supposed the players were giving their share as their gift to the church."

"Were you?" Master Kyping asked Basset.

"No, sir. We were not," Basset answered smoothly. "I believe it's written that the workman is worthy of his hire. Besides that," he added, "our tenth was from the full profits of the day, not simply from our playing."

Father Hewgo turned his glare from the bailiff to Basset while Joliffe thought at him, You lying disgrace to your priesthood, and Gosyn said, "I say they should have their full tenth and no quarrel about it. They were that good they had me in tears."

"You and a good many others," Master Ashewell said. "I agree there's no room for quarrel about it."

Everyone looked at Medcote, whose agreement should have come readily, but it did not. To Joliffe it was almost as if he were thinking the chance to make trouble by arguing would be worth it. No, Joliffe corrected. By the glint in Medcote's eyes, he was not *almost* thinking that—he was very certainly thinking it, and Joliffe's tight hold on his anger at the man began to slip. The players had done far better work today than was asked or expected of them, and now they were threatened with being cheated by the priest's greed and Medcote's love of trouble.

There was no telling whether, in the end, Medcote resisted the temptation to make trouble or simply decided that irking Father Hewgo would be more diverting, but he said, "I agree. They should have full payment and no quarrel."

Balked of his last hope of an ally, Father Hewgo folded his arms across his chest and stood glowering at them all, Medcote included, while Master Kyping went on with the counting-out.

This was the second time Joliffe had seen Father Hewgo's expectation of support from Medcote disappointed. Whatever alliance the priest thought they had was either ended or one on which he had better learn not to depend.

Master Kyping finished the full counting, then counted out the players' share to one side, all very openly and fairly.

While Father Hewgo brought a small but iron-bound box from a closed aumbry against the wall, Basset loosed his leather pouch from his belt, swept the players' share into it, latched it firmly closed, and refastened it to his belt. While the priest scooped the considerable remainder of the coins into his box as if expecting someone would yet try to "cheat" him out of even more, Basset and Joliffe bowed to the other men with more thanks given all around and then got themselves out and away from the sacristy, gathering speed as they left the church, wanting nothing so much as to be well away from the place. By the time they were outside and crossing the churchyard, they were at as full a stride as possible short of breaking into a run.

The village was nearly settled back to its usual quiet, with most of those come for the church ale well on their way home by now, to be there before dark or not long after. Joliffe wondered if Mary's husband had hired a horse for the day, or if she would be walking back to Faringdon, the child asleep in her arms, his head heavy on her shoulder. Or maybe her husband was a good enough husband that he would be carrying the boy, with maybe a hand free to be holding Mary's hand.

Joliffe was unready for the loneliness that shifted through him then, and he gave it a hard shove to keep it shifting right on and away. Choices made were choices made, with regrets and what-ifs to be left behind with the choice unchosen. Or else carried well back in the mind, to be brought forward and considered in the balance when time came to make new choices. And presently he had no need to make new choices or regret old ones, well settled as he was into the player's life and things going as they were for the company.

Basset waited until the village was behind them and the road all theirs, with the lowering sun throwing shadows long across the level fields around them, before he said a few sharp things about Father Hewgo, and then, "Saints! I don't know when I've seen so many ill-humours going so many different ways as we have here."

"Gosyn and Master Ashewell at least are friends, by the look of it," Joliffe said, "but neither of them much likes Medcote, and nobody likes the priest."

"Who returns the favor. And then there's the man who was quarreling with Medcote in the churchyard just now, with bad blood there, for certain. And those are just who we've noted the few days we've been here."

"You missed the fellow angry at Gosyn earlier today," Joliffe said. "And Gosyn angry at him, come to that. Let alone what had passed between Hal Medcote and Gosyn, and Nicholas Ashewell. You didn't see that either."

"Saint Genesius see us away from here tomorrow," Basset said from the heart. "When does that bailiff mean to talk with us? He should have heard by now from the steward or his abbess why we're here, but asking him in the church seemed a poor thought since I doubt he wants anyone here to know they've been spied on."

"That's likely it," Joliffe said. "Maybe he means to meet us on the road after we're away."

"However it is, it's his trouble to talk to us, not ours to find the chance to speak to him. No matter what, we leave in the morning," Basset declared.

"Amen!" Joliffe agreed.

By the time they came to the field, Tisbe was unharnessed and set to graze, and Ellis and Gil were just lifting the first hamper out of the cart. Basset stopped them with, "It was a great day in more ways than one! Before we do anything else, lay out the exchequer cloth, Rose!"

An exchequer cloth was painted in large squares—checkered—and used for counting out and reckoning money by large households and governments with money enough to need such accounting. The players did not have, had never had, any such cloth, and laughing at her father, Rose got her white apron from the cart and laid it on the grass beside the firepit. The players gathered around it, sitting down on their heels or on the grass. Basset emptied today's coins into a heap on the apron and with due solemnity counted them out in even shares, one share to each of them and a share for the company purse.

In the usual way of things, Basset would then write it all down on the small scroll he kept of the company's accounts, such as they were, give each of them a few coins from their share, and all the rest to Rose to hide in the cart in a place only she was supposed to know. There it was carefully kept and given out as needed, rather than wantonly spent, with the company's share kept to meet the company's day-to-day needs and any grievous necessity that might come, St. Genesius forbid. But this time with the counting finished, Basset sat back, looked at the separate gatherings of coins, and then shoved all of Ellis' toward him, all of Joliffe's toward him, and so on to the others, saying, "This you've all earned twice over. Today's work was more than I've ever asked of you, and you met my hopes to the full."

Piers whooped and scooped his coins into his belt pouch before springing to his feet and into delighted dance around the campsite. Rose put an arm around her father's shoulders and kissed his cheek. Ellis, Joliffe, and Gil thanked him heartily.

"My thanks doubled to you," Basset answered. "Without it was all of us together, we'd not have made it. Now let's finish the day and have our well-earned rest."

With a sense of high triumph, they set to their end-of-day work, the men and Gil making short work of hauling the hampers out of the cart, then leaving them to Rose, seeing to building up the fire and putting the bedding into the tent again, while Piers fetched water and Rose looked over the garb and properties they had used that day, finding nothing that needed washing and only the hem on Christ's robe in need of mending where it had pulled out. That was something easily done and could wait for a better time, because by the time everything was folded and packed away to her satisfaction, dark was drawn well in. It was by firelight and the sunset's last glow that the men reloaded the hampers into the cart along with everything else except what they would need tonight and in the morning.

With that their day was done except for supper, and after their good meal in the village, they settled now for simply bread and cheese and ale, no work for anyone, most especially Rose. At his grandfather's bidding, Piers had built up the fire against the coming darkness and cooling night, and they gathered around it, fairly tired past much talking, simply eating and drinking, with it becoming clear that Medcote had done one good thing today. While Rose sat with one arm around Piers, who was leaning against her more asleep than not, on her other side she was leaning against Ellis, his arm around her. The comfort he had given her today, and her anger and fear at Medcote, had brought down the wall she had set between herself and Ellis. It was maybe forgiveness between them now, or maybe it was only her need of him, but by the look of it, Ellis had hope she would take more than comfort from him tonight, Joliffe thought.

Then for a few days all would be well. Until her conscience began to shove against her happiness again.

The only thing worse than a woman with a conscience, Joliffe thought, was a man without one.

And that was not true and he did not believe it. It was merely one of those things that sounded more clever than it was. And he immediately wondered how he could sometime use it in a play.

Then he wondered if it might be more than his life was worth if Rose took it badly.

Tisbe had grazed herself to the edge of the firelight,

maybe wanting their company, but now she raised her head to stare into the darkness toward the gate as if seeing something there. An instant silence fell among the players, and into it Basset said quietly, "Joliffe."

Joliffe needed no more. He was nearest the cart. With seeming ease, he rose and went to its open back as if to fetch something of no great matter but putting himself in reach of the thick wooden clubs kept in a rack against the cart's inner wall, to be quickly in reach whenever there was need. Let him see a need and he'd have them tossed one after another to the other players in seconds. He couldn't juggle but he could toss clubs, and his hand was already resting on one when Master Kyping walked into the firelight.

Joliffe left the cart and sauntered back to the fire as the rest of the company stood up, bowing with the rest of them as Master Kyping reached them, nodded in return, and asked, "May I join you for a time?"

Basset waved to his own cushions and stepped aside, saying, "By all means, sir."

Master Kyping waved him back to them and sat down cross-legged on the other side of the fire, holding his hands out to the warmth and saying, "There was no good time to talk to you today. I've had word from my lady abbess of St. Mary's that Lady Lovell had offered the help of her players in learning something about our troubles here, and since I suppose you'll be leaving early come the morning, tonight seemed a good time to ask if you'd had any success."

"Indeed, sir," said Basset. He and the rest of them had all sat down again with every outward sign of ease, Piers with his head now on his mother's lap and already mostly back to sleep. "Lady Lovell did honor us with that task. I hope that gave no offense." Because not every man would care to have unasked help thrust on him.

"No offense at all," Master Kyping answered with a

smile. "I take what help I can and gladly. Have you learned aught beyond what's openly known?"

"We think we have," Basset said.

"And guessed some things, too," Joliffe added.

Master Kyping looked to him. "I take guesses." He looked back to Basset. "So?"

"So I don't know that we've learned anything you don't already know. There's little secret about all the dislikes running every which way among folk here, that's sure."

"Too sure," Master Kyping agreed.

"Master Ashewell seems the least trouble among them."

"He is. He's done well beyond the ordinary, but has a lighter hand and maybe more wits to him than either Walter Gosyn or John Medcote."

"He's good friends with Gosyn, though?" Basset asked.

"They've known each other all their lives here, yes."

"But despite that, the servant-talk is that Master Ashewell is thinking of marrying Nicholas to Medcote's daughter," Joliffe said.

Master Kyping snapped his head around to look at him, eyes narrowed. "What?"

"So an Ashewell servant says," Basset said. "That Medcote wants it and Master Ashewell is maybe thinking to do it, and that neither Mistress Ashewell nor Nicholas is pleased about it."

"I wouldn't think they would be," Master Kyping said. "There's no love lost between the two families. Young Nicholas married to Eleanor? That would be more like throwing a baby to a wildcat than a marriage. But you say there's talk that way among Ashewell's servants?"

"Some talk, yes," Basset said.

From the side of his eye Joliffe tried to tell if that reminder had made any harm between Rose and Ellis but could not tell, while Master Kyping said thoughtfully, "Something

is wrong there, right enough, if Master Ashewell didn't refuse out of hand an offer like that from Medcote. If he
hasn't, I have to wonder why. It would go far to explain-
ing something of what I've felt building here without being able to put hand to."

"I wonder if Gosyn knows about it?" Joliffe said mildly.
"I'd have thought a match between his daughter and Master Ashewell's son more likely."

"Yes. That's what we've all thought." Master Kyping
looked back and forth from Joliffe to Basset and around at
the others. "Aught else?"

Basset answered, "From something said between
Nicholas and Claire, it seems Hal Medcote is angling for
her and she doesn't like it."

"Her father won't like it either, if Hal Medcote means
more than a jest about it," Master Kyping said grimly.

"She seems to think he does, but from what was said, his
father favors it no more than Gosyn is likely to," Basset said.

"That helps." Master Kyping was grim about it. "There'd
be three kinds of hell let loose if Medcote and Gosyn set up
to quarrel over something like that. Not that Hal Medcote
can't make hell all by himself. You're sure Claire wasn't
taken with thought of him? He's good-looking enough to
turn women's heads."

"I think she said he made her flesh crawl," Joliffe offered. "And she didn't look pleased with his attention today, if you saw that."

"Yes. I did see." Master Kyping gave a sharp nod, as if
satisfied of something. "Good enough. And anything else?"

"Nothing else that isn't open for everyone," Basset said.

"Well, you've given me more than I had before and
enough to go on, certainly. My thanks." Master Kyping rose
to go. The players stood up, too. "I'll see to Lady Lovell
knowing you've done well by things here. Good journeying
tomorrow."

Basset thanked him for that, adding, "Good fortune to you, too."

"With this lot I'll likely need it," Master Kyping said with a grim half-laugh and walked away into the darkness.

The night was clear; beyond the firelight there was starlight enough for him to see his way, but, "I wonder where he's going to," said Joliffe. "He didn't ride. I heard no horse."

"Just so he's gone and tomorrow we can go," said Ellis. He stretched his arms wide and yawned. "I'm for bed."

He held his hand out to Rose, who took it and let him draw her close. He said something softly in her ear. She nodded, and while the others did their final readying for sleep, he brought his bedding and hers from the tent and went to spread them under the cart.

No one was fool enough to say anything. Leading Piers, more asleep than awake, Basset and Gil went to their own blankets in the tent, while Joliffe lingered to bank the fire for the night, bringing the darkness in around him, so that he stood for a few moments, waiting for his eyes to grow used to only starlight before turning for the tent himself. With the fire out, the stars were a thick wash of pale light across the sky, and when he looked toward the hills, the White Horse was faintly there, and he raised one hand in salute to it before ducking into the tent.

he slept heavily and only reluctantly came awake to pale light through the tent's canvas when the others began to stir and shift and crawl from their blankets. He resisted doing as much himself until Gil set back one flap to go outside, and said, "Oh. Euw."

Basset echoed that, and Joliffe unburrowed his head to see a thick mist hiding the world beyond half a dozen yards away. The only brightness was from the flames that Rose was encouraging under a pot hung over the fire. "Something warm to set us on our way, I thought," she said as Basset, Joliffe, Gil, and Piers joined her. "Even if only oatmeal."

Basset gave a yawning stretch and asked, "Where's Ellis gone?"

"Down to the stream. I'm supposing he'll find his way back through this."

"If I find him wandering, I'll point him the right way," Joliffe promised, took a towel from the two warming on the drying rack beside the fire, and set off to where he had to suppose the stream still was. The mist wreathed lightly among the trees and he heard the purl of water well before he saw it. Ellis, coming toward him, loomed dark-shaped out of the gray-whiteness, and Joliffe said as they passed, "It turned chill last night. Did you keep warm enough?"

"Shut it and put the bar across it," Ellis said pleasantly and kept going.

"Double that from me, whelp," Basset said cheerfully, closer behind than Joliffe had thought he was. He lightly slapped the back of Joliffe's head, and Joliffe grinned, neither harmed nor chastened but making show of rubbing his head.

The morning's first necessities seen to, the players mostly gathered around the fire to their breakfast of oat pottage. Only Piers among them was enjoying the damply shrouded morning, running in long loops out of and into sight through the mist, making strange noises for the sake of hearing what the mist did to them, until he came too close and his grandfather collared him, saying, "Finish eating so we can clear and get on the road."

"It's too hard to see for us to start out yet," Piers protested.

"We're not going at a mad gallop," Basset said. "We'll do well enough."

"And if need be," added Ellis, "we can always send you

ahead to fall into any pits there may be before we get to them."

Done with eating, they did what little was needed to be on their way. The tent, heavy with damp, was the worst part of it. Wherever they stopped and however they stayed to-night, they would have to have it out to dry lest it mold. While the others wrestled with it, Joliffe got Tisbe into har-ness and hitched to the cart. She showed her displeasure at that by butting her head into his chest, but he assured her, "No, truly, you know you'll be glad to be on the road again. You were starting to find all this eating dull, weren't you?" She butted him again, and not as if she agreed with him, but when the time came she leaned into the harness and pulled the cart bumping out of the field and into the lane willingly enough, turning to the left at Joliffe's lead.

Behind them, they left the pasture near to what it had been when they came, with the grassy turfs replaced in the firepit and nothing to show they had been there but the matted-down grass of their camp and the cropped stretches of Tisbe's grazing. The first would soon straighten and the rest grow and there would be nothing to show they had been there, nothing left but their memory of the place, and that would soon blur and be lost among fading memories of uncounted other places they had been. Walking at Tisbe's head into the white wall of mist that obscured their way as surely as time obscured the future, Joliffe admitted to himself, not for the first time, that it was an odd life but it suited and satisfied him.

For now.

His stride did not falter but his mind did.

For now?

From where had that thought come?

And if not this life, then what? He knew full well how many might-have-beens he had slid away from in his life thus far because none of them had been what he wanted, nor had he seen any others that would suit and serve him better than this one did.

So why the "for now"?

They passed Master Ashewell's manor gate without see- ing anyone except a dog that came out to bark at them with all the gladness of having something to do, but by the time they were going steeply up into Ashewell village, the mist was thinning and people in the street called out and waved as they passed, with no sight of Father Hewgo to spoil any- one's pleasure. On the village's far side, with the mist fast vanishing and the sun beginning to break yellow through it, they took the road westward, their plan being to perform at Swindon before the day was out and spend the night there. None of them took particular note of a horse closing on them at a canter from behind. There was room enough on the road here for a rider to pass them without trouble.

Except the rider slowed to a trot as he passed them, then swung his horse into Tisbe's way and brought his horse to a stop.

He was no one they knew. Tisbe stopped without need of Joliffe telling her, and he knew that behind the cart Ellis, walking with Rose until then, would be moving closer to the cart's back, ready to grab out and toss the clubs to them if need be; but on Tisbe's other side Basset was saying with no apparent alarm at all despite he would be as ready for trouble as the rest of them, "You want us for something, sir?"

"You're the players were in Master Ashewell's pasture last night?" the rider demanded.

By now Joliffe had taken in the fellow had no sword, only the usual dagger at his belt. Nor was there any sound of other men moving in ambush on them. Whatever this was, it wasn't likely robbery or assault, and with probably the same thought, Basset asked somewhat more boldly, "You are . . . ?"

"Master Kyping's man. He sent me to find you. You *are* the players?"

"We are," Basset said.

"Then on Master Kyping's order you're to go back to the field where you were and stay there."

"What's happened?" Basset asked sharply; and well he might, because something surely had.

And back at him with matching sharpness, the man said, "John Medcote was found murdered this morning hardly half a mile from where you were."

Chapter 11

There being neither point nor use to making trouble about going back, the players made none, and when the man saw they were going to give him no argument, his manner eased enough for him to offer, "If we go on a little way and turn off the high road the next chance there is, I can show you side ways and save you turning right around and going back on your tracks."

"Will they be wide enough for our cart, sir?" Basset asked.

"They're wide enough for haywains. Should do for your cart."

Joliffe was weighing as fast as Basset surely was how much trouble they might be in, with Medcote dead and close to their camp. Strangers were always better to blame for trouble than someone everyone knew. Even with a lord's name to their company, they were still folk not in the right way of things to most men's minds, and therefore likely capable of anything and therefore always easiest to blame. But Basset always held that it was best to be at least outwardly friendly to anyone with possible authority, pointing out—sometimes through gritted teeth—"It's being better they like us than not." So here and now, as Joliffe set Tisbe forward again and the man brought his own horse around to walk beside them, Basset asked easily, "You're from around here, then, you know the ways so well?"

"Born and bred over Uffington way and in Master Kyping's service these three years."

"So you know who doesn't like whom around here," Basset said.

The man barked a short laugh. "What you're asking is who didn't like John Medcote, yes? Ha! I'd be hard put to it to say who *did* like him around here. You've not much to fear there. Master Kyping'll be looking at more than you."

"Medcote didn't seem to get on well even with his own priest," Joliffe prompted.

The man short-laughed again. "Only when it suited the pair of them to make someone else miserable between them."

"His own household didn't seem pleasant with itself either when we were there," Basset said.

"It wouldn't be. Medcote and his son were like Medcote and the priest—hell on everyone else when they worked together, hell on each other when they fell out. Here's where we turn."

The lane he showed them into dropped at a long slant and talk stopped until they had Tisbe and the cart at the bottom and on level again. But then the man took up where he'd left off with, "Not that Hal Medcote doesn't raise hell fifteen different ways that have nothing to do with his father. I wouldn't care to cross either of the women either. It's said Anela Medcote has a hand like a man when it comes to whipping a servant."

"Must make it hard to keep servants," Joliffe said.

"Medcote has—had his ways. He'd get someone in debt

to him and then make them work it off in his household. Cheap wages, that. That's how he kept some of them there, anyway."

"Must make for an angry household," Basset said.

"From what I've heard and seen, Medcote liked angry. Got someone *too* angry this time, though, it seems."

So there would be suspects enough besides themselves, and plenty of them with better reason for wanting Medcote dead than could be found for them. With luck, Kyping wanted them back only for the form of the thing, to ask his questions and then let them go on their way.

With luck and the weight of being Lord Lovell's players on their side.

Kyping's man left them at the gateway to Grescumb Field with promise that Master Kyping would be along when he could be. A promise open-ended enough to mean there was no telling how long they would be here now they were back, and as he brought Tisbe to a halt with their cart where it had been before, Joliffe felt slightly unsettled at the wrongness of being here at all so soon after leaving. They never turned back on their tracks like this. A place left behind was a place left behind until maybe they came that way again some other month or, more likely, year. Here they had been gone so short a time that the grass had not begun to straighten around their erstwhile firepit.

Joliffe shook his head to shake the strangeness of it down to the bottom of his mind and asked Basset, "Shall I unharness Tisbe or not?"

With no need to seem at ease and pleasant now Kyping's man had gone, Basset openly grouched, "May as well, since there's no saying how long we'll be kept here."

Ellis knelt and started to pry the turves out of the firepit with his dagger, muttering angrily, "May as well plan to be here for the night at least. No one's likely to make hurry over us."

Very quietly, Rose told Piers and Gil, "Firewood and water, please."

Piers, unusually silent and with no bounce to his step, headed toward the trees. Most of his growing up had been spent in the company's dark years, when they had been without a lord's protection. He knew how bad trouble could be for players.

Gil, older by a few years but far younger in the company, cast uncertain, uneasy glances among them all but asked no questions as he took the bucket hanging under the cart and started for the stream.

Rose, still very quiet, said to her father, "I was going to buy food along the way today. We're somewhat short. Should I go into the village, do you think?"

Basset shook his head against that. "Best none of us go anywhere. And maybe especially into the village just now. Whatever you have at hand will have to do for today at least."

Ellis was wrong, though, about no one making hurry over them. The morning's mist was all burned away but the sun was not nearly to its midday height when Kyping rode into the pasture. The man who had fetched the players back was with him, but Kyping stopped just inside the gateway, dismounted, gave his reins to his man, and came on alone and a-foot.

Joliffe was away to one side, brushing Tisbe more for his comfort than hers. Giving her a final pat, he strolled back to join Basset, Ellis, and Rose beside the small fire and the kettle where some of their dried beef was gently seething, both to soften the stuff that otherwise was hardly better to chew than plain leather and to add a little savor to the dried beans seething with them. On the other side of the cart, Gil and Piers broke off their game of mumble-the-peg—a game even Piers found it hard to cheat at—and came to join the others.

Kyping began well enough, saying he regretted having to order their return, but it was easier for him than having to ride after them, not knowing when he'd be free of other questioning to do so.

"Besides it being better to have your best suspects close to hand," Basset said evenly, there being no use in letting Kyping think they were fools.

"Yes," Kyping agreed, accepting that as evenly as Basset said it.

"A question of our own before yours," Basset said. "Why are we talking to you rather than whoever is constable here?"

"Because he went six days ago with his wife to show off their newborn to his mother in Swindon. I've sent someone to fetch him, and none too happy he's going to be about it. Meantime, I'm serving in his place and am none too happy about it either."

"Your man said Medcote was murdered close by here," Basset said. "Shall we start off by our declaring we heard nothing."

"You may as well. It's not likely you would have heard anything. It happened half a mile away and in the woods along the stream and I doubt there was much noise about it. So, where were all of you last night?"

"Here," Basset answered. "All of us. All night."

Kyping gave a one-sided grin. "The expected answer, yes. You didn't see anyone, hear anything? Last night? This morning?"

Mostly they all shook their heads, but Piers said, "I did. This morning I saw a man go past in the lane. Going that way." He pointed toward Ashewell's.

The players all looked at him in surprise. "You did?" said Rose. "You never said."

"How?" Joliffe asked. "Until almost before we left, the mist was still so thick that way we couldn't see the hedge or the lane."

"He was running around," said Ellis. "Remember? Making stupid noises."

Paying that no heed, Piers said to Kyping, "I was close to the gate and this man went by. He stopped and stared at me half a moment, and I stopped and stared at him. Then he went on. He walked fast."

"So would I if someone came capering madly out of a mist at me," Ellis muttered.

"Did you know him? Was he someone you'd seen before?" Kyping asked.

"No. I didn't know him and I hadn't ever seen him."

"Can you tell me what he looked like, what he was wearing?"

"He was wearing a yellow tunic," Piers answered with firm confidence. "He had a brown—I think it was brown; dark but not black anyway—sleeveless surcoat over it, and plain shoes."

"Nothing on his head?"

Piers frowned into his memory and finally said, "A hood. You know—the kind that just covers the shoulders and comes up to cover the head. It was brown like the surcoat, only not the same brown."

"That was a lot to see in so little a while," Kyping said.

Proud of himself and enjoying being the center of things, Piers said, "I like clothes, so I note them. Not that these were much. Just common and not very good." He hesitated, then added, "Or maybe they were good once but they're old now. But maybe still his good-wear ones?"

"Why didn't you say you'd seen him?" Basset asked.

Piers shrugged. "He wasn't anyone. Just someone off to his morning work."

"Can you say better when this was?" Kyping asked.

Piers shrugged again. "The sun was a little up so there was light all glowing through the mist, but the mist wasn't shifting yet."

Kyping nodded as if he were thinking as much as listening. He thought a little longer, then asked, looking from face to face at all of them, "Why haven't any of you said anything about how she"—he nodded at Rose, not knowing her name—"was supposed to meet with Medcote last night, there where his body was found?"

Quickly, Rose said, "Because none of them knew about it. He wanted it. I didn't. I refused him and didn't see need of making trouble by telling it to anyone else."

The others' turns of head toward her in surprise at the lie served as well to seem the surprise of men who had known nothing about the business at all.

"You didn't go?" Kyping prodded.

"I did not," Rose answered firmly.

"How do you know of it?" Joliffe asked.

"His son told me. And his wife."

"His wife?" Ellis echoed incredulously. "She knew and she told you?"

"Seems Medcote didn't trouble to make secret his doings that way." Kyping swung a sharp look around at them all as he added, "Hal Medcote says he and his father were here three days ago. Friday, it would have been."

Joliffe felt Gil stiffen beside him and guessed his fists had clenched because Kyping looked down at them and then at Gil's face and asked, "Yes?" in a way that told he meant to have an answer.

Gil, looking surprised at having betrayed himself, stared back at him.

Kyping prompted him, "You were here?"

Gil looked at Basset, who nodded and said, "Just tell him."

Looking back to Kyping, Gil answered, "They thought Rose was alone here because I was gone to the stream. When I came out of the trees, Medcote was being lewd at her. She was frightened and backing away from him and Hal

Medcote was sitting on his horse, laughing. When they saw me, when they saw she wasn't alone, they left off and rode away."

Kyping looked to Rose. "That was the way of it?"

"Yes. Except I was angry as well as frightened."

"Were threats made or blows given?"

"There was nothing like that, no."

Kyping looked to Basset. "You played at their house that night. Was there any trouble then?"

"None," Basset said.

"Nor any other trouble with Medcote since you came?"

"None. Nor would I say what passed on Friday or yesterday was 'trouble' so much as the kind of bother we meet with sometimes. Nothing new and nothing to kill anyone about."

With a wry turn to one side of his mouth, Kyping looked around at them all again and said, "That all seems well enough so far as it goes. The trouble is you're players, aren't you? It's your business to seem other than you are. Yesterday I saw just how good you are at that, so how am I to know you're not all lying now?"

There was hardly a safe answer to make to that, and none of them said anything, merely went on looking back at him.

Kyping gave almost a laugh, shrugged, and said, "So. Unless I learn you're in some way lying to me, that's the end of it so far as the business concerns you."

"And we can go on our way?" Basset asked.

"Better if you don't. The crowner will surely want to ask these same questions all over again for himself." The crowner being the king's officer charged with deciding whether a sudden death was accidental or should come under the law. "I've sent for him, but it's never easy to say where my man will find him or how long he'll take to come." Since a shire had few crowners, they were often from home about their work. Kyping hesitated, then said, "Besides that, I'd like you to do more of what you've done already—ask questions and see what you can learn of things not likely to come my way."

So he wanted them to be his allies as well as suspects, Joliffe thought, and bowed with everyone else as Basset said, "Gladly, sir."

With a slight bow of his own head, Kyping said, "My thanks. Until later, then."

He turned and started back toward the horses and his waiting man. Joliffe took a step after him, then sent a quick, questioning look at Basset. Basset nodded for him to go on, and Joliffe overtook Kyping midway across the field. Kyping stopped, turning toward him with a questioning look, and Joliffe asked, "Where were you last night, that you came here on foot?"

Kyping showed grimly humoured understanding of the question. "Well asked, I suppose. I live somewhat beyond Faringdon and chose to stay last night at Master Ashewell's. His wife is a cousin of my mother's."

"Did you ask him about Medcote trying to force a marriage on Nicholas and why he hadn't refused it out of hand?"

"Not then. Not yet. I wanted to find out what else might be a-foot before I started that hare."

"Now you'll have to."

"Now I'll have to."

"At least, since you were there last night, you can say Ashewell safely was, too, and he can do as much for you," Joliffe tried.

"Not surely, for either of us. After we all went to our beds, I don't know who can say where anyone was."

"Not Mistress Ashewell for her husband?"

"She'll say he was with her and never left, won't she?"

"Probably. But you never know with wives. Or husbands,

come to that. Do you suppose she was no happier than Master Ashewell was at thought of her son marrying Medcote's daughter?"

"I've never noted anything friendly that way. The Medcotes are not a well-liked family, as you've surely noted. Which means, unfortunately, that I don't lack people who were maybe willing to kill him."

"Your best way to go, then, is to find out who knew Medcote would be where he was last night."

"You're telling me my business?" Kyping asked it with curiosity rather than heat.

"If we're going to work for you in this, won't it be better we work *with* you?"

"I somewhat guess," said Kyping, "that it will be *you* more than the others working in this."

It was fair enough that Kyping had been taking his measure while Joliffe was taking his, and Joliffe nodded for answer and said, "If that's to be the way of it, I need to know more than I do. For one thing, how was Medcote murdered?"

"He was drowned."

"Drowned? Just drowned?"

"How many ways do you want him killed? There's hardly 'just' about drowning. Keep a man's head under water long enough, it works as well as any other way to kill him."

"True," Joliffe agreed. "But most men give small cooperation to having it done to them, and Medcote was neither small nor looked to be a weakling. Was there any sign he was knocked senseless first?"

"By the looks of the scuffled ground and the bruises on his jaw, there was a fight."

"There's something to look for, then. Someone with bruises on his hands, his knuckles." Then, regretfully, Joliffe added, "Unless he was wearing gloves. Riding gloves or a workman's heavy leather ones. That might have kept down his own bruising."

"But it's something to look for, yes," Kyping agreed.

Joliffe circled back to, "They fought and Medcote was knocked senseless and then dragged to the stream and drowned."

"He was dragged to the stream, yes. There's marks of that. But he got back wits enough to struggle then. The marks of it are there on the muddy bank. Whoever it was, they knelt straddling his back, pinning his arms under their knees, holding him down while they forced his head under the water and kept it there until he was dead. Then," Kyping said even more grimly, "they left him there, his head still in the water. The fish had got at him some before he was found."

First to last, it was an ugly picture. "Someone strong then," Joliffe said. "Another man surely."

Kyping's gaze flicked away toward the other players, toward Rose, and back to him. "Who's her man here?"

"We share her among us," Joliffe said sharply. Then as Kyping's eyes started to widen, he said even more sharply and with disgust, "No, we don't. She's Master Basset's daughter. The boy is his grandson. She's widowed and has nowhere else to be except here, mothering the lot of us whether she likes it or not."

"A hard life for an honest woman," Kyping said.

"And made the harder by people like Medcote thinking she's easy for any man who wants her."

"I ask pardon," Kyping said as if he meant it. He started for the gate again. "It was a question I had to ask."

Going with him, Joliffe said, "I ask pardon in return for being sharp about it." Then he pointed out, "The man Piers saw this morning was dressed like that Jack Hammond was dressed yesterday when he quarreled with Medcote in the churchyard."

"So I've thought, too."

"It wasn't a new quarrel between them either."

"It wasn't, no."

"Piers didn't see them quarreling. He probably never saw Jack Hammond at all, to take any note of, to be saying he saw him this morning."

"But you and Basset saw Jack quarrel with Medcote. One of you could have told the boy to say all that he did."

That told Joliffe that Kyping was not letting loose of them as suspects, but seeming as if he had not noted it, he said, "True. But what time was Medcote killed? It was dawn when Piers saw Hammond. Surely Medcote hadn't been waiting all night for Rose, for Jack Hammond to happen on him at dawn and kill him. What hour was he killed? Do you know?"

"Not for a certainty, but Medcote left his place just at dark, they say there, and the body was well along with stiffening when I saw it this morning."

"He wasn't killed by Jack Hammond at dawn then."

"There's nothing to say Jack hadn't done it earlier and for some reason only came past here hours later, unlikely though that is. What I want to hear is why Jack was going past here at dawn when his holding is on the other side of the village. When I've heard what he has to say, then I'll find out whether or not he's telling the truth."

Heartened that Kyping looked willing to keep his mind open all ways, Joliffe asked, "What was the quarrel between him and Medcote?"

"Jack was his tenant. Jack's father held the land before him, and back in Francis Brook's time, his father paid Francis a fee to have the holding put in his name and Jack's. That was so that when Jack's father died, Jack would have to pay no heriot or fine for inheriting. But when Jack's father died two years ago, Medcote demanded not only that Jack pay the fine to inherit but he set it at twice what Hammond's father had paid when he inherited the property twenty years earlier. On top of that, he claimed that Jack owed him not one but three of his best animals as heriot because Jack has three holdings from him. Jack claimed back at him that it's not three holdings—he has but one split into three parcels and there's never been three animals taken until now. Most folk in the village said likewise and I took Jack's side so far as I could. He only had to give up one of his cows, but Medcote was still fighting him over the fine to inherit."

"That might make me mad enough to kill," Joliffe said.

"More than that," Kyping said grimly, "it's stirred up every man on every manor around here who's displeased about anything. Even Lionel Ashewell, who's fair as can be to his folk, is being troubled, and an old quarrel between Walter Gosyn and Wat Offington has flared up again."

"They were yelling together at the ale yesterday," Joliffe said.

"You saw that? That was Wat right enough. He's taken to refusing his villein duties. Claims that if Gosyn can buy out of being a villein, so can he. But he's a wastrel; has never had and never will have the money to do it, so he settles for behaving as if he has. He and Jack Hammond sit around drinking together and damning all landlords."

"Why hasn't the manor court ruled about Medcote's claim against Jack Hammond?"

"It's tried. Four times. But the juries have always locked between those too afraid of Medcote to stand out against him and those so angry they're spitting fire. I've been set to take it out of their hands and to the steward, and none too happy he's been to hear that."

"Now you won't need to."

"I'd not wager on it. Hal Medcote isn't likely to be better than his father was."

Joliffe had no trouble believing that. "Who else did Medcote have quarrels with?"

"Pick anyone who's ever come in shouting distance of him and you'll be right." Kyping started onward to the gate and his horse. "Now, if you'll pardon me."

"One more thing. Who found Medcote's body?"

"Hal did. When his father wasn't home by dawn, Anela Medcote sent him looking for him."

"How did he know where to look?"

"Apparently it's a place both he and his father are familiar with," Kyping said in a way that told more than the words did.

Preferring not to think too deeply into what that meant, the bare words sufficient, Joliffe asked what he should have thought to before: "What do the new widow and bereaved son and daughter say about where they were last night?"

"The daughter, too?" Kyping asked, somewhat mocking.

"Why not?"

"True enough, I suppose," Kyping granted. "They all say they were nowhere but at home last night, and no one gainsays them."

But they all slept in separate chambers, surely, and after some time in the night could not for a certainty say where each other were. Joliffe would wager, too, that servants there knew better than to notice anything, may have become truly blind to anything beyond what they were supposed to see and know.

Kyping was waiting to see if Joliffe had another question. When none came, he slightly nodded farewell and went on leaving, with Joliffe's slight and belated bow only to his back.

Chapter 12

Joliffe slowly crossed the pasture back to the other players, carrying his thoughts with him and surprised out of them by Ellis, who demanded of him edgily, "So. Am I still his first, best choice?"

"Ellis," Rose protested.

"Well, am I?"

"As far as Kyping knows," Joliffe answered, "there's nothing particular between you and Rose. I told him she's here as Basset's daughter and spends her time mothering the lot of us."

Rose gave a snort of agreement to that.

"What about the rest of you?" Ellis demanded at them. "Do you think I did in Medcote?"

"Ellis!" Rose protested again.

"Well, do they?" Ellis said. "Because I *am* most likely, aren't I?"

"Not really," Joliffe said easily. "The best you can do is join what seems quite a list of people who've, most of them, probably been wishing Medcote dead for years and for more reasons than you had. His own wife and son and maybe his daughter first among them, for all I know; but assuredly any number of his neighbors." And then, as if it had just now come to him, he added thoughtfully, "Nor do I see you likely to leave Rose's warm arms in the night to go groping through the chill dark to kill a man she doesn't even want." He looked to Basset, Piers, and Gil and asked as if serious about it, "What do you say? Wouldn't that be more trouble than Ellis is ever likely to put himself to?"

"Well," Basset said with apparent deep consideration, "put that way I have to say it's doubtful he killed Medcote."

"Of course I didn't kill him!" Ellis yelled.

Rose laid a hand on his arm and said, "Ellis, they're having at you. They know as well as I do that you didn't do anything to Medcote."

Ellis grumbled something under his breath.

Basset came forward and laid an arm across his shoulders. "Of course we know you didn't do it. And, Joliffe, leave off," he added, although he was not looking at Joliffe and could not have seen him just beginning to open his mouth. Joliffe closed it and Basset went on, "No. What we need to do is nothing. We stay here quietly. We answer what questions are put to us. We wait until we're told we can go." His voice hardened. "And if it looks like things are going to the bad, one of us rides like a hellwind back to Lady Lovell to tell her what's happening and ask for rescue."

That last was a defense they had lacked all the years they had been lordless players. They had small choice but to stay, to wait and see how things went here. But knowing there was Lady Lovell to take their part if need be made the staying easier. Not that Joliffe meant simply to wait, and he said lightly, "So, Rose, where is this place you were to meet Medcote?"

On the instant he had everyone's suspicious stares along with Rose demanding, "Why?"

"I thought I'd go to see it. To see what's to be seen that maybe Kyping didn't see or think about."

"And?" asked Basset.

There were disadvantages to being known too well. "And maybe ask a few questions if there's anybody there," he admitted.

Ellis said sharply, "We've done what Lady Lovell wanted. Medcote's murder isn't any business of ours. Leave it."

Joliffe looked to Basset. "Basset?"

Basset regarded him in close-lipped silence, very plainly weighing one thing against another in his mind before sighing and saying, "Tell him the way, Rose."

Ellis made a disgusted sound and turned his back on them all.

Looking worriedly at Ellis' back, Rose answered, "Medcote said there's a place where the stream and trees swing closer to the lane about a half-mile from here toward his manor. He said he'd wait there for me."

Joliffe thanked her and started to leave.

"I'll come with you!" Piers offered.

"You won't," his mother said back at him before Ellis, turning sharply around, could.

Joliffe waved to them all and made his escape.

A half-mile walk was nothing much. It would have been a little farther from Medcote's manor, but even at night it would have been easily done under a clear sky like last night's had been, and when Joliffe came to the place where stream and trees came near the lane, with a break through the trees to what looked a cattle-ford across the stream, there was no doubting it was far enough from the camp that, no, the players would have heard nothing of a quietly done murder here. Nor did he have to wonder if this was the place; there was no other likely reason for the five men clustered beside the stream.

He started toward them while looking around. Where

had Medcote intended his sport with Rose? Joliffe wondered. Not in the open here, where the grass was scanty and the ground hard-trodden from passing cattle. If Kyping was right about this being somewhere used before now to Medcote's purposes, then Medcote probably had some particular grassy place among the trees. But last night while Medcote had waited for Rose, someone else had come and ended both Medcote's waiting and his life. Happening on him by chance, which seemed unlikely, or because they knew the place and his ways?

Two of the five men were come away from the stream to meet him, neither of them looking much like friendly. One of them never had been, and Joliffe said as they met, "Master Lynche, isn't it?"

Giving Medcote's steward even that much title of respect was hard when a solid kick to his rigid behind would have been more satisfying, but as Basset was wont to say, a little flattery can go a long way and take not a penny from your purse. Whether it helped here, Joliffe could not tell, as Lynche said at him roughly, "That's me, and you're one of those players. What are you doing here?"

As if he didn't hear the rudeness, Joliffe said easily, "Come to look. Like them, I suppose." He beckoned his head toward the three men still beside the stream.

Lynche looked back at them as if to make certain whom Joliffe meant, but it was the fellow with him who demanded, "What business is it of yours?"

"Master Kyping wants our company to stay for the crowner's coming," Joliffe answered evenly. "If we're going to have to hang about where someone's taken to murdering men, it's for our own good we'd like to know what we have to watch out for."

"Thinks one of you did it, does he?" the fellow asked. "It's more likely one of you we have to watch out for than anybody. Or all of you."

That manner of thinking was precisely what the players had to fear, but Lynche said curtly, "Let it go, Hod. They're Lord Lovell's men. If anything's done to them, it'll be Lord Lovell we'll be answering to."

That was sufficient to silence Hod for now, although he looked to be inwardly grumbling as Lynche said at Joliffe, "You want to look along with the rest of them? Medcote's still here."

"He is?" Joliffe said in surprise.

The law was that a body was to be left where it was found until the crowner could come to view it where it lay, that he might better judge what had happened. But since it could take days for the crowner to be found, wherever he might be in the shire, and then to come, people—especially those in grief—often preferred to shift the body and pay the fine for having done so. There had been time enough today to shift Medcote's body. Was his family going to leave it lying where it was? Why? Had they hated him that much? Or, there having been little love among them while he lived, were they indifferent now to respecting the dead? Or maybe they were just unwilling to "waste" money on the fine.

Whichever it was, Lynche didn't answer his surprise, just led him toward the stream and the other men, Hod trailing behind. As they neared, one of the men left the body, saying as he met Lynche, "I've seen enough. We can spread the word he's dead for sure."

"Try not to make too merry over it," Lynche said curtly.

"We'll not," the man said, but not as if he meant it. Over his shoulder, going away, he added, "We've not forgotten his whelp is still with us to make our lives hell."

One of the men still at the stream called out, "Still, one down, one to go!"

The man leaving laughed at that and kept going. Lynche said after him and at the others, "Damn you for vultures and Saint Erasmus take your guts." And at the two men still at the stream, "You've seen enough. Get out of here, too."

They laughed, no offense taken, and went the other way, by stepping stones across the stream, to disappear along a path into the field on the other side. Besides that as a way someone could have come and gone, Joliffe saw there was a path, too, running through the woods; and there was always wading along the stream running low between its banks and hidden by the trees.

But now he was come to Medcote's body lying on the stream's muddy bank. Someone had at least pulled it out of the water and thrown a coarse piece of canvas over it. Lynche, with outward indifference, flipped a corner of the canvas aside, uncovering Medcote's face. The dead man's mouth hung open in the usual way and no one had troubled to close his eyes. They stared, bulging and blank. And as Kyping had said, the small fish that flicked through the shallows of the stream had been at him before he was found.

The bruise along his jaw was plain enough, though, and Joliffe said, pointing to it, "Looks like he fought whoever did for him. Any other marks on him?"

"If there are, they're under his clothes and for the crowner to find out," Lynche said.

"That blow to the jaw maybe stunned him enough for the other man to wrestle him down, pin him, drown him," Joliffe said as if making unconsidered talk. He added more as if asking himself rather than either Lynche or Hod, "But why drown him, I wonder? Why not stab him?"

He guessed that both men would take too much pleasure in refusing to answer any straightly asked question. It was probably because he deliberately seemed to be not talking to them, only to himself, that Hod said, albeit glumly, "Stabbing? Stabbing might have been too quick for whoever did it, if they wanted it to last longer."

Coldly, Lynche said, "There'd be no outcry with drowning. No chance someone would hear. That's the more likely reason for it."

"How much likelihood was there anyone would be out and about to hear anything anyway?" Joliffe asked.

"Not much at that hour," Hod said. "A poacher maybe, but he'd move away from the sound of men, not toward it, likely."

"So it was well after dark it happened?"

"It was after dark when he rode out," Lynche said. "I closed the gate behind him."

"Rode out?" Joliffe looked around as if expecting suddenly to see a horse he had somehow missed until then.

Lynche answered his look with, "Master Hal brought it back when he came with word he'd found his father."

"How did he know where to look? Or was it only chance he came this way?"

"No chance to it. Hal knows this place as well as his father did and Medcote made no secret of why he was going out last night." Lynche was flatly, glumly sure of that. He gave Joliffe a suspicious sideways look.

"Never did, come to that," said Hod. "Liked to leave the kettle boiling behind him when he went, as it were."

That meant that Medcote's use of the place was as open a secret as Kyping had made it seem—and that almost any man in the household could have taken the chance to be rid of an unliked master. Joliffe would have liked to ask more questions that way, about the household and who might have been presently most angry at Medcote, but he'd have to leave those questions to Kyping or the crowner. Lynche was becoming restive with dislike at him being there. Joliffe doubted he'd have many more answers out of him and said with a shrug, starting to turn away, "Pity all the way around, I guess. Every time I saw him, he looked to be a man enjoying his life about as much as a man can."

"Nobody else was, sure," Hod muttered.

"What?" Joliffe asked lightly.

"Enjoying their life while he was around. Not that it's likely to be all that better now."

"That's enough, Hod," Lynche said, but Hod grumbled on, "Whether it's to be son or widow we answer to now, it won't be all that better and you can't say it will be, Lynche, unless you lie. The only help will be if Mistress Eleanor marries again and goes off soon."

"Oh?" Joliffe said easily. "I thought she seemed pleasant enough the little I saw her."

"Must have been very little and at an odd hour on one of her better days," Hod snorted. "As bad humoured as the rest of them she is."

"With more reason," Lynche put in stiffly. "She was well and away from here and then her husband dies and she's right back in the middle of it."

Given how short he was about most things, the steward's readiness to say that much to the good about Eleanor Medcote told more than maybe he meant it to, but Joliffe was not sure whether that more was about Eleanor Medcote or Lynche himself, and he said, still easily, "Ah well, there's trouble everywhere for everybody, isn't there?" and walked away.

He had learned more than he had thought he would and took his time along the road, in no hurry to rejoin the others while he thought about it. First, those nearest to Medcote—family as well as servants—were surely in no great grief for his death. Second, any number of people could have known where he planned to be that night, and not just his near and not-so-dear, because if he'd gloated to them, there was no knowing who else he might have gloated to. And any servants who knew what he purposed could have talked of it at the village alehouse last night if they'd gone there. Or someone might have overheard him when he told

Rose to meet him, with no need for anyone else to be told anything.

Add to that stretch of possibilities how many people would rather he were dead than alive—maybe beginning with his own family and certainly going outward from there—and the possibilities for who killed him spread out and out in a widening circle.

A circle that could even include Kyping, since his life would be far easier without Medcote stirring up constant trouble.

A circle that had to include Master Ashewell, quit of whatever had kept him bound to Medcote's desire for marriage between Eleanor and young Nicholas. Of course Nicholas, too, had reason to want escape from that marriage, but Joliffe doubted the boy had the weight to hold down a man of Medcote's size and likely strength.

Walter Gosyn had the needed size and strength, though. But if he had gone for anyone, wouldn't it more likely have been Hal with his unwanted heed of Claire?

Come to it, once Medcote was down, a well-sized woman could have held and drowned him. It needn't have come to fists between them. There was nothing to say a club or just a heavy branch couldn't have laid him out, couldn't have dazed him long enough for a strong woman to have him helpless and half-drowned before he recovered enough to struggle. Anela Medcote was not of a size to do it, but her daughter was.

But so were plenty of other women, common women grown strong with women's heavy duties around the house and with fieldwork, and there was no telling how many of those there might be wanting revenge after being wronged by Medcote. And then there were men whose women had been wronged by Medcote, as well as all the men with other quarrels against him.

Joliffe did not envy Kyping, or the constable, or the

crowner when he came for the questioning that was ahead of them. Before there was much hope of knowing who had killed Medcote, they would have to narrow the circle of possibilities down past who might *want* to kill him to who *could* have killed him, and that might not prove possible, given the difficulties Joliffe saw so far.

Altogether, he would settle for the players being given leave to go and never mind if they never knew who killed Medcote. Whatever Kyping said, they were still too easy to accuse, too readily at hand as a way to save everyone else the trouble of looking harder for a murderer. He'd maybe do well to suggest to Kyping to take note of whoever might first or most insistently point a finger their way, because the murderer might well do that, trying to end the matter before it came too near him.

He stopped at a gate into a ploughed field softly green with young shoots of grain. A lapwing was crying *pee-wit* from somewhere, but that was the only sound, and he bent and picked a small daisy out of the grass and chewed on its stalk for its sharp taste, leaning on the gate and gazing up at the White Horse on its hillside. Yesterday at this hour Medcote had been alive and now he wasn't. That Medcote wasn't a man to be mourned was beside the matter. Living and dying were a mystery deeper than any one man's murder.

A man or woman lived and then they did not and mankind fumbled on its way and still there was the Horse, lifetimes old, in its flaring gallop across the hillside, its being a mystery among other mysteries.

Why had Medcote been such a curse toward everyone? Apparently prosperous when he was a butcher in Wantage, his lot had only been bettered by coming into this manor by way of his wife, a comely enough woman. He lived more comfortably than most men, and there was nothing outwardly wrong with either of his offspring. So why had he been such a complete cur? Had he thought the power to

make folk miserable was a greater power than to play fair
with them? That was a mistake common to small-witted
people—to think good was a weaker thing than evil. From
all that Joliffe had seen, evil—in both its greater ways and
in such petty ones as bullying—was the weak man's way,
taking a fool's pleasure in his strength to destroy. To destroy was easy. To create was hard. And solid goodness to
others was harder still, with maybe the hardest thing being
to stand strong in the good against the anger and force of
those who understood only ugliness and destruction.
Against people like Medcote.

And like whoever had killed him.

Joliffe pushed back from the gate and went on toward
the players' camp, hungry for whatever was for dinner and
ready to be away from his thoughts for a while.

Chapter 13

At camp Joliffe found the tent up again, Tisbe grazing as if she had never left, and the players sitting, waiting while Rose cut bread and cheese on a board for them and a man Joliffe did not know. With the skill he had learned early as a player, he quickly judged by the way the man was sitting easily among them that he had likely neither brought nor meant trouble. That was to the good. Besides that, coming nearer, Joliffe saw that the man's rough hosen and plain-made, serviceable tunic were all of good enough cloth and meant to last but more what a master would provide for a servant as part of his wages than what a man was likely to choose for himself. Add to that there was no horse of his to be seen and he did not look as if he was worn out with long walking, and it was an easy guess he was someone's household servant and from nearby. Master Ashewell's, likely, or maybe Gosyn's.

Nonetheless, as Joliffe joined them and they all looked up at him, he made the man a low bow, complete with a sweep of his hat and, "My lord. You grace us with your company."

The man gaped at him a moment, then caught the jest and threw back his head with a roar of laughter. There must be few jests around here, he took that one so much to heart, Joliffe thought as the man said, "Aye, that's me. Lord Sy. Ya've seen through my disguise."

"Sy's come from Walter Gosyn," Basset said more temperately. "We're asked to his place to play this evening."

Joliffe glanced at Basset for his cue. Basset gave it by a shadow of a nod, and without missing a beat Joliffe said, adding another bow for good measure, "It will be our honor and our privilege."

Sy laughed again. "You're a merry lot, I'll say that for you. I wouldn't be so blythe, maybe, with a murdered man almost on my doorstep and the crowner's eye likely to be turned my way."

As if he did not know Sy was fishing for talk he could take back to the Gosyn household, Basset held his hands out, palms up and shoulder-high on either side, in a kind of shrug meant to show the players' innocence and unconcern. "We've gathered Medcote had men enough who wanted him dead for better reasons than we ever had against him, since we never had any. The crowner will have men in plenty to suspect without having to look at us."

"That's not always been known to stop a crowner," Sy said with unexpected shrewdness. "Pick who's likely to be the least trouble and settle on them to have done it. That's been known to happen."

"Ah," said Basset, still with easy confidence. "But you see we're not likely to be the least trouble. We're Lord Lovell's men, and he's likely to be loathe to lose us to a crowner's convenience."

"Aye. That's true enough," Sy granted. "You being Lord Lovell's men was why my master was wondering if you'd play for his folk at all. Though he said if you'd play for

Medcote, you'd play for anyone. Not that he meant that any bad way, look you," he quickly added.

Rose handed a thick-cut piece of bread and an equally thick-cut piece of cheese to Joliffe, saying, "These are from Master Gosyn's wife. She took thought we might be short of food, having been turned back on our way."

Joliffe took the food gratefully, saying, "If his wife sends us new bread and fine cheese, Gosyn can say whatever he wants about us, good or bad."

"She's a fine hand in the dairy," Sy said, proud as if her accomplishments were his own. But he leaned toward Joliffe with a different eagerness and asked, lowering his voice, "Ya've seen him, then? Medcote? He's dead, surely?"

"Dead surely," Joliffe assured him. Hungry, he would have rather eaten than talked, but to give Sy what he wanted, he told what he had seen. He would have been telling the other players by now anyway, so it made not that great a difference, except with a different audience, he put more into the telling than he otherwise might have.

Sy was pleased at the end, anyway, sitting back like a man satisfied after a full meal, saying with a shake of his head, "Drowned and dead. Who would have thought it?"

"Everyone's glad to be quit of him, I gather," Joliffe said.

"You'd be hard put to find a man—or probably a woman either—with a good thing to say of him," Sy said. "Nor will the rest of the Medcote lot be missed if they pack up after the funeral and take themselves back where they came from. But they won't," he added glumly. "They got their claws into Francis Brook's lands and won't be giving it up."

"I thought the manor came to Anela Medcote by right after her cousin's death," Joliffe said, half making it a question.

"It did." No matter how much Sy grudged granting it.

"Shouldn't ever have come to him dying, though. He was bettering from his hurt. You heard how that was?"

"Young Nicholas Ashewell wounded him by chance, yes," Basset said.

"By chance it surely was." Sy was as fierce on that as if Basset had said otherwise. "There's never been harm in that boy and everybody knows it. It wasn't even much of a wound, I heard, and Brook was bettering. That's what was being said. Then here come his kin, that Anela and the rest, and next anyone knows, Francis Brook is dead, his heart given out or some such thing and no one there to say differently."

"No one was there when he died?" Basset asked. "He was left alone, you mean? That can't be right."

"It was Our Lady's day in harvest. Most were gone to church, and when they came back, it was over with him."

"Most were to church?" Joliffe prompted.

"Save for a few servants and Medcote and young Hal." Sy laid a finger aside his nose with a knowing look. "Nothing to be proved then or afterward, but there was talk then and there's talk now. And whether there was anything untoward or not in Francis Brook dying the way he did, the Medcotes didn't waste more time on mourning than they had to. Were moved in, bag and baggage, before Holy Rood Day, just see if they weren't. Now if they'd just go as quickly, that would be something to sing about."

"Jack Hammond wouldn't be minding, anyway," Joliffe said easily.

Sy gave a crow of laughter. "Jack Hammond? He'd lead the rough music that saw them out of town."

"But doesn't Master Gosyn have his trouble, too, with a villein who doesn't want to know his place?" Joliffe said, still easily.

From the corner of his eye he saw Ellis start and cut short a gesture probably meant to tell him to shut up, but Sy answered without hesitation, "Wat Offington. Him and a few others, too, that think Gosyn has made what he has of his life over their backs, not seeing the fault is theirs, not Gosyn's, if he's made much of what was his and they've made little with theirs."

"Instead of stirring each other up to trouble," Basset said.

"That's the way of it," Sy agreed heartily.

"Folk don't seem to resent Master Ashewell, though," Joliffe said.

"Ah, well, he's another matter, isn't he? He went off to war and made his fortune and nobody can quarrel with that, can they? He's a quieter man, too. Always trying to cool things instead of stir them up."

"You'd think that would be Father Hewgo's place," Joliffe said innocently. "Him being the priest here and all. Peace and God's love and all."

Sy bent over on another loud laugh and had to straighten and catch his breath before he could protest, still laughing, "Ah, you've seen enough of him to know better than that! Coals to kindling is that man. What Medcote doesn't stir up, Father Hewgo does. He's forever at Jack and Wat and George Lamb to 'cease to trouble their masters,' as he puts it. Like that'd be enough to settle those three."

"George Lamb?" Basset asked.

"He's fellow with Wat Offington in thinking he's hard done by. Wants to buy out of his boon work but hasn't the money for it. Might have if he and Wat didn't spend so much at the alehouse washing their wrongs in ale. Thinks Gosyn ought to let him have what he wants for what he can pay, not what the work is worth." Sy stood up. "Ah, they're all of a kind, those three, but maybe matters will settle a bit without Medcote to stir them up every chance there was."

"Why would Medcote be doing that?" Joliffe asked from where he still sat. "If Wat and this George aren't his men?"

"For the sport of it. To keep old Gosyn stirred up. No love lost there."

"So," said Basset, "we'd do as well with a merry play tonight as a sorrowful one?"

"No need for sorrow with us over Medcote's death," Sy assured him and started away.

Ellis called after him, "Will there be supper in it for us?"

"Sure to be," Sy said over his shoulder cheerfully. "There's nothing mean about my master!"

The players held silent among themselves until Sy had disappeared into the lane. With him gone, Joliffe was about to say that Walter Gosyn looked to be liked by his household folk, anyway, but Ellis burst out at both him and Basset, "Lord god of madmen, you two never give it up, do you? We've done what Lady Lovell asked of us. All we have to do now is keep our mouths shut and our heads down until we're let go from here. But there you sat, asking every question that came into your heads!"

"It was just friendly, common curiosity, that's all," Joliffe protested.

"Hah!" Ellis returned.

"Leave off. The both of you," said Basset. "We all want to be somewhere else other than here, but here is where we are, and since we are, it's better that we know more than less."

"On the chance we'll need to know that more," Rose said quietly.

She laid a hand on Ellis' knee. Looking to her, he laid one of his own hands over hers, then clasped it, stood up, and pulled her to her feet with, "Let's go for a walk, you and I. But not you," he added at Piers.

Before Piers, already half-way to his feet, could protest that, his grandfather caught his hand, pulled him back down, and clamped him firmly to his side with an arm around his shoulders, saying, "That's right. You and Gil can help Joliffe and I argue out what play we'll do tonight."

"Brave Bevis!" Gil said promptly, he having a well-sized part in that one.

"St. Nicholas and the Boys!" Piers returned on his own behalf.

"I do like the part in that one where the evil innkeeper grinds the two boys into sausages," Joliffe said, then added thoughtfully, "though I've thought it would be even better if we left out the part where St. Nicholas turns them back into boys."

"Hai!" Piers protested.

Ellis and Rose had disappeared down the path toward the stream by then. Basset tossed possibilities for tonight's play back and forth with Gil and Piers for a while but ended by saying, "I'll make up my mind in a while. For now, Piers, why don't you finally show Gil how you cheat at merels."

Gil crowed, "Ah-ha! I thought you must, you win so often at it!" while Piers protested, all vast and injured innocence, "I don't! I'm just better at it than anyone else, that's all." Free of Basset's hold, he stood up and started for the cart where the merels gameboard was kept with his own few things. "Come on. I'll show you."

Gil shared a grin with Basset and Joliffe, and they returned it, all of them knowing the diversion would keep Piers happily occupied a goodly while. But neither Basset nor Joliffe made immediate use of being left to themselves; instead they sat in silence a while, Joliffe finishing his share of the bread and cheese while Basset gazed away at the sky in apparent idleness. Gil and Piers were well into their game on the far side of the cart before Basset said, still gazing at the sky, "So. What do you think about Medcote's death?"

"Rose and Piers and probably Gil are safe from suspicion of doing it. They haven't the weight or strength."

Basset cocked his head and a look at him. "Which leaves you and me and Ellis if the crowner wants to turn on us. Except we can each claim none of us left here last night."

"Not that anyone need believe we're telling the truth about that," Joliffe pointed out, although it was a thing Basset knew as well as he did. The little silence between them came back until Joliffe added, "I do like our company being Lord Lovell's."

Basset nodded on a sigh of unspoken agreement with that. In their years without a patron they had had more than one narrow slide out of trouble, and sometimes they had not made that slide unscathed. But being shielded by Lord Lovell's name did not mean they should rest easy, and Joliffe said, "At least by everything we've heard it's sure there are plenty of others willing to have Medcote dead."

"What you're wondering is which of them it was did for him," Basset said.

"So are you," Joliffe returned.

Rather than deny that, Basset began to count on his fingers, "Jack Hammond, Walter Gosyn, Master Ashewell, maybe Nicholas Ashewell—"

"If I was threatened with marrying Eleanor Medcote, I'd be tempted to murder, surely," Joliffe said thoughtfully. "Though it would make more sense to kill her than her father, I would think."

"Shut up, Joliffe," Basset said without heat and went on with his count. "Medcote's wife, tired of his ways."

"Eleanor, tired of her father making use of her to his own ends?" Joliffe suggested. "She looks to be a strong young woman. More likely than her mother to match Medcote's strength, I'd think."

"The same can be said, and more so, for her brother."

"He and his father didn't seem at odds, though. Seemed even to work hand-in-glove together. Why would Hal kill him? And why now?"

"To inherit? With us at hand and readily blamed? After all, Hal is the one who'll gain the immediate most by his father's death."

"True enough. I'd like to know where he was last night."

"And where Gosyn, Ashewell, and Jack Hammond were, and all the others who don't mind Medcote is dead," Basset said. "Kyping has his work cut out for him."

"It would help to know if the murder was planned and Medcote was stalked to where he was killed, or if someone merely happened on him and took the chance."

"Which isn't something anyone is likely to know until the murderer is caught."

"Too true for comfort. Still, it would help to know who knew for certain where Medcote would be last night. I wonder, too—" Joliffe broke off. What he had suddenly wondered was whether the murderer had meant to kill Rose, too, if she had been there, to make both deaths look more surely Ellis' doing. That being altogether a thought best left unsaid to Basset, he said instead, "—who gains besides Hal Medcote."

"The rest of the family, glad to be rid of him," Basset said. "Not every murder has to be for a large reason. Quite a small reason will do as well for some people."

"Being rid of Medcote would seem a large reason to me." Joliffe thought for a moment, then added, "It seems less of a gain for both the Ashewells and Gosyn. Hal is all too likely to keep on with his father's demand for the Ashewell marriage for Eleanor, and now he's clear to move openly for Claire for himself."

"As you said, for the Ashewells at least, killing the daughter would have been better sense," Basset said, with no jest to the thought.

"What about her?" Joliffe said.

"What about her?" Basset echoed.

"For the murderer. We've agreed she might have the strength to hold Medcote down, if she got that blow to his jaw in first."

"That's hardly a woman's blow. A fist to a man's jaw?"

Joliffe touched his own jaw lightly in memory and said, "There's some women who do. If they mean business enough."

Basset's face lightened with interest just short of open laughter. "Who? When?"

"A long time ago," Joliffe said with dignity, "and that's all that I'm telling."

Basset did laugh then.

Ignoring him, Joliffe went on, "Or else Mistress Eleanor has a lover. Someone she wants who also wants her. And she got word to him of where Medcote would be last night, and this lover killed him in the hope that with Medcote dead he'll have Eleanor."

"Unless Hal still wants the Ashewell marriage," Basset pointed out.

"That's something I've wondered on," said Joliffe. "She's a widow. Why wasn't she free to marry as she chose? As a widow, she should have her own say over her life."

"Maybe she does want to marry Nicholas Ashewell."

"Or she may think Hal will be better to sway than their father was. Medcote kept a heavy hand on everybody. Maybe the only way past him was—"

"—over his dead body," Basset finished. "Unfortunately, we've no thought of who this putative lover might be, do we?"

"Um. No," Joliffe granted, then waved an easy hand. "We'll have to find out. Well, find out if he exists and then who he is. Along with where the Ashewells and Walter Gosyn were last night."

"That's something Kyping will surely see to. As well as already knowing how many others besides Jack Hammond will be dancing most merrily now Medcote's dead."

"Of those there's no lack, and because Medcote made no secret of what he was intending last night, there's no way to know how many of his servants knew it and who they may have told over ale in the alehouse." Joliffe shook his head with deep dissatisfaction. "It's a hard thing when a murdered man was hated by nearly everyone who knew him. Even Father Hewgo didn't look very liking of him by the time we finished in the sacristy yesterday."

"True," Basset agreed. "They're said to be two of a kind and to work as one, but yesterday was the second time we saw Medcote cross him."

"And with Medcote that means there were likely other times, and Father Hewgo had maybe had enough. Or maybe he thought it was his Christian duty to put a stop to Medcote's fornications. No," Joliffe corrected himself. "Given what I've seen of Father Hewgo, he'd rather have the sport of imposing heavy penance on Medcote for his sins and setting the bishop on him if Medcote didn't comply. Or maybe Medcote knew something Father Hewgo didn't want him to know. Or maybe Medcote knew something someone else didn't want him to know. Or—"

"Enough," Basset said, running his hands through his hair and clasping them together at the back of his head. "My brain is overheating. Let's drop Medcote and decide what you'll all play tonight for the Gosyns."

Joliffe caught that "you" and asked, "What about you?"

"I'm thinking someone should stay with the cart and it shouldn't be Rose," Basset said grimly. "Or not Rose alone. Besides," he added with his Evil Sheriff smile, "what's the use of being master of this company if I can't order someone else to do all the work once in a while?"

Chapter 14

The Gosyns' manor lay farther out in the Vale. Drained by reedy ditches between the road and the broad fields and pastures, the land here was rich both for crops and grazing, Joliffe thought as he, Ellis, Gil, and Piers walked along. There was the hopeful green of young growth across the ploughed fields, but that was a promise of harvest-to-come that had proved false these past two years of wet summers and harsh winters, and there were not so many cows or even sheep at graze as there might have been. That had been true everywhere the players had traveled so far this year. When the haying failed in a rain-drenched summer, fewer cows could be over-wintered and that meant fewer calves come the spring and that meant fewer cows in years to come. And if too little was left from a ruined harvest to feed a family through the winter, then what should have been saved to plant the next year's fields too often went to ease present hunger, lessening even further the next year's hope. And because when all this happened, the hunger was everywhere, there was nowhere to go to escape it, nothing to do but stay and see it through until the fat years came again. Or die where you were if you didn't last that long.

Joliffe had seen how that trap went when he was very young and had taken his first chance to slip free and away from it, first by one way, then by another, and then into being a player. But he was older now and knew there was no true going free. For one thing, all in life was too much bound piece to piece to piece, was too much a whole, for anyone to be wholly free while they still drew breath. For another thing, whatever sort of life someone might choose, there were burdens to it, and any manner of "escape" left an emptiness where the might-have-been would have been, with sometimes—after some "escapes"—that emptiness a burden in itself.

Not that Joliffe had any wish to go back on the choices he had made, but neither was he so cowardly as to try to deny their costs. Nor was he so young anymore that he thought life could be lived without burdens. In truth, he had found that in bearing a burden honestly and with a whole heart there was often a surprising freedom.

What was needed, he had long since decided, was to find the balance between burdens rightly accepted and burdens stupidly borne, between escapes rightly made and the fool's escape that led to nothing but worse burdens than those left behind.

He had also decided there were few people able to tell one choice from the other until too late—and he wasn't at all certain he was any better at it than anyone else.

But he also knew that on the whole he would rather starve as a player than as something else, so here he was and, thanks to the vagaries of fortune and Lord Lovell's favor, less close to starving than the company had been for years.

The road curved and sloped down to cross a stream,

probably the one that ran past their camp. It was wide and
shallow here, with an easy ford for cart or wagon, and stepping stones by which Joliffe, Ellis, Gil, and Piers crossed dry-
footed. Beyond it, the road curved again, bringing them into
a scatter of perhaps ten houses. There were signs there had
been more of a village here upon a time. Between the present
houses there were here and there wide gaps that told where
other houses had likely stood, with some of the gaps now
made into someone else's kitchen gardens but others simply
left bare, one with the stub of housewall still standing, while
in another what looked to have once been a house was turned
now into a byre or barn.

A dying village, its life draining away to other places, Joliffe thought. The players came to such now and again. Time
was past when men and women were tied to one place for
life. More and more lords found it easier to take money in
place of services, and then money in place of a man or
woman altogether, letting villeins buy themselves free to try
their luck elsewhere, leaving the lord able to hire others to
whom he owed nothing but their wages and none of the tangle of rights and privileges that his erstwhile villeins had ac-
quired through the generations. In some ways it was a freeing
of the lords as much as it was a freeing of ordinary folk—
which of course was why the lords were willing to do it.

Of those peasants who stayed where they were, many
did simply because they could not imagine doing otherwise, could see no further than where they already were.
Others stayed because they saw how to make use of what
new chances there were, and from what Joliffe had heard,
Walter Gosyn was one of those—an up-coming man and
resented for it by the likes of Wat Offington who wanted
what Gosyn had but, lacking the wits to get it for themselves, settled for being angry about it.

Of course, Joliffe added to himself, Gosyn's ways might

be as likely to kill off the village's life as other men's igno-
rance, but that was the way things went—chance and foolishness happened to all men.

From Sy, the players knew Gosyn's place was on the
village's far side, the last house, and Ellis had said as they
walked along, "Shall we give the villagers something, too,
as we pass through? Just for the sport of it?" The others
had agreed, knowing more than sport was part of it. Villagers made friendly now could be villagers friendly in the
future for other players who might come this way—though
any players come this far from any main way were probably in more need than could be helped in a place like this.

Aside from that, it was easier to pass through a village
doing something other than simply walking with everyone
staring, maybe none too friendly, wondering why they
were there. So as they came up from the ford, Piers began
to tootle on his pipes and rat-tat on his tabor, leading the
way for Ellis and Gil, who set to making a show of juggling
the bright-painted leather balls, while Joliffe thumped the
curved bottom of his lute and sang an idiot song to let folk
know the players were come to town, tra-la, to sport and
play today, hey-hey.

In the clear early evening, folk were at work in their
gardens or sitting in ease by their doors, so the players had
audience enough for their going, as well as a merriness of
children who gave up some circle game they had been
playing in the street to dance and laugh around the players
for the hundred yards or so to Gosyn's gateway. At the gateway, though, they spread aside and fell back from the players. Ellis gave the word, and Piers, just gone into the yard
beyond the gateway, left off his pipes and tabor while Ellis
and Gil deftly caught all the juggling balls. Together with
Joliffe they all turned back to their following of children
and a few men and women who had joined them, and bowed

deeply, with Joliffe and Piers sweeping off their hats with flourishes and Joliffe saying, "Our thanks and more, good folk, for your good welcome . . ."

"Judas!" a child yelped, pointing at him.

Joliffe bowed again, smiling, and said, "Nay, that was yesterday and only for the while. Today I am myself. Though mayhap in a while I may turn into a devil. One never knows." He twisted his face into a mocking, leering grin at the child, who yelped with delighted fear while others laughed or pretended to be frightened with him.

With more bows and flourishes, the players turned away, toward the house and its open doorway where at least a servant should have been waiting for them by now to see them in. They had made noise enough that no one could be ignorant of their coming, but no one was there, and that surprised Joliffe.

The house itself was set back from the street on the other side of a small, dusty yard flanked by the usual byre and barn and separated from the street by only a waist-high wattle fence. While beyond argument the house was the best in the village, it was a far lesser place than either Medcote's or Ashewell's. Reed-thatched and half-timbered, with white-plastered daub walls, it had plainly been only a small yeoman's house of probably two rooms and a loft until, at one end, a two-floored short range of rooms had been added, end on to the yard, not so long ago—both timbering and thatch were still golden-new, not weathered to gray with time and weather—with what had been the house probably made into the hall.

"There's someone else here," Ellis said with a nod toward one side of the yard where three saddled horses were tied to posts.

"So we're to play for more than only the Gosyns," Joliffe said lightly. "The two bay rouncys look like Ashewell's."

"But the gray is Medcote's," Gil said tautly. "I remember it from when he was at our camp."

"Damnation," Ellis growled. "It has to be Hal Medcote is here."

"No trouble," Joliffe warned.

"My quarrel wasn't with him," Ellis said sharply. "But I doubt him being here will add to the merriment, do you?"

Joliffe did doubt it, but before he could answer, Sy came out of the house door and scurried—that was the only word for it—toward them with much the frightened hurry of a hare pursued by hounds.

"Damnation," Ellis said, this time in a mutter.

Joliffe silently agreed, but drawing together, the four of them kept on across the yard, Ellis pulling Piers by the shoulder back and a little behind them as if out of harm's way as Sy reached them, urging as he came, "Come in, come in. Mistress Geretruda says come in, you'll maybe help. They'll maybe stop if you're here."

"Who'll stop what?" Ellis demanded.

"Master Gosyn, Master Ashewell, and that Hal Medcote. They're quarreling horribly. Mistress Geretruda doesn't know what to do. Nor does Mistress Ashewell."

"Neither do we," said Ellis. "We're here just to play, not put ourselves in the way of anything."

"What are they quarreling about?" Joliffe asked, earning a furious look from Ellis.

"I don't know!" Sy exclaimed. "Come!"

Ellis surely would not have, but at that moment the girl Claire came from the house and toward them, nearly but not quite running, her skirts lifted out of her feet's way and fear very open on her young face. "Sy, hurry them!" she said. "It's Mother. I'm afraid . . ." But she gave up on Sy without a pause, going past him to Ellis, so desperate that she laid a hand on his arm as she pleaded up at him with

fear and tears in her eyes, "Come and make her think of
something else. She's so frightened, listening to them.
She's going to make herself sick. Please come."

Joliffe knew they were lost. Ellis would likely have held
out against Sy and almost any other man, but a pleading
girl with tears in her eyes . . . In fairness, Joliffe had to admit that he started toward the hall in the same moment Ellis did. Nor was Gil behindhand, or Piers. Though Piers did
not count. He liked trouble. But for the rest of us, Joliffe
thought, we're idiots. He also thought it was unfortunate
that understanding they were idiots was not the same as
stopping being idiots.

With a gasped, "Thank you," Claire let go of Ellis and
made to lead them inside, but Joliffe put out a hand to pause
her, asking, "Where are they quarreling at? In the hall?"

"In the orchard. Beyond the garden. Father took them
out there to be away. But we can hear them yelling."

Joliffe wanted to ask again, "About what?" but more to
the necessary point Ellis said, "Where's your mother?"

Claire was going forward again and they followed her as
she answered, "In the solar. Will you sing to her or something? Anything to turn her mind."

She had them into the hall now. With its old hearth in
the middle of the floor and smoke-blackened beams, it was
raised above its former humbleness by a table set across its
upper end, covered with a white linen cloth and set with
good pewter dishes, waiting for a meal that had not happened yet. At the hall's other end two women servants were
standing by a doorway to probably the kitchen, hand-
wringing and looking worried. Claire pointed Sy toward
them, saying, "Make sure they don't let supper spoil," but
headed herself toward a door that had to lead into the new
range of rooms where the solar would be.

"Wait," said Ellis. "We need a moment."

They surely did, having no thought of what they were

going to do, and they clumped together, heads close in quick talk. It was always best to have a thing practiced and certain before they played it, but they were also practiced at making up something on the moment—a needed skill when playing the streets with no certainty of what could happen next—and it took few words before Piers handed the tabor and pipes to Gil and hitched at his tunic and hosen to be sure they were loose enough, while Ellis said to Claire, "The solar is right through there?" beckoning his head toward the door beyond the table.

"Yes."

"You go in first," Ellis said. "Say, 'The players are here,' step well aside from the door without looking back, and after that go along with whatever we do. Yes?"

Tears gone and eyes wide, Claire nodded.

"Go on then," Ellis said with his warmest smile. The rest of them smiled, too, all showing cheerful confidence and no sign of how much of it was feigned.

Claire nodded again and went. They heard her say stiffly, "The players are here, Mother," and saw her step aside. Ellis tapped Piers on the shoulder and Piers darted through the doorway, paused for a quick bow that gave him time to see where everyone and the furnishings were, then flung himself forward into a somersault that ended with him walking on his hands, legs up in the air. There were women's startled gasps and half a laugh, but by then Ellis had strode into the room in Piers' wake. He slapped Piers' feet, toppling Piers into a sprawl on the floor where he sat glaring up at Ellis as Ellis declared, one hand flung out, the other laid on his heart, "Ladies fair and ladies fine, I come . . ."

Behind him, Gil set up a firm *rat-a-tat* on the tabor and a *tootle* on the pipes and jigged into the room, followed by Joliffe with his lute at the ready. The solar was a long room, with unglazed windows at either end and against one wall steep stairs leading to the room above it. Through the nearer window streamed the evening's last light, warm over the brown-tiled floor, the bright, tasseled cushions on a bench, the polished pewter pitcher and goblets on a small table. Little might have been done to change the old house into the hall, but much had been lavished here to make this new room into a place of comfort.

But through the far window—toward the orchard, Joliffe presumed—two men's raised, angry voices battered at what should have been the room's ease. Near the room's one chair, Geretruda Gosyn stood with her hands wringing at each other while Mistress Ashewell looked to be either steadying her or else urging her to the chair.

What Joliffe instantly wanted was to be where he could hear what was being said so angrily between the men, but Gil was busily jigging around the room, drumming and tootling, and Joliffe carried onward as he was supposed to do, elbowing Ellis aside in mid-declaration and hitting a firm strum across his lute as he did, saying louder than Ellis, "Ladies fair and ladies fine . . ."

Ellis, outrage in every line of him, first turned a glare on him, then gave him a hard shove on the shoulder. Joliffe tilted sideways, teetering on one foot. His arms flailed briefly to bring him back to the balance he was never in true danger of losing, and then he made a return shove at Ellis, who made to shove him back, but Piers had "recovered" from his sprawl and now, still sitting on the floor, grabbed hold of Ellis' near leg and pretended to sink his teeth into it. Ellis jerked free with a yell and began to hop around on one foot, holding his "hurt" leg. Joliffe tossed his lute to Gil, who was already thrusting the pipes through his belt to have his hands free to catch it skillfully just as Ellis "blundered" into Joliffe and they both went down in a tangled heap, almost on top of Piers, who yelped and scrambled away, then dove back in to grab Ellis' leg again and worry at it like a determined puppy.

While they were busy at that, Gil, well aside from the fray, struck a fine pose and a pretty flurry of notes from the lute, and began to sing the sweet spring song of summer coming in with cuckoo's call and lambs and all. That brought an end to Joliffe and Ellis' "fighting." Still entangled, they glared up at Gil, then struggled to free themselves from each other, trying to recover their dignity and taking up the song in round as they climbed to their feet. Only Piers remained determinedly oblivious, still clinging and pretending to puppy-worry at Ellis' leg until Ellis took him by the belt and lifted him bodily from the floor, breaking Piers' hold. Piers, defeated, gave up and, hanging there, began to sing, too, his clear, bright voice blending with the rest of theirs. Ellis set him on his feet, and with all discord vanished, the four of them finished the song, with first Gil dropping away, then Ellis, then Joliffe, leaving Piers to sing alone, sweetly bringing it to an end and silence.

By then Geretruda had sunk onto the chair and now held out a hand to Piers, saying, "Sweet boy. Come here."

Used to women being charmed by his fair curls and sweet face—"Fooled like birds by a snare," was how Ellis put it—Piers went forward, bowed, and then knelt on one knee before her, looking up at her, all bright eyes and innocence. She laid a hand on his curls and said again, "Sweet boy."

At the church ale yesterday Joliffe had thought Geretruda Gosyn looked frail. Today she was gone past frail to outright ill, was gray-faced, with the skin drawn in and hollowed under her cheeks and at her temples, and the hand she put out to Piers' curls more thin, ridged bones than flesh. Whatever was amiss with her, it was not something come on her suddenly but was an old foe in a fight that she was losing, Joliffe thought.

But for that moment she was smiling, her eyes soft with the pleasure of laughter and Piers' singing, and Claire and

Mistress Ashewell, too, were both smiling, maybe more at the sick woman's pleasure than with their own but eased along with her out of the tautness there had been.

And then Walter Gosyn slammed in through the doorway at the room's far end, saying backward over his shoulder as he came, "No! Once more and finally, *no*! The only thing you're welcome to is to get out of here and not come back!"

Behind him, Hal Medcote came in far less vehemently, no sign of anger on him, saying, "I'm only saying it as something for you to think on." He smiled. "Before the crowner comes."

Gosyn turned on him. "So you've said, and I'm saying right back at you, if that's a threat, it's a threat you can keep to yourself. You're not laying hand on a single thing of mine."

Geretruda started up from her chair. All her ease and pleasure gone, she went toward them, crying at her husband, "Please don't! Please!"

Claire went after her as Gosyn turned from Hal Medcote to say, still raging, "Do you know what he wants now? He wants Claire!"

Geretruda clutched one hand to the base of her throat. "What?"

Ashewell, just come through the doorway behind Hal, said with anger only barely more controlled than Gosyn's, "And he still wants that Nicholas should marry Eleanor. He's as mad as his father was."

The players had all drawn aside and toward the room's far end when the men had burst in, but not so far that Joliffe did not see the desperate look that passed between Claire, now holding to her mother to steady her, and Nicholas Ashewell, just come in behind his father.

"He says it doesn't even matter to him," Gosyn stormed, "that maybe one of us—Ashewell or me—killed his father!"

"Haven't I thought of doing it myself sometimes?" Hal said lightly. His voice took on a slightly harder edge. "Nor did he ever let anything stand in the way of his own profit, did my father, and what man doesn't want his son to follow in his footsteps?"

Joliffe had to admire Hal Medcote's boldness. Not many men would seek a bride while saying he thought her father was possibly a murderer, and on the same day that he'd found his father's murdered body. That could be dim-wittedness rather than boldness, of course, but Joliffe doubted there was anything dim about Hal Medcote's wits.

"Besides," Hal went on, smiling, "if we settle this before the crowner comes, then we'll all be family together, with less suspicions likely to fall our way."

Gosyn's hands were fists, kept at his side only by harsh will, Joliffe thought, but whatever answer Gosyn might have made was stopped by Geretruda saying, her hand still clutched to her throat, "Is it truly so ill a thought? If Nicholas is going to marry Eleanor, why not Claire for Hal?"

Claire cried out in protest, Nicholas jerked forward a step, and Ashewell's face darkened with the answer he was going to give that, but it was Gosyn who swore, "By God's beard, are you gone mad, woman?"

Geretruda began to cry weakly.

"I'll leave you to it, shall I?" Hal Medcote said to every-one, all friendliwise, then came away from the men and to Claire and, before she could stop him, took her hand, raised it, and kissed it. She tried to twist free, but he kept hold on her long enough to make her meet his gaze as he said, "It's all for you, my lovely. Be sure of that," before he let her go.

As Claire snatched her hand behind her, safe away from him, he made a bow to Geretruda; and despite he likely saw from the corner of his eye that only Ashewell's grip on

Gosyn's arm was holding Gosyn back, he made a bow to Mistress Ashewell, too, and left the solar with the easy assurance of a welcomed guest.

Geretruda began to sink toward the floor. Gosyn wrenched free of Ashewell, not to follow Hal but to go to her. So did Mistress Ashewell, and between them they helped her to the chair again while Claire hurried to pour what looked to be cider from a pitcher into one of the goblets. Her mother took the goblet gratefully but Claire had to steady and help her lift it so she could drink.

Ill as she was—and everyone knowing it—why had Gosyn been foolish enough to have his quarrel with Hal Medcote within her hearing and afterward bring it into the house? Joliffe wondered.

Almost as if Rose were there, he could hear her saying, "Men!"

The cider had brought a trace of color into Geretruda's face. She let Claire take the goblet and reached a hand to take hold on her husband's sleeve, asking faint-voiced and a little querulously, "But why not Hal for Claire? He's well-formed, well-mannered, has lands enough. If Nicholas is to marry Eleanor . . ."

Claire and Nicholas shared another desperate look across the room, while Gosyn said with muted fury, trying for gentle with his wife but mostly failing, "I wouldn't sell a dog to Hal Medcote. He's . . ."

Mistress Ashewell cut in over him, saying clearly and firmly, "Supper must be ready by now. Shouldn't we go to it?" It was a question with command behind it as she came to take Geretruda by one arm and around the shoulders, helping her to her feet while adding gently, "You'll feel the better for food, Truda. We all will. Come now. All this talk will keep for later." She sent a look past Geretruda to the husbands that dared them to say otherwise.

Neither man took her dare. With something like good

grace, however forced, they left the solar for the hall, save at the doorway Geretruda said something to Mistress Ashewell, who nodded, gave her into Gosyn's keeping, and turned back to the players, who were keeping very quiet as well as out of the way.

"Fellows," Mistress Ashewell said, and they all bowed and Ellis stepped forward, asking, "Mistress?"

"You'll still play for us tonight, I hope?"

He made her another low bow. "We will."

"Since I doubt our talk will be worth much, you can begin as soon as the food is on the table. You're going to divert us with something light of heart, I hope?"

Again there was more command than question in that, and Ellis answered, "Assuredly, my lady."

She bent her head in approval and left them. They looked at one another in a silence that admitted nothing of their thoughts. Then Joliffe said, "Well then, let's go make merry, shall we?"

Chapter 15

As the players had found out often enough before now, it was one thing to "make merry" themselves and altogether another thing to make others merry. That evening in Gosyn's hall they succeeded very little at the latter. The fall-about excesses of *The Baker's Cake* brought some of the servants at the lower table to quickly smothered laughter and wary glances up the hall at Gosyn at the high table where almost the only laughter was from Geretruda and not so much as if she were truly diverted as that she was determined to be.

Mistress Ashewell attempted laughter, too, and seemed to try to bring her husband to it as well, laying a hand on his arm, but while he put one of his own hands over hers it was only briefly. Mostly he dug at his food, frowning at either it or his thoughts. Gosyn did the same. Nor did Joliffe ever see either young Nicholas or Claire more than glance up from their plates.

What else he noted was that, unlike the supper at Ashewell's manor, when Nicholas and Claire had sat side by side, here they were set at opposite ends of the table from each other, well apart. Was that a sign that decisions were already being made by someone as to how things were going to go?

The players made their bows at the end to some happy clapping and some table-rapping from the servants but only scattered, half-attending applause from the high table. Gosyn did stand, though, and hold out coins that Ellis went to take with thanks and a deep bow.

"They were well-earned," Gosyn said.

They had been, Joliffe thought, though the work looked to have been mostly wasted, especially on Gosyn.

Smiling with determined pleasure, Geretruda said, "If you go to the kitchen, there'll be supper for you, too."

Ellis bowed again with more thanks, rejoined the others, and with much bowing and flourishing of hats by Ellis, Joliffe, and Gil, and with Piers doing back-flips after them the length of the hall, they made their retreat, escaping out the door at the foot of the hall into a small room that looked to serve as butlery and pantry together.

One of the women servants at the lower table had scurried out of the hall ahead of them and now stood at another door on the other side of the room, smiling and beckoning them to come in, leading them through to the kitchen itself. Beginning to bustle around it, she said happily, "That was great good sport. I could have laughed myself half-sick if they weren't all so down and dark-humoured up the hall."

Ellis, Gil, and Piers sat themselves on a bench, watching with interest as she sliced thick pieces of bread on the worktable. Joliffe stayed on his feet, leaning against the wall, and asked, "Are they often that down-mouthed?"

The woman said with a regretful shake of her head, "No. It's only this little while, what with one thing and another, things have gone so sour."

"Your mistress being ill can't help," Joliffe ventured.

Beginning to spread soft young cheese on the bread slices, the woman made a *tch*ing sound. "That's sad, that is. We've all been hoping it was a winter thing and it'd pass off, that she'd better with the spring and be herself again. Seems more and more she won't though. Master will be beside himself if she . . . if it goes to the bad."

"Pray God it won't," Joliffe said, certain though he was, by every sign, that it would.

"We've prayed, right enough. In Lent, Master even sent one of the men to Saint Swithin's shrine with an offering, but we've seen no help from it. Here you are."

She handed the slices of bread and young cheese to them all, with a particular smile at Piers and a quick tousle of his fair curls. He smiled his sweetest smile at her, then looked with faint longing toward a pot on the hearth and said, "That smells right good, mistress."

The woman laughed at him. "That's next, and some cider to follow."

Piers gave her his best bright-sweet-boy smile and she tousled his hair some more before she turned away toward some wooden bowls on a shelf. She wasn't to know he hated having his hair tousled, but the players all did and Joliffe grinned at him behind her back. Piers stuck out his tongue. Ellis made a hissing sound at both of them and Gil smothered a laugh.

The bread and cheese were good. So was the thick bean pottage and the cider that came after it. It was simple food but filling, and generously given. While the players were thanking her as generously as she had fed them, the other servants began coming into the kitchen, done with their own meal in the hall. Still saying their thanks, the players retreated out the door and into the yard, not wanting to wait for someone to ask them to perform something more there in the kitchen. Sometimes that was worth their while, but not now when they were already tired and with the walk back to camp waiting for them, although Ellis jibed at Joliffe as they crossed the yard toward the gateway, "A little short on questions in there, weren't you?"

"And the ones I asked were only friendly ones," Joliffe said.

Ellis snorted his doubt of that.

They were just out the gateway into the road when raised voices behind them turned them all around. Across the yard Gosyn and Master Ashewell were coming from the hall, and whatever they had been saying before, the first clear words that reached the players were Ashewell's angry, "So Nicholas can be sacrificed but not your Claire?"

"That's not the way of it at all!" Gosyn flung back. "Whatever Medcote was holding over you—"

Ashewell made a harsh silencing gesture at him, and the players turned hurriedly away, as one in their instinct to be away from trouble that wasn't theirs, though to be sure of it Ellis and Gil took Joliffe by either arm to help his hurry.

They were just across the ford when they heard the canter of horses behind them and stepped aside to the road's grassy verge, out of the Ashewells' way as their horses splashed through the stream, Mistress Ashewell riding pillion behind her husband, Nicholas on his own horse a little behind them. From what Joliffe could see of their faces in the evening twilight, none of them had the look of folk who had just spent a pleasant evening with friends. Then he and the others were bowing and the Ashewells passed, and after that, with the road to themselves and the first stars coming out in the cloud-wisped, darkening sky, the players walked in silence for a time until Gil said lightly, maybe as a way of shrugging off everything, "I thought we played well enough, but that lot made more work of it than need be, didn't they?"

"That they did," Ellis agreed wearily. "Pulling a laugh out them was like trying to pull my own teeth." He shifted his shoulders as if they were sore. "I'm telling you, too, that we're nearly done with that 'pick up Piers by the belt' business. He's getting too big for it."

Piers threw back his own shoulders and strutted. Ellis gave him a light clout to the back of his head and growled, "You can stop that. Any fool can grow."

Piers staggered forward as if he had been truly hit, clutching the back of his head and whining, "I'm telling Mam!" Not meaning it. And a little farther on, with darkness more around them, he drifted to Ellis' side and, a little after that, slipped a hand into one of Ellis' and they walked on together.

Joliffe, lulled by a full belly, the fresh coins in Ellis' belt-pouch, and the gathering peaceful night-sounds of settling birds and other unseen things in the hedges and fields around him, let weary contentment much like Piers' settle on him. The evening's work had been disappointing, surely. A good player learned early on that the lookers-on were a large share of any performance, and if they could not be drawn into the play—whether through their own fault or the players'—then the whole business became a pushing against a wall with little satisfaction on either side. It had been that way tonight, and not by the players' fault but all that of the ill feelings and angers seething at Gosyn's before they ever came there.

The troubling thing was that neither the angers nor ill feelings seemed to have faded after Hal Medcote had left. Instead, to judge by Ashewell's and Gosyn's anger at each other outside the hall, they were now turning on each other despite what Joliffe guessed had been a long friendship. It seemed that John Medcote had thrown some manner of rock into all the lives around him, had set waves spreading outward that might have smoothed and disappeared now that he was dead, except his son looked to be set on following his father's way.

Joliffe was sorry to find his contentment slipping from him. His too-much thinking was yet again taking him where he did not need to go. Nothing here was any business of his now. It was Kyping's and the crowner's, and what he should be thinking on was hope that one or the other would soon give the players permission to go, to leave everything and everyone here well behind them.

Yes. That hope was what he needed to think on. Not the rest.

By the time the players turned through the open gateway into what was become the too-familiar field, the last narrow band of yellow sunset was gone from along the horizon and stars were swathed across the sky. Cart and tent and Tisbe grazing nearby were no more than black shapes in the darkness, but small flames were dancing merrily orange from piled wood in the firepit, showing Basset and Rose sitting beside it, warm light cast up and moving on their faces.

Ellis called out, "Hai!" and Basset called back, "Ho!" in return. He did not sound as if there had been trouble while they were gone, thank several dozen saints, Joliffe thought. They were all too tired for trouble tonight. Or tomorrow. Or any other time, he added silently. He shivered, suddenly aware of the damp chill that had come with the sun's going. Piers left Ellis and ran ahead to Rose, who did not rise but held out an arm and, as he tumbled down beside her, gathered him close and asked, "It went well?"

Piers nodded, his head tucked against her shoulder. "Except Ellis says I'm too big for the carry-by-the-belt."

"Oh my," said Rose, smiling up at Ellis. "Is it you're too big or he's too feeble?"

"Both," murmured Piers. He cuddled nearer to her, his eyes closed.

"You've eaten?" Rose asked the rest of them as they settled around the fire.

"Very well," Gil said. "They paid us, too."

Rose held out her free hand to Ellis, who had the coins ready and gave them to her. She looked at them approvingly and then to her father. "Save or share?" she asked.

"We'll use them for buying food in the village tomorrow," Basset said. "There's no knowing how long we'll be here, or when we'll earn more. We've fairly well played out the neighborhood."

They all nodded understanding and agreement. It was why all players were traveling players—there were no towns, not even London, large enough for a company to make a living all in one place.

Not that traveling always served that much better. Their own small company was fortunate at present. With their quarter's pay from Lady Lovell still untouched, they were in no immediate peril of poverty, and just now, all of them settled around the fire, they were content with how things were and silent together for a while, until Basset asked without looking away from the fire, "So, how went it at Gosyn's?"

Ellis, Joliffe, and Gil all traded looks among themselves.

"Ah," said Basset to their silence. "Like that, was it?"

Joliffe nodded at Ellis to go ahead and tell whatever he wanted to tell. Ellis did, making short work of it, and at the end, Basset sat considering the fire for a moment more before saying, "So. No fault of ours if things went flat."

"No fault of ours," Ellis echoed.

"The servants enjoyed it," Joliffe offered.

"There's something," Basset granted dryly.

The contented silence came back among them. Piers had slipped down, was lying with his head on his mother's lap, surely more asleep than awake. Rose was smiling down at him, for once all at ease, her face peaceful as she gently stroked his hair. Ellis was beside them, idly poking the unburned ends of logs into the fire's heart with a stick. Gil was sitting with his knees drawn up, his arms around them, staring into the flames after thoughts of his own, or maybe not thinking at all, and Basset, too, was still simply sitting, watching the flames.

Joliffe, watching the fire with the rest of them, found his weariness was a good weariness. He was glad his blankets were waiting for him, but here and now beside the fire and among the others was too pleasant to leave. With all the wood burning now, Ellis had dropped his stick into the fire and was watching Rose still idly stroking Piers' hair. Gil now had his head laid on his knees but had turned sideways to go on watching the flames, as Joliffe and Basset still simply were, until Joliffe said out the slow drift of his thoughts when he would have rather they stayed quiet, "If I were Hal Medcote, I think I'd take to watching my back very closely just now."

"No one's asked what you think," Ellis pointed out without looking away from Rose.

But Basset granted, eyes still on the fire, "He does look ripe for being murdered next. Unless he's his father's murderer, of course."

"Even then I'd watch my food and drink," said Joliffe. "His sister would inherit if he died, wouldn't she?"

"Christ's blessed bones, you've a twisting mind," Ellis said with no particular heat.

Basset straightened and laid his hands on his knees. "I'm for bed. The rest of you can sit here while the chill creeps in on you if you want."

None of them wanted, and when Basset climbed somewhat stiffly to his feet, Joliffe and Gil stood up, too, Joliffe stretching his own stiffened back and legs. Rose waited until Ellis had lifted sleeping Piers from her lap. Then, with Piers on one arm, limp against his shoulder, Ellis held out his other hand to her and she took it, letting him help her up, and hand in hand they went toward the tent, following Basset. Joliffe looked at Gil, who gave a rueful nod that he would stay and bank the fire. Joliffe nodded back and strolled after the others. With Rose and Ellis among them tonight in the tent, they would all at least sleep warm. He just hoped that wasn't rain he smelled on the small wind beginning to come fitfully from the hills.

Chapter 16

The rain came whispering across the tent some-time near to dawn. With no need to rise early, the players did not; and when necessity finally forced Joliffe to rise first, he came out into a softly dripping morning, with low gray clouds almost skimming the hedgerows' tops and the hills vanished as if they had never been. The rain was only misting, though, and the clouds were drifting on a steady wind, well likely to be carried away before the morning was done.

Too used to weather to make much of it, Joliffe put up his hood and went to see how Tisbe did. She paused in her grazing to shake her head at him, spraying him with rain from her mane. "Very friendly," he told her, wiping his face. Giving her a squishing slap on her rump, he went to do what he could about rousing the fire with some of the wood that was stacked dry under the cart, so that by the time Rose joined him, wrapped in her own cloak and hood, the little blaze was going well enough to hold its own in the damp morning. "This is your way of saying you're hoping for a warm breakfast?" she asked. "There's only what's left of the bread."

"Warm is warm," said Joliffe easily. "What if I toast the bread?"

"There's nothing to go on it," Rose warned.

"Cheese?"

"Not unless you want to go without it later in the day if no one goes into the village."

"I'm not going to starve on Medcote's account. Come what may, I'm going to the village for food today."

She gave him something of the look she gave Piers when she doubted she was hearing all the truth from him. Understanding her look perfectly, Joliffe added, grinning, "And there'll be talk to be had in the village."

"Yes. I thought that might be it." She handed him the bread and cheese and the board to cut them on. "Let it be toasted bread and cheese this morning, then."

By midmorning the rain had stopped. The clouds were tattering to show blue sky, and a swathe of sunshine had just passed across the meadow, drifting with the clouds, when Master Kyping and his man rode through the gateway. Tisbe raised her head and stared as if worried there might not be grass enough for three horses here, while the players gathered from whatever tasks they had been doing to beside the fire, facing Kyping as he dismounted, gave his reins to his man, and came toward them, leaving man and horses behind him.

Judging by his thoroughly rain-darkened cloak, he had been out and about for some hours already this morning, and if he was happy about it, his face did not show it. But there was no way to tell if his displeasure was at them or at life in general, nor did he greet them, only said, "You played at Walter Gosyn's yesterday."

"Four of us did, yes," Basset said in courteous agreement.

Ellis, Joliffe, Piers, and Gil each held up a hand, smiling, Ellis saying as courteously as Basset, "We did." Then, with sudden suspicion, "Has something more happened?" saving Joliffe the trouble of asking.

"Not yet," Kyping said. Joliffe eased a little: Kyping's displeasure seemed general, rather than at them in particular. "You saw Hal Medcote there?"

"We did," Ellis said. "He was quarreling with Gosyn."

"And with Master Ashewell?" Kyping asked.

Ellis frowned with thought. "Not so much. It seemed mostly between him and Gosyn. After he left, Gosyn and Master Ashewell quarreled with each other, though."

"About what?"

"About the same thing Hal Medcote and Gosyn had been quarreling over," Ellis answered. "About the marriages."

"Either Gosyn knew before, or else he'd just heard that Medcote wanted Nicholas for Eleanor," Joliffe said. "Why he and Ashewell were angry at each other about that we never gathered, but Gosyn was angry at Hal Medcote because Hal wants Claire. You'd heard that before."

"From you and elsewhere, yes," Kyping said tersely.

Before Joliffe could guess why he sounded angry at that or whether he was angry for another reason, Kyping asked Ellis, "You agree Hal Medcote and Gosyn were quarreling because now Hal wants to marry Claire, yes?"

"Yes."

"Does it seem Hal still means for his sister to marry Nicholas Ashewell?"

"Yes," Ellis said again.

Maybe deciding that too many words was better than too few, Kyping asked Joliffe, "You've no thought of why Gosyn and Master Ashewell quarreled?"

"It seemed to be because Gosyn was set and certain he won't marry Claire to Hal, and somehow Master Ashewell took offense," Joliffe said readily. "Maybe because he had some hope of having Nicholas free from marrying Eleanor now Medcote is dead, and he was out of humour at finding Hal means to hold him to it. Which means Hal must know whatever it is his father was holding against Ashewell and must be holding it, too."

Joliffe waited, hoping Kyping would say something about that.

Kyping looked at him, giving nothing away.

Joliffe prodded, "You've not found out what it is, have you?"

"No."

"Have you asked Hal Medcote about it?"

"Yes."

"And Master Ashewell?"

"Yes."

Kyping was becoming as miserly with words as Ellis had been. Hoping to loosen him, Joliffe tried, as if the thought had only just now come to him, "In their way, both marriages make sense. It's a reasonable joining of lands to everyone's good in the longer run, I'd say."

Sharp with dislike, Kyping answered, "I'd not wish Hal Medcote on any daughter of mine for any reason, and Eleanor Medcote deserves better than some stripling who doesn't want her."

Interested in how much Kyping had betrayed with that, Joliffe went altogether another way, asking, "What about Jack Hammond? Have you questioned him?"

"Yesterday. To give him a better fright I had him brought to me under guard as if I was about to arrest him. He talked very willingly."

"To any use?" Joliffe asked.

"He claims he was at his uncle's overnight. That they went together from the church ale and Jack stayed the night with him, trying to talk out his anger and to borrow money.

Claims he started home as soon as there was light enough to see his way. 'To be in time for his god-bedamned boon-work for the god-bedamned priest,' was the way he put it."

"Seems he didn't talk out much of his anger," Joliffe said dryly.

"Nor he didn't get any money out of his uncle either."

"Who, I suppose, lives in a direction that makes it reasonable Hammond should be going home by way of here," Joliffe said.

"He does, and though I'm sure I got to him before any word passed between him and Jack, he tells the same tale and I have to think he's told me straight."

"Pity," muttered Ellis.

Kyping's somewhat bitter smile agreed with him. So, silently, did Joliffe. Jack Hammond as Medcote's murderer would save everyone a deal of trouble. But aloud he only said, "And I suppose Jack saw neither Medcote's body or even his horse as he passed, what with the heavy mist and all."

"He did not," Kyping said resignedly. "Nor is it likely he would have raised the hue-and-cry if he had." Because few men wanted to be first-finder of a dead body and have all the irk of duties that came with it. Kyping shrugged. "Ah, well. There's still others I'm asking questions after."

"Including Master Ashewell and Gosyn?" Joliffe asked.

"And you lot," Kyping said. "There's only your word for each other that none of you left camp that night."

Joliffe acknowledged that with a small bow of his head. "True. But if it wasn't one of us, then isn't it likely the murder was not by someone coming on Medcote by chance but done deliberately by someone who followed him there? Or knew he would be there? You've asked to find who from his manor went anywhere that night?"

"Servants seen talking in the village, you mean. Someone who said too much to the wrong person," Kyping returned.

"Or a servant who claims he was in the village or some-where, but no one remembers seeing him there."

"I've been asking those questions, yes, but going at it the other way, too—trying to sort out who couldn't have killed Medcote, no matter how much they may have wanted to, from all those who disliked Medcote enough to maybe do it."

"Who couldn't have?" Joliffe asked.

Kyping nodded at Rose. "Her. Anela Medcote. Gosyn's wife. Mistress Ashewell. Eleanor Medcote." He was seem-ingly keeping to the thought that no woman could have killed Medcote the way he had been killed, but Eleanor Medcote was altogether another matter from the other women. She had surely known as well as the rest of the household had where her father was going, and she was quite sufficiently built that, if once she had him down, she might have been able to do the rest. Curious why Kyping dismissed her with the others, Joliffe asked, "You think Eleanor Medcote couldn't? Or is it that you think she wouldn't? I saw no love lost between her and her father."

"If she hadn't murdered Medcote before this," Kyping said somewhat too sharply, "she's unlikely to have done it now."

He sounded ready to leave it there, but Rose—bless her, thought Joliffe—asked, "Why? What had he done to her before?"

"Her first husband." Kyping bit the words off short and angrily.

This was where Kyping had the advantage, Joliffe thought. He knew these people and about their pasts in ways the players could not match.

But that was maybe against Kyping, too. Knowing too much too nearly maybe made it hard for him to sort what mattered from what did not—the grain from the chaff—and to see what else he could get him to say, Joliffe said, "I take it her first marriage was bad. You don't think being forced to another marriage was more than she was willing to bear? Or does she want this marriage?"

"She doesn't want it," Kyping said.

Rose asked, "Then how could she be forced to it? She's a widow, with say in her own life. She surely has dower that she could live on if that was the only way to be free of her father."

That had to be true enough, it being unlikely Medcote had married her the first time to a poor man. And while a woman brought a dowry of goods or land or money to her husband when they married, he in his turn settled a portion of his own land or goods or money on her in dower, to be hers should he die first, to see her provided for as much as might be in her widowhood. Poor men left little; rich men left much. But either way it was all of it likely to be laid out in the marriage contract that careful couples—or their parents—saw made before ever the Church's blessing came into the matter.

But Kyping said sourly, "She had dower, right enough, but Medcote drove a twisted bargain with her first husband and he was a twisty mongrel in his own right and crabbed with years into the bargain. They settled it between them that nothing was to come into Eleanor's own hands until she's thirty years of age. Until then she was to be dependent on Medcote for everything. Including another marriage."

"And now she's dependent on her brother," Joliffe said.

"On him now, yes," Kyping agreed.

So killing her father would not have been enough to free her, and Eleanor must have known that. Again Joliffe thought that Hal Medcote had best look to his back, because even if she hadn't killed their father, she might have less scruple against him. He kept that to himself, though, and asked, "What about men who might have done for Medcote? I take it you fully think Jack Hammond is clear."

"Unless his uncle and a quarter of his uncle's village are lying together for him."

"Could they be?"

"I doubt it. Hammond isn't that well-liked by his uncle. Or by anyone else there for that matter. I'm still prying about other men who wouldn't mind Medcote dead, but even of the ones I don't know for certain where they were, it's hard to judge how they could have known where he would be. I've had no satisfaction from the Medcote servants that way, yet, try though I have." Kyping looked at Rose. "Could someone have overheard Medcote when he was with you?"

"No. There was no one close by."

"You're certain?" Basset prompted.

"Yes," Rose snapped.

Kyping was watching her too carefully for Joliffe's ease; nor was he any way eased by Kyping saying at her consideringly, "Being asked about it makes you angry," as if finding something particular about that.

Sharply, giving no ground, Rose said back at him, "It's having even to think about him makes me angry. He was a mind-befouling kind of man."

Kyping made a small sound that might have been agreement, and Joliffe asked, to take Kyping elsewhere than Rose, "What of Master Ashewell and Gosyn? Is it certain where they were that night?"

This time Kyping did not try to hide his thought behind a straight face but said, his mouth as wry as his words, "They claim they never left their own places after they came home from the church ale, and I've found no one to gainsay them."

"Then maybe it's true," said Basset. "There's usually someone ready to make trouble for someone if they can."

"True enough in Gosyn's case for certain," Kyping agreed. "Maybe less likely with Master Ashewell."

"What of Father Hewgo?" Joliffe asked.

Kyping showed surprise at that. "The priest? What would he know of where Master Ashewell or Gosyn were?"

"I mean would he have had chance to know where Medcote was?"

Kyping held quiet, his stare brooding on Joliffe but his thought apparently on the priest because after a moment he said, "There was less love lost between them all the time, I've noted, and there was maybe more wrong than has shown on the surface. But I doubt Father Hewgo's such a fool as to think Hal Medcote will be any great improvement over his father in dealing with one matter or another."

"Unless Medcote knew something Father Hewgo didn't want him to know," Joliffe said.

"But he'd have to worry that Medcote had shared something like that with Hal, as Medcote seems to have done with whatever he's holding over Ashewell."

"Father Hewgo might have thought the risk worth the taking, if there was chance Medcote hadn't told Hal," Joliffe said.

Kyping held that thought for a long moment, frowning on it before he said, "I'll ask some questions that way, too. So. Now you know fairly well all that I do. What have *you* learned?"

He asked it of Basset and Joliffe both, and Joliffe looked to Basset, who looked back at him and said, "It's yours to tell."

Joliffe accepted that with a slight shrug and said to Kyping, "We've told you the only new thing we had—what we heard at Gosyn's last night."

"How deep do you think the quarrel is between Master Ashewell and Gosyn about these marriages?" Kyping asked.

"I would guess fairly deep. If there's peace kept between the families, it will be because of the wives, and I don't know if that will work either. I don't know what Mistress

Ashewell thinks of any of the business, but we heard
Gosyn's wife say she didn't see why Claire shouldn't marry
Hal if she couldn't have Nicholas."

"She must not know much about him, then," Ellis
muttered.

"She maybe doesn't," Kyping said. "Or chooses not to.
She's never been a sharp-witted woman. Good-hearted and
a good wife, but never with much reach beyond her kitchen
yard and never any heart for trouble—either making it or
seeing it."

"And now she's dying," Joliffe said.

"Has been this past half year, now anyone looks back on
it," Kyping said regretfully. "She'll see summer in but
likely won't see it out."

"How will Gosyn take that?" Joliffe asked.

"Joliffe," Rose said, disapproving.

But Kyping answered, "Hard. There's no one will say
she hasn't always been the better side of him, keeping him
safe from his own ill-humours as much as anyone could.
Gosyn is going to be the worse man for her being gone."

"That's maybe why she'd like to see her daughter safely
married while she still can," Rose said. "Except marrying
her to Hal Medcote has nothing 'safe' about it, does it?"

"Nothing," Kyping agreed. "By all the look of it, he's
his father over again."

"What I'd like to know," Joliffe said, "is what Medcote
was using to force Master Ashewell to this other marriage."

"So would I," said Kyping grimly. "I've been hoping to
learn something along the way that would add weight to
my asking him again, but I haven't."

And he probably believed no more than Joliffe did that
Ashewell was likely to give away whatever it was unless he
was forced to it.

Kyping was looking at them, one after the other, as if to
draw some useful answer out of them. Joliffe kept his own

face blandly unhelpful, knowing the others were matching him. Even Gil in the months he had been with them had learned the usefulness of a blank face when faced with someone's questions that couldn't, or else shouldn't, be satisfied. Just now they were none of them lying. There was nothing else to tell. Whether Kyping believed it or not was hardly their fault, and his terse sigh only betrayed his impatience as he seemed to accept there was nothing more to be had from them and said, "Well enough. I still can't give you leave to go, not until the crowner comes. If you learn aught in the meanwhile . . ."

He looked at Basset as he broke off. Basset somewhat bowed and assured him, "You'll know whatever we know, sir, as soon as may be after we know it."

The rest of the players matched Basset's bow, and Rose made a small curtsy. Kyping nodded in reply and made to turn away toward his waiting man and horses, but Joliffe took a step forward and asked, "Have you learned anything about who gains from Medcote's death?"

Kyping stopped. "Who gains?"

"Besides everyone by being rid of him," Joliffe said.

"No one in particular," Kyping replied. "His wife more than anyone except Hal. She'll have her dower and her freedom, I suppose. Hal has the rest and looks to be taking up where his father left off and that's surely no surprise to anyone nor any gain. If it was change the murderer wanted when he killed Medcote, he needs to be rid of Hal, too."

So Joliffe wasn't the only one to see that. He wondered if Hal did, too, but said, "Then likely Medcote was killed not to change things but because he knew something his murderer didn't want him to know."

"You're thinking of whatever we suppose he was using to force the Ashewell marriage," Kyping said.

"Not foremost," Joliffe answered. "If his murderer had any sense at all, he had to suspect that whatever Medcote was using as a lever against Master Ashewell, he was all too likely to have shared with Hal and maybe his wife."

"Which he did," Kyping said. "With Hal anyway. Anela gives no sign of knowing anything. What you're thinking is that there's some other secret he was killed for. A secret we've not thought of."

"A secret so new the murderer had hope Medcote had so far kept it to himself."

Kyping's eyes widened a little with sudden speculation as he took in that thought. Slowly he said, "Yes." Then gave a short, bitter laugh. "But good luck to us finding it out."

"Still, it won't hurt to look," Joliffe said mildly. "It would likely be something come up of late. It might pay to look twice and thrice at everyone he's lately had dealings with, of whatever kind. Anyone he maybe had some new falling out with but not yet a full and open quarrel. Father Hewgo, say," he added, to help Kyping along.

Staring down at the grass as if revelations were to be had there, Kyping nodded slowly. "There might be something to find out going that way, yes." He looked up suddenly and sharply into Joliffe's face. "So. Anything more you've thought on?"

Joliffe smiled, all outward easy friendliness. "Not a thing. All I can do is wish you luck with it all."

Kyping did not bother with smiling back, just nodded, turned away to take his horse from his man, mount, and ride off with no other farewell.

Chapter 17

Until Kyping and his man were well gone, the players stayed standing where they were, no word among them. Then Piers said at Joliffe, "He doesn't like you," at the same moment Ellis said bitterly, "Seems one of us could still turn out the first choice for hanging for lack of anyone better."

Ignoring Piers, Joliffe said more lightly than he felt, "Then we'd best set to finding someone better for him. I do feel a need to see what's being said in the village among ordinary folk. Fair Rose, what would you like for us to bring from there?"

"Bread," she said promptly. "There should be that at least, but I don't know what else is likely. Whatever was to spare would have gone at the church ale, I'd think. You'd not rather go to Faringdon, I suppose?" That being a market town, there would be more to be bought in this lean time of the year when the winter stores were run low or out and little was to be had yet from field, flock, or herd.

"Tomorrow maybe," Joliffe said, going toward the cart to fetch his lute. "Today we'll have to feast on local talk."

"Famine on it, more likely," Ellis muttered.

"Take Gil with you," said Basset.

"And me!" Piers cried.

"No," said Rose, Basset, Ellis, and Joliffe all together.

Despite Piers had to have known they would say that, he glared at them anyway. Basset handed Joliffe coins from his belt pouch to pay for whatever food he might find, while Ellis got the leather bottle for ale and tossed it to Joliffe with, "Get some fresh ale, too. There should be that to be found at least."

Joliffe tossed the bag to Gil, took up his lute and swung it around to carry on his back by the strap over his shoulder, saying, "Gil will see to the ale while I see if sweet music will bring sweet words."

"If it's sweet music you want, you'd best let Gil sing," Ellis growled.

"Come on, Gil," Joliffe said with more outward cheer than he had inwardly. "Time to sing for your supper."

As he and Gil headed away, he waved over his shoulder at everyone without looking back and his stride was light; but outside the gate and hidden by the hedge from everyone but Gil beside him, he let his walk flatten to match his thoughts, and Gil asked, "As bad as that?"

Joliffe quirked one corner of his mouth, acknowledging the sharpness of the question. Gil did not rattle-talk as much as the rest of them did, but he saw things well enough. There was even the chance that—unlike most people in the wide world—he thought about what he saw, rather than merely jabbered about it, and so Joliffe answered him fairly with, "It's bad enough. Not so bad as Ellis has it. I don't think Kyping is bent and set on finding one of us guilty unless we are. He's willing to have us not be his first choice anyway, and that's something."

"You think it but you're not sure. Is that it?"

"I don't know Kyping well enough to be sure. Maybe if no one better is found, he'll settle for one of us being guilty. And anyway, there's nothing sure in life, no matter what we do. How's your ankle? No trouble with it?"

Gil admitted to twinges but nothing that mattered, he said, and after that they walked in silence that was companionable enough, leaving Joliffe to his own thoughts that were not good company at all. Even if Kyping was as fair as he seemed to be, there was still the crowner to come, with no way to say aforetime if he was someone willing to take the easiest way to closing a murder of a man who, after all, had not much mattered in the general way of things.

Of course if he did look to be that way, then Basset would send someone fast-footed to Lady Lovell, who would make plain the players were not easy prey, and then all would likely be well enough, but even a disproven charge of murder had a way of dragging after a man. Talk went from village to village to town easily enough, and scandal attached readily to players at the best of times. Would Lord Lovell want to keep a company of players that was burdened with that kind of talk about them? Maybe, since he—and now his lady wife—had found other uses for them than merely as players.

And that was another uncomfortable thing to think about, because he had an unsettled feeling that this question-asking the Lovells had sometimes asked of the players could lead to more than it had. If he let himself, he could worry over what that "more" might be. He thought Basset thought the same but they had neither of them said as much to each other, and if the others had any thought about it at all, they had all likewise kept it to themselves. After all, there was more than enough to worry about in the usual course of a day without brooding on "maybes" that might never happen.

Besides, if he wanted something to worry on, there was the more pressing worry about what anger or suspicion he and Gil might meet in the village, and despite giving no outward sign of it, he kept a wary eye around them as they arrived there. This hour of the day, most folk were gone to the fields or were busy at their work at home. The few they passed in the street gave them looks only maybe a little longer than was usual and nods that were ordinary enough. Somewhat encouraged, Joliffe said, "The alehouse first. That's where there'll be talk."

"And ale," said Gil readily.

What there was not in the alehouse were any drinkers or men loitering, which likely accounted for the warmth of the alewife's greeting to them. But to Joliffe's question as she urged them to a bench she assured him she had new ale ready. "Just passed by John Greene, who's been ale-taster here for the assize since before I was old enough to walk. He knows his ale, he does, and he says it's a good batch. So sit you down and I'll bring you some."

"Where are all your customers, then?" Joliffe asked as she went to fetch two clay cups and a pitcher from across the room.

"That Master Kyping," she said, sounding somewhere between approving and irked. "He's been at it to see to it everyone is out and at work, to get as much done in the fields as can be while the weather holds, he says." She laughed as she handed Joliffe and Gil each a cup. "He even has the old men out. Said they could keep an eye on the children if nothing else. You should have heard old Will going on about that."

"What's Master Kyping's reason for it all?" Joliffe asked, despite he could guess.

"My guess is he and the reeve—that's Master Ashewell, you know—hope it will lessen troublemaking talk if everyone's kept to work and be a way of being sure where everyone is, too, until things are settled about Medcote's death."

Joliffe held out his cup and said, "So there's no one suspected more than anyone else yet?"

"Not that I've heard."

"Does your business no good though, having everybody out."

She laughed while pouring the ale. "Won't hurt it, likely. They'll all be here come evening, full of talk and wanting to drink. I'll be busy enough then if not now. Where's the rest of your company?"

"Too slothful to walk so far, even for your fine ale," Joliffe said. When that brought another laugh from her, he ventured, "Truth is, we're all somewhat worried over how folk might be toward us here."

She paused at pouring Gil's ale. "Be toward you?"

"With the murder and us being strangers and all."

She went back to filling Gil's cup. "No need for any of you to worry about that. Medcote had enough people angry at him that folk are more pleased he's dead than looking to blame strangers for it. Come to it, there's no one looking all that hard for who did for him. Save maybe Master Kyping because it's his duty to."

Joliffe took a long swallow of ale and made a deep, satisfied sigh as if it were the best of ale he'd ever had. It was not, but a friendly alewife willing to talk was the quickest way that he knew to learn about a village and he held out the cup to be refilled before he asked, making a jest of it, "Everyone's easy, then, thinking his murderer is maybe here among them?"

"It was Medcote that was murdered," the alewife said, filling his cup. "Who's to care or worry? Not even his own people, it seems, from what's being said." She rested the pitcher on her hip. "Except his wife is angry that Hal

Medcote won't let the body be moved before the crowner comes. She'd have it done, fine or no fine for it."

"From what I saw the time we played there, I'd not think she'd care that much, one way or other," Joliffe said.

"From what was said here last night, that's just one more thing they're quarreling over, her and her son. What had us in whoops was that Father Hewgo is taking her side about it when she's not been able to stand him these three years and more since they quarreled over tithes and Medcote took his part against her. Not for any good reason, mind you. She was in the right of it, most of us think. He just liked to set against her, and besides, he and Father Hewgo were thick as thieves until just lately."

"They had a falling out?"

"The way thieves do, yes."

"About what?"

"Nothing certain that I've heard. Maybe just because they were both quarrelsome men. Now Father Hewgo's siding with Anela Medcote over moving Medcote's body, but I doubt he'll have much joy of Anela in the long run. She's never been able to bear him. But then I mind Father Hewgo's not doing it so much for a good reason as because he and Hal Medcote are already at odds and quarreling. Over Medcote's dead body, as it were."

"How?" Joliffe asked with the readiness of anyone wanting to hear a good story. "Why?"

She laughed. "What I hear is that Father Hewgo asked more money for the funeral Mass and all than Hal thinks saving his father's soul is worth."

Joliffe laughed with her and asked lightly, "How do you hear all this? They surely don't come in here to do their quarreling in front of you."

She tipped him a wink. "No need they should. Their servants aren't as quiet about things as they might be. What Medcote cheated them in wages they took out in talk against him. Are still taking out in talk. We know more about who's mad at whom and about what in that household than Anela Medcote would like, I'd guess."

"Did Medcote know they talked? Or does Hal?"

"Who's to say? Even if they knew, they weren't likely to care. If anything, Medcote went out of his way to stir up talk while he was alive, and Hal isn't more than a hairs-breadth different from his father, the devil take him, too. Nor I doubt that Eleanor cares a penny about what anyone thinks or says. Cold as old stone, that one is. If anyone, it's Anela who wouldn't like it. Grew up here, she did. Was Francis Brook's ward after her mother, that was his sister, see, died."

"Francis Brook," Joliffe said while Gil held out his cup for more ale. "That's the man that Nicholas Ashewell killed by chance, yes?"

"No, that was Francis Brook the younger as was killed. His father is who I mean. Francis Brook the elder. He was a few years dead when his son was killed; that was Anela's cousin, see. They grew up like brother and sister. That's why young Francis put up with her husband when she married, though he and Medcote got on no better than Medcote did with anyone else."

"They were here when Francis Brook was hurt, weren't they?" Joliffe asked, though he knew that wasn't what he'd heard.

"Anela was," the alewife corrected him. "And Hal and Eleanor. Visiting, like. Getting out of Wantage for the summer when there was a bit of pestilence about, as I remember. When Medcote heard Francis Brook was hurt, he came fast enough, though. Then Francis died and there are those as have thoughts about that," she added darkly.

Joliffe feigned choking halfway through a sip of ale, swallowed hurriedly, and said, "Thoughts? You mean . . ." He broke off, preferring she say it.

"I mean the word was that Francis Brook was on the mend. The bird-bolt had no more than scraped along the side of his neck. It was the blood he'd lost was the trouble and that's why he was kept to bed. But he was getting his strength back, see, and then he was dead and nobody was in the house when he died but Medcote and some servants. And young Hal as was a half-grown boy then."

"Where was everyone else?"

"It was Assumption Day in harvest. Everyone was gone to the church who could be. The servant that had been tending Brook went out to the well to draw some water, it being hot and Brook a little fevered. She had some trouble with the rope being in a tangle somehow, and when she came back, there was Brook lying dead in his bed. Heart failed him, it was said, and there was nothing to prove differently. Nor could she say Medcote had been near him while she was out."

"But folk thought otherwise," Joliffe said.

"Folk thought otherwise."

"Why wasn't Medcote or Hal at church with the rest?"

"There was another priest here then, and Medcote had already quarreled with him, so Medcote wouldn't go, and little Hal was already his father's boy and wouldn't go either. A pair they were even then, and no good at the core, either of them."

"What became of the servant?"

"Her? She moved on that next Michaelmas when her hire was done. Went Swindon way, I think. Nor was she the only one not to linger there, then or since. The Medcotes don't keep servants long."

"How are the present ones taking Medcote's death?"

The alewife gave a throaty chuckle. "There's no great grief going on there, that's sure. Not among the servants nor the rest of them."

"Has there been talk about how Medcote came to be where he was when he was killed?"

"Gone out to meet some woman," the alewife said scornfully. "That's what they're saying he said. Me, I can see him saying that just to goad his wife, when all the time he was up to some other devilment, though I don't know what."

That was good, then, if there was no talk of Rose, just of some woman and apparently doubt about even that. To see what else there might be, Joliffe tried, "I've heard there was a quarrel between Medcote and his wife the night he was killed. What's said about that?"

"Nothing particular that I've heard. Bitter words may have been passed, but from what's said, those were common enough. I'd have thought they were long past outright quarreling. Why waste the time when she knew his ways well enough to know there was no changing him?"

Joliffe had a moment's pity for Anela Medcote, cursed with a quarrel-hearted husband, a son who matched him, and a cold daughter. Despite them all, she had dealt fairly enough with the players that one time, which was reason enough for Joliffe to consider better of her than some might. Come to that, though, her daughter had seemed none so harsh either. So maybe it was best to remember it was easy enough to talk about someone, but knowing what was in their heart was another matter altogether.

Though he had a fairly sure thought of what was in Hal Medcote's heart and did not like it. Where his father's death could have been a chance to begin a healing of all the angers and wrongs Medcote had done, Hal looked set instead on deepening and spreading the ugliness.

He was forming a question about Hal when Gil set his emptied cup aside and asked, "Should we be seeing about food now?"

He sounded so much like Ellis when Ellis had had

enough of Joliffe making questions that Joliffe had to hold
back from laughing while obediently turning the talk toward
food and where they might buy some in the village. The
alewife was as helpful there as with her ale, glad to fill their
bottle while telling them who had done baking that morning
and that her daughter-in-law had some new cheese from a
cow that had calved early. Paying her with coins and thanks,
they went on their quest and had better fortune with it than
Rose had hoped for. The only loaves anyone would sell them
were a coarse mix of rye and barley, but this end of the year
few in the village were likely to have better, and they were
surely better than none. Besides that, the daughter-in-law
was pleased to sell some of her new cheese and she was even
persuaded, by Joliffe's ready talk and a few more coins, to
part with some meat from a newly butchered lamb she had
been readying for her household's supper.

"So you'd better get yourselves away with it, before
they find out what I've done," she jested at them as she
gave it over, wrapped in rhubarb leaves.

Taking it with a bow like a courtier receiving largess
from royal hands, Joliffe said, "It is the more precious for
being received from your fair hands. I will betray you to no
one, good my lady."

She blushed and laughed and told him and Gil to get on
their way. They went and were well outside the village before Gil said of a sudden, "That was a lot of talk you had
from the alewife. You set out to find things out and you
did." He grinned. "It's a good thing it was me instead of Ellis with you."

Joliffe matched his grin. "Yes."

"Did you find out anything? That helps, I mean."

"Nothing that helps. Not yet anyway. Maybe if I have a
chance to learn more there'll be pieces that fit, but nothing
does yet."

"Oh."

Gil was disappointed by that, but it was the truth. If he had found out anything that helped, Joliffe did not know it yet, and what surprised him was how little he cared. If the players were given leave to go within the hour, he would go with a free heart, completely willing to leave Medcote's death unsolved behind him.

He only hoped they were given leave to go before someone murdered Hal Medcote, who looked as likely to it as ever his father had been.

With the field hidden from the lane by the hedge, it was only as they came to the gateway that Gil said, "Uh-oh," and Joliffe silently echoed him.

Midway between gate and camp, Basset and Ellis were standing in talk with four riders. New trouble—that was Joliffe's first thought, before he saw two of the riders were Kyping and Kyping's man. Old trouble then.

Or maybe new to go with them, because the third rider was Eleanor Medcote. The fourth, though, looked to be only a servant, probably companioning her.

Joliffe handed the share of the food he had been carrying to Gil, saying, "Take this to Rose," who was still at the fire, tending to something in the pot on its trivet over the coals. Piers was nowhere in sight, and Joliffe added, "Find Piers if you can," following the players' sure urge to draw together when there might be trouble.

Gil obeyed without pause or question, circling the riders to go to Rose while Joliffe went forward to join Basset and Ellis. Kyping was just gathering up his reins as if to go but returned Joliffe's bow with a bend of his head while saying to Basset, "That was all. I just wanted you to know word is the crowner will be here before sundown."

"Hopefully in time to view my father's body so we can move it today," Eleanor Medcote said.

Joliffe could not tell whether it was bitterness or restrained anger in her voice. But why not both? he thought.

Why limit her when she had reasons enough for both? And
wanting to know more of her mind, he bowed to her and
said, "May I offer regret for your loss, my lady?"

As a player, he had small business offering her anything
but his service and not even that at present, when such other
matters were in hand, and she looked at him, surprised, before saying, graciously enough, "Thank you."

Kyping was starting to turn his horse away and she gathering up her own reins to go with him. Ignoring that, Joliffe
said in the bright voice of someone too stupid to know he's
saying the wrong thing at the very wrong time, "But perhaps we'll be asked back to play at your wedding and your
brother's? A double wedding perchance?"

The sudden, sickened look on Eleanor's face betrayed
much. So did the sudden anger on Kyping's. Seeming to
misread hers and not see his, Joliffe said with distress, "My
apology, my lady. Is your brother's suit likely to go astray,
then?"

Eleanor's sickened look hardened on the instant into
anger deeper than Kyping's. Her voice raw with bitterness,
she answered, "Oh, Hal will get Claire if he wants her. Hal
generally gets what he wants." She harshly pulled her horse
around, adding as she set heels to its flanks, "Even to having Father out of his way."

She rode off, her servant behind her, and Joliffe, despite
feeling the daggers of Ellis' gaze on him, said to Kyping in
seeming contrition, "I'm sorry. I should have thought better before saying anything."

Turning his horse to follow Eleanor's, Kyping said
curtly, "Best have Basset tell you the rest." Then he was
away, too, his man with him.

Joliffe, watching them go rather than turning to meet Ellis' glare, said thoughtfully, "I'd not say she's deep in grief.
Would you?"

"What I'd say," Ellis snapped, "was that you need your

head held in the stream like Medcote's was. Leave off with the questions, can't you?"

Joliffe gave up patience and pretense, looked at him, and snapped back in matching anger, "I will when you give up womaning your way across the countryside."

Ellis' head jerked back as if he had been slapped and his mouth opened but no instant answer came; and Joliffe turned on Basset and demanded, "So what 'rest' did Kyping mean you were to tell me?"

In his usual way of "oil on troubled waters," Basset said evenly, as if there were no anger anywhere around him, "Kyping has just found out—and it seems Hal Medcote took delight in telling him—that his father a year or so ago saw to all his property being put in his name and Hal's, so that despite he's dead, Hal will have to pay no fine for having everything, being owner with him instead of heir."

"But isn't that what Jack Hammond and his father did?" Joliffe asked. "And Medcote refused it and was forcing Hammond into paying the fine to inherit anyway and doubling it or some such thing?"

"Yes," Basset said.

Ellis had apparently decided answering Joliffe was not worth it. He was stalking away, not back to the cart or Rose but toward the woods along the stream. To wear off his ill-humour by thrashing the trees or water or something, Joliffe hoped, but was more interested in saying to Basset, "So Medcote had done the very same thing for himself and Hal that he was refusing to allow to Hammond. 'Hypocrite' doesn't come close to describing him, does it?"

"It doesn't," Basset agreed. He started back toward the fire, asking as Joliffe fell into step beside him, "What did you bring back in the way of food? Rose looks happy."

Joliffe told him how well they had succeeded in the village and took pleasure in Rose's delight at fresh meat. She had sent Gil and Piers to find some wild garlic and any other herbs to make the lamb more savory in the cooking. While Joliffe set up the spit to roast the meat, they came back with what they had gathered, and in a while Ellis returned, too, not openly angry anymore and bringing a piece of wood that he settled to carving. With Piers hanging over his shoulder making suggestions of what he should be making and Rose happy at her cooking and the rest of them sitting at rest, there was a contented time then—one of the small times when nothing of great matter was happening, when simply being was enough. They were together and at ease and for just now in need of nothing but what they had.

For the sake and pleasure of that peace, Joliffe kept quiet. No one wanted to hear the questions still wandering in his mind. In truth, he was tired of his questions, too, and why not leave off them altogether, because what was the point of them? The crowner was finally here, would ask his questions, hold his inquest, and maybe as soon as sometime tomorrow give them leave to go. Then they would be away from here within the hour, even if they had to travel by moonlight, Joliffe thought, and that would be the last he would need ever even to think anymore about all this ugliness. The people to whom it mattered would sort it out or sink in it, however it might happen to go, but assuredly none of it would matter to him anymore.

They had finished eating, had praised Rose until her face glowed more with pleasure than with the fire's warmth, and were all still sitting around the fire, too satisfied to bother with any tasks so late in the day, when the sound of more than several hoof-falls in the lane turned all their heads that way, to watch as several riders, then a flat, horse-pulled cart with a long, canvas-wrapped bundle on it went past the gateway, headed villageward.

"The crowner, his folk, and Medcote's body," Basset said.

"Kyping was with them," Ellis said.

Several more riders followed the cart, Hal Medcote riding alone, his mother and sister riding side by side behind him. Two servants brought up the rear. A small procession seeing Medcote's body to the church. If the inquest did not get in the way, the funeral and burial would likely be tomorrow.

Had best be tomorrow, given how long Medcote's body had lain out, waiting for its grave.

As hoof-fall and the creak of the cart disappeared, the players all faced back to the fire where the flames were beginning to show brighter as dusk came on; and despite everything he had intended, Joliffe asked, "Did Eleanor Medcote and Kyping come here together this afternoon?"

Everyone looked at him. For a moment no one answered. Then Basset said, "He was here. She came afterward. She must have had some purpose for coming, but maybe because he was here she never said."

"No," said Rose. "I saw her. She didn't mean to come here. She was riding past when she looked through the gateway and saw Kyping. She drew rein, hesitated, then turned in." Rose paused, then added, "If I was asked, I'd say she was pleased to see Kyping. I could almost think she had been looking for him."

"She was more likely going to the Ashewells," Ellis pointed out. "To see her boy-husband to be."

"She would have ridden on then, not come in," Rose returned. "Master Kyping hadn't seen her. There was no need to turn in."

"And she rode away with Kyping," Joliffe said. "They went the same way away and it wasn't toward Ashewell's place."

"Because she was hoping to see Nicholas Ashewell secretly, and couldn't once she'd met Kyping," Ellis tried.

"No one meets anyone secretly by taking a servant with

them," Joliffe said. "And she didn't have to turn in here when she saw Kyping."

"Good enough," Ellis said grumpily. "She wasn't bound for the Ashewells. She was looking for Kyping and she found him. You've some sharp thought as to why, probably."

Joliffe did not. It was Rose who said, "Because she'd rather have him than Nicholas Ashewell. And Kyping wants her." She gave a hard look around at them all, daring them to disbelieve her, adding with open scorn, "It's not my fault you're blind. You could see it in how they tried not to look at one another and couldn't help themselves."

Ellis foolishly made a small snort of disbelief, but Joliffe said slowly, "And there was the way Kyping talked this morning of the wrongs her father had done her. He was angry about it. Yes."

"He cared," Rose said. "You could hear it. He cared more about it than there was need to, I thought. Then seeing them here together, I saw more. The caring is on her side, too."

Joliffe started to say, "Then that . . ." but broke off, deciding his next thought was best left unsaid—that if there was something between Eleanor Medcote and Kyping, then Kyping was one more man with good reason to want John Medcote dead.

Chapter 18

In the morning, not much past first full light, Kyping's man came with word that Medcote's funeral would be at midmorning and the inquest directly after it.

"Seems the crowner doesn't want matters to get any more cold than they already are," the man said. "He's driving everyone double-fast about it and has Father Hewgo's back up at his wanting the inquest in the church if the weather doesn't hold." They all cast eyes at the lightly clouded morning sky that might or might not turn to rain, depending on which way the wind veered, and the man added, "Otherwise, it's to be in the churchyard for the press of folk there's likely going to be."

When he was gone, Basset said, "Probably best we're there for the funeral as well as the inquest. Surely best we wear our Lovell tabards, too, and, Rose, your Lovell gown."

This past winter she had made herself a gown particolored in Lovell red and yellow like the men's tabards, to make better show of their arrivals at any place greater than a village. This time it would serve to keep clear in the crowner's mind that she was as surely in the Lovell service as the men.

"Who's to stay with the cart and Tisbe?" Ellis asked.

"Piers and Gil," Basset answered.

"Hai!" Piers protested. "Why should we miss everything?"

"Because you're the youngest and least needed at the inquest," Basset said.

"But the funeral!"

"You're not needed there either," Joliffe pointed out. "It's not you they're burying."

Gil helped with, "We'll play at merels, Piers, and this time I'll win more than once out of ten."

"You won't," said Piers with satisfied surety, and by the time the rest of them left, he and Gil were quarreling happily over the gameboard.

As Kyping's man had supposed, there was a goodly crowd for the funeral, more than enough to fill the church. The Ashewells and the Gosyns, as near neighbors to the deceased, were surely in the church itself, but the players willingly stayed outside, keeping together in a corner of the churchyard. Some questioning looks were thrown their way, but no one showed especial suspicion or anger at them and they were left to themselves. All that was to the good. Either none of them were favored to be Medcote's murderer or else, as the alewife had said, everyone was too pleased to have Medcote dead to care much who had done it.

Joliffe kept that thought to himself, it not being good to goad Ellis when the players were keeping the solemn but unworried faces of innocent people at a sad occasion.

On the other hand, they might be the most solemn people in the churchyard. In the wide space used for the plays three days ago, a table, a tall stool, and some benches, probably brought from nearby houses, were being set for

the inquest, but with the black-draped solemnity of the funeral Mass shut away in the church, there was much easy
talk among everyone waiting in the churchyard, no one
looking to be cast down in grief. In token of the time,
voices were mostly held low and what laughter there was
brief and rare. Too, heads stayed turned away from the
mound of newly dug earth beside the open, waiting grave
at the far end of the churchyard.

Whose choice had it been for Medcote not to be buried
in the church—family's or priest's? Joliffe wondered. Maybe
it had been Medcote's own, made sometime and remembered now. At least his grave was close outside the chancel,
in what some thought was more holy ground than other in
a churchyard, being close to the altar and the Mass. If that
were true, Medcote would be far closer to holiness in death
than he had been in life, Joliffe thought, then tried, briefly,
to repent of that uncharitable thought, failed, and let it go.
There were some things not worth the struggle, and repent-
ing of uncharitable thoughts about Medcote was one of
them.

He had been looking for Jack Hammond but did not see
him. He would have to be here for the inquest, surely, if
only to testify he had seen nothing and no one when he
passed along the lane on Monday morning, so very likely
he was among those who had been able to crowd into the
church. Wat Offington was in sight, though, clotted together
with several other men and some women who looked to be
their wives just outside the churchyard gate. Whatever they
were saying, it was not to anyone's good if their sullen
looks and sometimes angry gestures were anything by which
to go. Certainly, solemn was not what they were or were even
pretending to be, and Joliffe's thought was that they would
have done better to stay at home at their work than be here,
maybe hoping for trouble.

They made none, though, nor did anyone else. When

Medcote's body was carried from the church in solemn procession, quiet fell over the whole gathering and people drew back, clearing the way to the grave. Joliffe noted with mild surprise that although Master Ashewell and Gosyn were among those who came from the church, neither Mistress Ashewell nor Geretruda Gosyn were there, nor Claire, nor Nicholas. Geretruda might be too ill to come and Claire had stayed with her, he supposed. Or maybe, for all of them, avoiding Hal and Eleanor Medcote was worth the risk of offending Anela Medcote by their absence.

The crowd's quiet held while Father Hewgo went through the graveside ceremonies, his voice crabbed and terse across the churchyard as if Medcote offended him as much in death as in life.

More likely, Joliffe thought, was that Father Hewgo had no charity of heart for anyone, dead or living. How did such a man become a priest?

Or had becoming a priest made him that way?

There was another thought on which Joliffe would rather not dwell because the less thought spent on Father Hewgo the better. But it did not go away. Had Father Hewgo at some time wanted his priesthood, only to find too late that he was wrong for it and then lacked the grace to make the best of it, once his priestly vows were taken and irrevocable? A bad choice badly kept had been the damnation of many a man and woman. To keep a bad choice well despite everything took more courage than many people had. Lacking that courage, they often took the weakling's way instead— taking vengeance on their life for their pain, looking not for healing but to make others hurt as they were hurting.

Joliffe could remember when he had come too near to making a bad choice for his own life. He had escaped and therefore never had to learn how well or ill he would have done at living with that wrong choice. He could pray to all the saints there were that he would have made the best of it instead of the worst if he had come to it, but because he didn't know how he would have done, he had no right to despise those who did choose wrongly—only those who willfully made the worst of their wrong choice.

Across the churchyard, Medcote's body was lowered into the grave. As was expected of her, his widow took up a handful of dirt from the waiting mound and dropped it into the grave. With how much regret? Joliffe wondered. Or was it with relief to be done and rid of him?

Anela turned and moved away from the grave, her daughter and son on either side of her. Way was made for them but not out of the churchyard as it might have been if Medcote's death had been an ordinary one. Instead, they went to take their places on one of the benches set for the crowner's inquest. That was a courtesy given to the bereaved family. The other benches were taken by six village men and Master Kyping, to serve as jurors because they were presumed to know enough about such facts as there were to make a judgment. Everyone else had to stand, with the crowner's men and Master Kyping's seeing to it that those who would be witnesses were brought to the fore, including the players.

That done, the crowner, who had been waiting out of the way at the church door, came forward to take his place at the table. He was a well-bulked man with sharp eyes and a thin mouth who was surely already well-informed by Kyping of who everyone was and their part in the business. He eyed the players with especial interest, particularly Ellis, which was worrying. Joliffe had encountered crowners both careful in their office and not, and even one who had preferred to send facts altogether to the devil if he could, choosing who was guilty by who best suited him, then trying to ram his decision down a jury's throat.

If things went that way here, then Gil would be away to Minster Lovell before sundown, Joliffe supposed, having

seen Basset take him aside and talk to him a while this
morning with several nods toward Tisbe. Joliffe did not
envy him that ride, if things came to it. Tisbe had the gait
of a spavined donkey. And afterward so would Gil if he
had to ride her very far.

But it seemed this crowner played fair. He took charge
of the inquest and moved it forward as if he were someone
with no time to waste, never trying to make them say what
he might want to hear but giving no one encouragement to
wander in what they had to say. Even his questioning of the
players was no sharper than of anyone else, with the matter
between Rose and Medcote never brought up, only questions about whether any of the players had left the camp
that night and whether they had heard anything or seen
anyone. Since all they could say was "No" to all of that,
the crowner was soon done with them. Either their Lovell
tabards stood them in good stead or the man was fair-
minded enough not to want to find someone—anyone—
guilty, whatever the facts or lack of them were. Joliffe
found himself thinking the latter was the more likely. But
he was also thinking that in all likelihood the murderer was
still here, either simply looking on or else among those the
crowner actually questioned.

It was a disquieting thought, the more so because if he
or she was, they were playing their part of innocence as
well as the players had played their parts on Sunday in this
same place, because despite having listened and watched
carefully, Joliffe heard and saw nothing from anyone under
the crowner's questioning that could not be put down to understandable unease at being there at all. In truth, if the
crowner had wanted to go by outward signs of guilt, Jack
Hammond would have been most in trouble, veering between badly hidden fright at being questioned by an officer
of the king, resentment at being there at all, and unsteady
anger at mostly everything and Medcote in particular. But

his account of where he had been when Medcote was killed was repeated by his uncle and several others, and the crowner dismissed him with what Joliffe would have sworn was a deep and regretful sigh. But dismissed he was, and the crowner kept the business moving firmly forward, so that even with a pause for him to take his dinner at Father Hewgo's, all was done—or as done as might be—before the clouds had finished thickening toward the promise of a late afternoon rain.

In all that while Joliffe heard mostly what he had already heard for himself or from Kyping, and such new things as there were made no great difference before finally the crowner, with a glance at the dark blots of the first raindrops scattered on the table in front of him, asked the jurors what was their decision. With very little talk among themselves and glances of their own at the lowering clouds, the jurors declared that John Medcote's death had been undoubted murder but they could not say who the murderer might be. The crowner accepted that, declared that the murderer was still to be sought by all means possible, let no man hide the truth should it be learned, on peril of his soul and the law's displeasure. He waited for his clerk at the table's end to finish pen-scratching, then declared, in the king's name, the inquest at an end.

As the gathering began to scatter, Basset went forward, hat in hand, to bow to the crowner and ask if the players had his leave to set on their travels again. Ellis, Rose, and Joliffe kept back, out of hearing, but by the crowner's nod they guessed he gave his permission and were assured of it by the brightness of Basset's eyes in his solemn face as he returned to them. They shared no words about it there, though, and they were well away from village and villagers and alone on the road, the rain misting too lightly down to make them hurry, before Basset said, "So that's that. We're done and free and clear."

"We're on our way tomorrow, yes?" Ellis asked.

"As soon as we can see the road," Basset answered.

Ellis did a few quick steps of one of the dances with which they sometimes ended a play. "Away, away, for a merry day. I won't mind seeing the last of this place."

Nor would Joliffe, but despite he knew he should not, he said, "We still don't know who killed Medcote."

"Nor do we care," Ellis returned. "Medcote is a problem I'll leave behind me without a second thought."

Rose, walking between Ellis and Joliffe, said, "It's odd the crowner had no questions for Master Ashewell or for Gosyn, isn't it? They were both there."

Basset answered, "So far as we've heard, Kyping found nothing that put them anywhere near Medcote that night. Lacking that, there wasn't any point in asking them anything."

"By everything that was said at the inquest," Joliffe said, "there wasn't a more blameless lot of folk to be found anywhere in the world than here the night Medcote was killed."

"Just let the crowner keep us included among the blameless and I've no complaint," Ellis growled.

Basset declared, "Amen and thanks to Saint Genesius for that!" with a look at Joliffe that told him to agree or keep silent.

Willing to let worry go, Joliffe heartily agreed, "Amen!" while Rose, smiling, slipped her hand into Ellis'.

He lifted it and kissed it, and with all of them smiling together, they walked on, taking the good news back to Piers and Gil.

They were not so quick away in the morning as Basset had declared they would be. First, they sat up somewhat late, all together in the tent once supper was done, out of the small rain and the evening's growing chill, in high enough good spirits they started to debate changing the way they meant to go from here. Since they were already off their usual way, Joliffe was for going farther away from it, maybe all the way to Gloucester or even swinging south to Dorset and Somerset for the sake of a change. Basset was half-inclined to agree but at the same time, "Maybe we're better to curve back to our usual way and be satisfied with what lies different between here and there."

Ellis swung one way and another, and no one else had a firm thought on it, or much worry either. They were all merely enjoying the easy, unworried talk of familiar things, until at the last Basset declared he would decide in the morning which way they would go, and they settled contentedly to sleep under the light patter of rain on the tent's canvas.

The rain was still with them in the morning, making no one in haste to leave their blankets. Basset gave in first and only because necessity demanded it, and once they were all up, the gray, dripping morning gave no reason to linger over being on their way. Joliffe quickly downed his cold breakfast of bread, cheese, and ale, and left the others to theirs while he went to wipe Tisbe as dry as might be before putting on her harness.

She was welcoming his attention to her when he heard Ellis say, low-voiced, "Damnation and the Devil's tail," and he looked around to see Kyping and his man riding through the gateway. He didn't need to see Kyping's face to echo inwardly Ellis' oath. Nobody was likely to be riding out for pleasure in this dripping morning, and he left Tisbe and went to join the other players as Basset moved forward to meet Kyping, who did not dismount but sat grim-faced, looking down at Basset, then at the rest of them, then at Basset again before saying, "I suppose you've all been here all night and all together?"

"We've been, yes," Basset said, as grim as Kyping was. "What's happened?"

Flatly, angrily, Kyping answered, "Walter Gosyn was murdered last night."

Chapter 19

asset ended the long silence that followed that by saying to Gil, "You'd best build up the fire after all." And to Kyping and his man, "Will you join us at something warm to eat? You look as if you need it."

They did look it. Both were shadowy gray in the face and neither was making any effort to sit straight in their saddles. Their hoods and the shoulders of their cloaks were dark with soaked-in rain, and their horses were mucked to the knees with mud. Men and horses all looked to have been out and about for hours and miles, and after a moment, Kyping said, "Yes. Something warm would be welcome. Thank you."

That much was to the good anyway, Joliffe thought. If they were suspect in Gosyn's death, Kyping would likely have kept greater distance.

Or mayhap he was just being cunning, hoping to learn something by seeming friendly when he was not.

Either way, he and his man dismounted, tied their horses to a wheel of the cart, and while Gil awoke the banked fire and fed it carefully to life with the last of their gathered wood, and Rose unbundled the bread and cheese she had already readied to store in the cart, Basset asked the in-evitable question, "What happened that Gosyn's dead?"

Kyping wiped rain from his chin and said, "He went out while the household was settling for the night and never came back in. It was his way to walk for a while every eve-ning in that orchard behind his house."

"It was raining steadily at nightfall yesterday," Basset said. "He went out anyway?"

"He went out whether there was rain, snow, cold, heat," Kyping said. "It settled him for sleep, his wife says. My own thought is he wanted the peace of being alone for the while, especially now. It can't be easy watching your wife die. You know she's dying?"

"We thought it, seeing her," said Ellis.

"She'll likely die the quicker now," Kyping said darkly. "Grief will tear her heart out, the way she presently is."

He must be even more tired than he looked, to talk that freely, Joliffe thought, and took the advantage to ask, "What of the daughter?"

"Claire? From what I saw, she's all torn between her own grief and her mother's need."

"She's very young to see to all of that," Rose said gently.

"Mistress Ashewell is with her," Kyping said. Rose handed him a thick cut of cheese and a thick slice of bread. He thanked her. "And Master Ashewell is there, too, to help."

"And Nicholas?" Joliffe asked quietly.

"Nicholas, too," Kyping agreed around a mouthful of bread and cheese. "Claire Gosyn sent to the Ashewells at the same time she sent someone to find the crowner and me. They were there long before I was."

That Claire or her mother would send for their near

neighbors and friends was understandable, Joliffe thought, but for her and Nicholas to be together at such a high-wrought time was maybe not a good thing. Not with the Medcote threat still hanging over them both. And why was Gosyn the one murdered when Hal Medcote was so much the more likely one?

"What happened?" Basset asked again.

"Part of it's plain enough. He went out to walk in the orchard in his usual way, at what would have been sundown if there'd been any sun. With the rain it was just a deep gloaming, of course, but that's never been enough to stop him. He went out and he didn't come back, and when he didn't come to bid Geretruda good night—they no longer share a bed because of her pain; there's a servant sees to her in the night—Geretruda became fretful, so Claire sent one of the men to find him, to remind him to come in. Instead the man found him dead at the far end of the orchard."

"How was he killed?" Joliffe asked.

"Stabbed," said Kyping's man. With the fire now beginning to lick more strongly among the wood, he and Kyping were come close to it. Taking the bread and cheese Rose now held out to him, he added, "Right through the throat."

"It was more than that," Kyping said with angry weariness. "He was first knocked to the ground. There's a bruise along the side of his face, jaw to temple, where he was hit with something hard. A length of wood probably. Something sufficient to fell him. Then while he lay there on his back, stunned, whoever it was ran a dagger through his throat at the base. Through it and slantwise to miss the spine and pin him to the ground with it, then straddled his chest and arms and held him there while he kicked and scrabbled and died. The grass was torn up where he kicked, and when I saw the body, his fingers were still dug down into the dirt with his final death spasm."

Kyping said it flatly, his voice as uncolored as the gray and dripping day, but the ugliness of it coiled like a venomous snake in Joliffe's mind, and with his own voice as flat as Kyping's, he said, "That's much like Medcote's death."

"It is," Kyping agreed, the thought plainly one he had already had.

"Please," said Rose. "Say that neither his wife nor daughter saw him that way."

"The servant who found him kept his wits about him. He saw to it they were kept away."

"It's a pity Gosyn didn't grab something off his murderer," Joliffe said, watching Kyping to see if that were true.

"It's likewise a pity we haven't found anyone as soaked in blood as his murderer had to be," Kyping said and did not sound as if he were making even half a jest of it. "We found the dagger, though. It was dropped in a neighboring field. It's maybe Wat Offington's."

"Maybe?" Basset asked.

"He's the first one I went to see, wasn't he?" Kyping said. "He had no dagger on him and couldn't say where it was. He tried to swear the one in the field isn't his, but at least two other men say differently."

"And now Offington claims his was lost or stolen," Joliffe said.

Kyping gave him a sharp look while answering, "Aye. That's what he claims. That it went missing yesterday at the church or churchyard. That he didn't miss it until he was almost home."

"Do you maybe believe him?" Basset asked.

"It's too useful, isn't it?" Kyping answered, not as if it made him happy. "He's in known quarrel with Gosyn. Gosyn is murdered. Offington's dagger is there, carelessly dropped after doing the murder. It's too useful by half."

"But you've arrested him anyway," Ellis said.

"I haven't, no."

But the crowner likely would. For simplicity's sake if nothing else, Joliffe thought. Because a thing was too useful by half did not mean it was false.

"There were others besides Offington angry at Gosyn of late," Kyping was saying. "I want to know about them before doing anything to anybody. Even if Wat Offington was seemingly the only one maybe angry enough to kill him."

"We've not been angry at Gosyn," Basset pointed out.

"No," Kyping granted.

"But we're not going to be able to leave today, are we?"

"No. You're strangers and a strange thing has happened, so you'll have to stay somewhat longer, for the look of the thing. Just as, for the look of the thing, I've come to question you. My thanks," Kyping added as Ellis held out a cup of ale to him.

His man's thanks were likewise grateful when Ellis handed him a cup. Piers nudged his mother's elbow and said hopefully, "The fire's fit for toasting us some bread and cheese," looking up at her with a small boy's hungry pleading.

He was grown too large for that to work quite so well as it had, and it had been a long while since it had worked on Rose, anyway. Like all of them, she knew him too well. She also knew how much bread and cheese was left and she refused him with a shake of her head, while Joliffe said to Kyping, "Who else has been angry at Gosyn lately?"

"Aside from other of his own tenants, he's quarreled lately with Lionel Ashewell over these marriages. Then there's Hal Medcote, who maybe thought his way to Gosyn's daughter would be clear with Gosyn dead." Kyping rubbed a hand tiredly at his eyes. "Then there's talk that Gosyn was lately saying he was going to take his ongoing quarrel with Father Hewgo over tithes to the bishop's court, along with some other things against him."

"I'd not heard that last one," Joliffe said.

"You'd heard of the rest?" Kyping asked, then answered himself, "Right. You saw some of it at Gosyn's when you played there."

And only Mistress Ashewell had kept it from turning truly ugly then, Joliffe thought, while Ellis said, "None of it looked murdering-angry, though."

"Things fester," Kyping answered. "Who knows who might have a long anger against him that everyone else has forgotten? They might take this chance to kill him when there are so many others angry at him as would cover why it was done."

That was too altogether possible to be put fully aside, but Basset asked, "Is that likely?"

"Is it likely the murderer just happened to be there in the orchard at just the time Gosyn happened to go for an evening walk there?" Joliffe returned. "In the rain."

"There was no 'happen' about Gosyn being there, remember," Kyping said. "It's when he was usually there."

Already regretfully sure of what Kyping would say, Joliffe asked, "How widely was it known he did that?"

Kyping gave a small laugh that had no pleasure in it. "Widely enough that even if we did set ourselves to learning how far it was known and to whom, we'd hardly be further ahead."

"Why?" Rose asked. "Why did it matter so much to him to walk in his orchard every evening?"

That was not a question Joliffe had thought of. It was maybe a question he would *not* have thought of, he realized with surprise, it seeming aside from the matter of Gosyn's murder. But Kyping answered, "The orchard was the first land he bought for his own. Maybe walking there helped him feel how far he had come from where he started."

And now he had died with his hands dug into that same land, as if he would hold to it in death as he had in life.

There would surely, in years to come, be stories told of his ghost seen walking there.

Kyping had finished eating and drinking. He and his man had even dried a little beside the fire and maybe somewhat warmed. Giving their cups back to Ellis, they both thanked him and Rose and Basset, and started to leave, walking their horses back toward the gateway. Joliffe traded a look with Basset. Basset nodded agreement and Joliffe went with them, falling into step beside Kyping to ask when they were away from the other players, "If it comes to no one else, will the crowner be content with simply finding Wat Offington guilty?"

"I doubt it. He's a great one for both the law and his own dignity. He's furious there's been a second murder, and done while he was here, as if to spite him." Kyping's face went heavy with greater gloom. "He's going to ride this into the ground. He's going to tear at things until he has everything out into the open. Things that have nothing to do with either murder. What with that and everybody's fears already raised, the whole parish is going to be torn apart before he's done. Then, when he's done and satisfied, I'll be left to put the pieces back together."

"Besides all that," Joliffe said, "Medcote's murder was one thing; Gosyn's is another."

"It is that," Kyping agreed heavily. "There was nothing false or foul about Gosyn. Even most of those who didn't like him will grant you that. People can understand Medcote being murdered. Not Gosyn. Supposing his murderer isn't found, everyone's suspicions are as likely as the crowner's questions to tear the parish apart."

It was shrewd of Kyping to know that, Joliffe thought. Not comfortable, but shrewd, which was to the good because there were times when being comfortable was dangerous. This looked to be one of them, and aloud he asked,

"So, would I be welcome, do you think, if I went to play quiet music for the widow and all?"

Kyping, about to swing into his saddle, stopped to look at him. "You mean today?"

"Today. Yes." While everything was still raw enough that someone guarding what they said and did might show against others too lost in grief to protect themselves. Untoward wariness could betray as much as open guilt.

Kyping held quiet a long moment—whether thinking that or not, Joliffe did not know—before saying, "It's not your business."

Joliffe made a small gesture back at the players, Tisbe, and the cart. "So long as we're trapped here by it, it's our business."

Kyping considered that before finally saying, "You might be welcome at Gosyn's. You can try anyway. If you learn anything . . ."

He left that hanging, but it was enough. They understood one another.

Chapter 20

By the time Joliffe walked into Gosyn's yard, the rain had dwindled to a stop and the clouds thinned enough for hope there would be sun before the day was over. There could be little work in the fields yet, but the village was oddly empty of people, even children, as Joliffe walked through it. He expected at least a clot of folk at the manor gateway, standing about in the useless way that people had, as if they hoped something worth seeing would happen now that the worst had, but the gateway was empty.

In the manor yard the several tethered horses by the barn showed neighbors were come, but such servants as he saw were glumly quiet, neither speaking to him nor making an effort to stop him. He even stood for several minutes on the hall's threshold before anyone there took note of him, and he took the chance for a long look at who was there and how they were among each other. He learned little. Except for a servant standing at a table where food and drink had been set out, only a few men were gathered, Master Ashewell and Nicholas among them and the others of like kind, to judge by their clothing and bearing. None of them were plain villagers anyway, but looked to be folk like the Gosyns and Ashewells—yeomen on their way into gentry and all the more sure of themselves because there were no near-neighbored high gentry or lords to overbear them and make them feel their place.

Joliffe supposed that, if he tried, he might know some of their faces from the church ale's crowd or yesterday's funeral and inquest, but he did not particularly try. He wondered if their low-kept voices and strained faces were entirely for grief at Gosyn's murder or if they were thinking, too, of how they could come to like sudden end, all hopes and ambitions gone to nothing between one minute and the next.

He wondered, too, as he had to, if any of them had had quarrel with Gosyn.

But Kyping was the one who could ask questions. The most he could do here himself was see and hear what there was to see and hear, and presently that did not seem likely to be much; there was little talk going on among the men. But there had been pads behind some of the saddles on the horses in the yard for women to ride pillion. Mistress Ashewell was surely here, and other women must be, too, and probably in the solar, giving Geretruda what comfort could be given. Or else in the bedchamber if Geretruda had been laid completely low by this blow.

He could walk into neither solar nor bedchamber without bidding, but since no one was troubling to give him greeting or even heed here, he went aside from the hall's doorway and toward the solar, to a bench against the wall there that gave him somewhere to set one foot so he could rest his lute on his knee while putting it in tune. Keeping watch on the gathered mourners, and especially the Ashewells, he began to play, at first drawing quiet notes at almost random, letting them fall beneath the low-kept voices, only slowly after a while weaving them into a softly sorrowing song.

He did not sing. For one thing, the lament was one familiar enough that the words would be in people's minds without he sang any of them. For another, singing would draw too much heed to him and he was here to note things, not to be noted himself. Or, rather, to be noted just enough to be taken to soothe Geretruda.

His hope of that looked like it was happening when Claire shortly came from the solar and toward him. The black mourning gown she wore must have been made for her for someone's death a few years ago; it was short in the hem and too tight, showing how far she had passed from girlhood toward womanhood between when it was made and now. But with her tear-reddened eyes and face blotched from crying, she looked very young after all, as well as deep in pain, and Joliffe stilled the lute strings, straightened, and bowed low to her in respect for grief that deep, despite that in her pain everything but pain was probably only a blur to her just now.

She was starting to say to him, "My mother would like . . . ," when her gaze shifted past him to the outer doorway and her voice died as if all air had been suddenly pressed from her lungs. Everyone else in the hall had turned toward her when she came from the solar. Now everyone else and Joliffe followed her look toward the doorway.

To see Hal Medcote standing much where Joliffe had paused, taking in, as Joliffe had taken in, everyone there.

But where Joliffe had had no more than a glance from anyone, Hal was greeted by an array of stares, and one corner of his mouth twitched toward what looked close to in-held laughter before his gaze, sweeping over everyone there, fell on Claire. He instantly sobered and started toward her. She took a small step backward, as if toward flight, then steadied and held where she was, only putting her hands behind her.

From the corner of his eye, Joliffe saw Nicholas Ashewell take a step forward and Master Ashewell take hold on his arm, keeping him where he was as Hal bowed to Claire, saying as he straightened, "I've come to say how sorry we are, my mother and sister and myself, to hear of your father's death."

Stiffly, Claire said, "Thank you."

Joliffe shifted his lute and said, seeming blind to any business but his own, "You were saying you wished me to play to your mother, yes?"

That was putting himself forward more than he should. Musicians, like players, were there to be ignored except when wanted, and Hal gave him an angry glance, but Claire said, short-breathed with relief at reason to escape, "Yes. She's in here," and fled more than led his way into the solar.

Joliffe gave a short bow at Hal and made to follow her, meaning to leave Hal to join the Ashewells and other mourners. But Hal flicked a hand at him, warning him back, and followed Claire himself. Joliffe, keeping to himself a small surge of anger, followed him in time to see Claire turn almost at bay between Hal and where her mother sat in her chair, hunched over with her arms wrapped around herself, rocking back and forth as if cradling her pain. Mistress Ashewell stood beside her, an arm around her shoulders, while another woman hovered near them, holding a cup she clearly wanted to give to Geretruda, who did not look up, either at them or at Claire, let alone at Hal or Joliffe.

The other two women, though, stared, startled, at Hal, and Claire looked to be trying to find words angry enough to use on him. But Hal, as if neither she nor the other women were there, went to Geretruda and down on one knee in front of her, saying, "Good lady, we're all in sorrow, my mother, my sister, and I, to hear your husband is dead."

Geretruda gave a shaken sob and rocked harder without raising her head.

Hal laid a hand on her knee, bold beyond courtesy, and said, "Good lady, I was willing to be your son before. Let it be some comfort to you that I'm still willing. Please know there's no need for you and Claire to bear everything alone, without a man here."

Mistress Ashewell hissed on an indrawn breath, but Geretruda was probably too far into her grief to understand much except her own pain. Joliffe's guess was that all she truly took in of Hal's words were "son" and "comfort" and "man." What she surely heard was a promise of someone else's strength to shelter her. She had been safe with her husband. He had been her strength, maybe always and surely since her disease came on her. If she understood she was dying, that must only add to her fear and need for comfort and someone's strength—the comfort and strength of a "son"— and with a soft sob and barely raising her head, she put out a trembling hand that Hal seized and held in both of his.

Claire, as if it were more than she could bear to see, turned and fled to the solar's far door, not the one back into the hall but the one Joliffe had supposed was to the garden. She fumbled the latch as if hardly able to see it, then was gone, leaving the door open behind her.

Hal, seeming to give Claire no heed, was rising from his knee, drawing a joint stool close to let him sit beside Geretruda, still holding her hand and saying something to her too low for Joliffe to hear.

Leaving Geretruda to him and the women, Joliffe followed Claire.

He had been right that there would be a garden there. It was a small one tucked along the back of the hall with a young growth of herbs and early flowers in its four square beds, but he hardly noted even that much about it because Claire was already gone from it, out the narrow gap in the

low withy fence along its far side and into the orchard
there. He saw her slender, black-gowned shape going away
among the black trunks of the trees under their spring froth
of pale blossoms, and he followed her, but not quickly now,
able to guess where she was going.

Like the garden, the orchard was not large, perhaps
twenty trees. As a young boy Joliffe had spent tedious af-
ternoons in an uncle's even smaller orchard, enforcedly listening to him go happily on at length about his cherry,
apple, and pear trees. Whether he wanted to or not, Joliffe
knew something about orchard-keeping because of that
and was able to see that here every tree was well-pruned
and in health. He remembered what Kyping had said—that
this had been Gosyn's first purchase of land when he began
to better himself. A small beginning, maybe, but one that
Gosyn had valued to the very end.

In truth, looked at against the wider world, all of
Gosyn's success could be measured as small compared to
some, but that did not lessen what he had done. Where
many others never tried at all, he had succeeded in bettering
his family's place in the world; nor was there way to say
how much more he would have done if he had been left to
live his life out. But he had not been left, and Joliffe found
Claire at a far corner of the orchard, standing at the edge of
a trampled stretch of grass not far from where a shallow
stream made the orchard's boundary, very probably the
same stream he had forded on the other side of the village
and the one that flowed past the players' field.

He had not tried to follow her quietly, but her back was
to him, and from several trees away he could guess by her
bowed head and shaking shoulders that her sobbing had
likely covered his footfall; and he stopped where he was,
slipped his lute around, and stroked a run of notes from it
as light as the petal-fall from one of the trees.

Claire instantly turned, almost as sharply as if it had

been Hal Medcote's voice she'd heard instead of the lute, but her alarm and anger faded as she saw Joliffe. Turning away from him, she said, "Go back to my mother. You're not needed here."

He was used to being spoken to as a servant. After all, he served. But he was not a hireling and that gave him some choice of which orders he obeyed and which he did not, and still stroking now-sad notes from the lute, he went forward, saying, "This is where your father died, isn't it?"

"It's where he was murdered," Claire said with bitter force. "Go away."

Much of the trampling had to be from after Gosyn's death, done by those who came to see and deal with the body. Because of it, Joliffe supposed he would have to depend on what Kyping had told him of what had happened between Gosyn and his murderer, but there was more than that to be seen. Just here, for perhaps a dozen yards along the stream that made the orchard's boundary, the willows and alders had been cut away instead of being left as usual to keep the stream's banks stable. Standing where he was now—a little behind and a little aside from Claire and looking outward and beyond the stream as she was—he had a clear view of an open field ploughed in long, broad strips where this year's young wheat was a green haze over the dark soil.

"Your father's land?" he asked quietly.

"My father's land," she agreed, not looking at him again but not ordering him away, either, as if he were not worth her bother to care whether he was there or not.

Joliffe was willing to settle for that. He had followed her here on an unthinking urge to help someone in pain, but the urge was faded. There was no help he could give the girl, she being who she was and he being no one to her. But since he was here, there was no reason not to see all that he could. From what Kyping had said, Gosyn had walked in the orchard every evening, and here, where the trees were cleared along the stream, he must have stood on most or all of those evenings, looking out at his land. In triumph that it was his? Or for always renewed assurance he had succeeded? Or with thoughts of what he hoped to do next? Or simply with the quiet pleasure of knowing it was his?

However it had been with him, Gosyn would never stand here again, with hope or fear or any thought at all.

Had whoever killed him planned on him being here? Or had someone simply been late at work in the field, seen him, and on the sudden taken the chance at Gosyn with no forethought at all? This was the time of year for the first hoeing out of weeds among the crops and likewise when everyone was behind at all their work, there being so much of it that needed doing. It was not beyond thought that someone had been there in the field yesterevening and seen Gosyn. They might even have meant nothing more than to talk to him but instead had argued and given way to anger and ended by killing him instead.

That would match with Wat Offington or someone else of his short-minded kind. Which part of the field was Offington's to work? And who else had strips in sight of here? Had Kyping asked questions that way yet? He needed to, because even if someone had been there but was not the murderer, they might have seen someone or something that had not mattered then but would now.

Joliffe's momentary excitement at those possibilities went dull. By yesterday's evening the rain had been small but steady. No one would have been at work in the fields. There very probably would have been no one outside to see anything. Only Gosyn taking his usual walk in his orchard no matter what the weather. Gosyn . . . and whoever had come to kill him.

With another thought, he went forward, past Claire to stand on the stream's bank, looking across at the other side.

Both banks were steep here, but not high. Hardly three feet, if that much. An easy drop into the stream, and to get out nothing more was needed than a hand braced on the bank for an easy vault up. Supposing the stream's bottom here was not sucking mud. It did not look to be. The water was flowing fast and somewhat high from the rain but he could see its green, streaming water weeds and what looked a graveled bed.

Behind him, not moved from where she had stopped, Claire said in a hollow voice, "There's going to be too much rain again this year. That's what my father thought. Another bad harvest."

Joliffe turned around. "We'll have to pray not."

"For all the good prayer is likely to do," said Claire with no particular feeling.

She was dull with grief and probably hopelessness, Joliffe thought; but it had been anger that drove her from the solar, and anger would probably serve her better in the while to come than dullness would, so very deliberately he said, "Do you think Hal Medcote will wait the year of mourning before he marries you?"

Claire gasped as if he had struck her. Color flooded her face and for a moment all the anger was there again, ready to be flailed against him. But either her control was better than so young a girl could be thought to have or she was further into hopelessness than she had seemed. Instead of an angry answer, she turned her head from him to stare away among the trees and said, "I told you to leave."

So she couldn't be goaded. That would likely serve her well in time to come, too, but meanwhile she needed more, and Joliffe tried, "That your mother takes what comfort he offers doesn't mean you have to marry him. You only have to refuse him and go on refusing him, no matter what anyone else chooses or does or says to you."

" 'Only' refuse him," Claire said with a bitterness that

showed she knew full well how harsh and sustained a struggle such a refusing could bring on her. Anger warm in her
voice and face again, she looked at Joliffe and mocked,
" 'Only' refuse him."

Lightly back at her, not feeling light at all—this was her
life they were playing at—Joliffe said, "Better than being
married to him, surely."

"Anything is better than being married to him!"

"Well then." Joliffe spread out one hand as if offering
her what was perfectly plain. "There you are."

"Where?" she said back at him, still with fierce mockery. "I'm nowhere! Nowhere is where I am," she said, and
spun away from him on a sob and went at a harsh walk
back toward the garden and the house.

He was left wondering if he'd done any good at all. She
had been a much-loved, much-loving daughter all of her
life. Would she be able to stand against whatever her dying
mother might want for her? If she remembered her father's
anger against Hal Medcote, maybe she would have strength
enough to hold out against a dying woman's wish. But only
maybe.

And if she didn't?

Then she would come to share, along with Nicholas
Ashewell, whatever hell it was the Medcotes lived in, leaving little to pray for except God's mercy on all their souls.

He let thought of her go and instead stood frowning
down at the trampled, torn ground between the trees nearest the stream. From what Kyping had said, Gosyn's had
been a messy death, but what blood there must have been
was washed away here by the night's rain. There was only
the torn ground and grass. The blood there must have been
on Gosyn's murderer must be long since washed away, too.
It was his bloody clothing that would be least easily rid of
its evidence. Kyping had said nothing about it, but surely

his men were questioning for anyone seen bloody as well as asking about bloody clothing or if someone had noted clothing unexpectedly washed.

Of course in the rain there had been—and was going to be, Joliffe thought, cocking an eye at the re-clouding sky—someone could have washed his bloodied clothing and no one been the wiser about why it was wet. Nor could Kyping count on someone being willing to tell that someone of their family had come home last night bloody or with bloody clothing or that some of someone's clothing was gone missing without explanation. So the chances of learning anything that way were slim, and the more that Joliffe thought on it, the more sure he was that Gosyn's murder was no matter of chance. Gosyn was known to walk in his orchard at about the same time every day, come what may. Yesterday's rain had served to make almost certain no one else would be out and about to see the murderer come and go, and that same rain had been enough to wash away any traces he might have left during that coming and going, as well as making no particular matter of his washed, wet clothing afterward to anyone who might have noted it. That was too many things working to the murderer's favor for Joliffe to be willing to say it had all happened by unplanned chance. It might have, but he had to doubt it. It was easier to believe that someone had thought all that through ahead of time and only been waiting for the time to be right. Or maybe not planned well ahead but suddenly seen everything was in place at once and very deliberately seized the moment.

"You. Player," Hal Medcote said behind him.

Behind him was not somewhere he wanted Hal Medcote to be, and with face and voice immediately both bland, Joliffe turned, saying, "Sir?"

"You were here with Claire. Why? What passed between you?"

There was both challenge and demand in Hal's voice, and despite himself, Joliffe matched him, saying, "Nothing more than words and none of them of concern to you."

"Only words?" Hal demanded.

"Only words."

Hal unexpectedly grinned. "Pity. You should try for more next time."

Too taken by surprise to hide it, Joliffe said, "What?"

"More than words." Hal came closer, dropping his voice as if they were suddenly friends sharing talk no one else should hear. "She thinks she doesn't want to marry me, so likely she can be a fool other ways, too. You've probably a way with words and women. If you can get her into 'trouble,' shall we say, I'll make no trouble over it."

Only with a sharp lurch of his mind did Joliffe follow where Hal was going and in answer shaped his face to a knowing leer and said in a voice to match, "Because afterward I'll be gone and you'll still be here and she'll have to marry you because there'll be no one else to have her."

"You have it."

"You'd take on another man's bastard for your own?"

Hal answered that with a long look that by its cold emptiness said everything.

No, he would not be raising anyone's bastard as his own.

Joliffe let a glitter come into his eyes that said he and Hal were men who understood each other. "I get the sport and you get the profit. Is that it?"

"That's it," Hal agreed.

With Claire no more than something to be used by each of them toward their own ends and never mind what happened to her because of it.

Joliffe slightly bowed, putting mockery into the bow, and sly mockery and lust into his face and voice as he answered, "I'll do what I can to serve you, sir. With pleasure."

Hal gave him a curt nod in return, as if accepting a servant's willingness to serve, said, "Good then," went away, back toward the house.

Watching him go, Joliffe thought it was pity that looks couldn't kill, because if they did, his own at Hal's back would have here and now assured another murder.

The one good thing was that if Hal Medcote believed he had set Joliffe on to wrong Claire, then he would not be immediately setting anyone else to it. Or taking steps himself—such as rape to insure she had no choice but to marry him as her ravisher.

On second thought, Joliffe was glad looks did not kill. Hal deserved to be dead by some way other than quickly.

Knowing that was a sinful thought did not lessen the heat behind it, and he moved away from thinking it, back to staring at the trampled ground, going again over thoughts he had already had about how the murderer had come and gone and about his bloodied clothing.

Or maybe there had been no clothing, he suddenly thought.

If the whole business had indeed been thought out beforehand, the murderer had surely forethought that part of the problem, too. And had probably seen as plainly as Joliffe now did how to solve it.

Chapter 21

By finding his way away through the kitchen garden and around the rear byre-yard, Joliffe left Gosyn's without encountering anyone except a surprised kitchen maid and a boy forking dung out of the byre. So there was that way into the orchard, too, but he wouldn't choose it as a way to go if he was on his way to do a murder, or to leave by, either, if he wanted to be secret at it. Besides that, the byre-yard opened onto the village street, in clear view of half the houses there.

He had his whole walk back to the camp to change his mind about what he meant to do. There was, after all, no need for him to do it. He could tell his suspicion to Kyping and let it be his trouble. He could forget the matter altogether as something with nothing to do with him and leave it behind him when they all moved on, which could be as soon as tomorrow if the crowner accepted they had nothing to do with the business and let them go. After that he would never come back here and all of it would fade from memory like so many other places the players had been and never returned to.

The trouble was that he knew his memory better than that. It was not kind enough to him. It had a way of suddenly tossing up things long unremembered that he would willingly have left unremembered. He still wished he could forget the time he had pushed his brother into mud and spoiled his new tunic and made him cry and their mother angry to tears. That had been when he was all of maybe eight years old, but the memory still rose up sometimes and made him feel his guilt and shame all over again. If he did nothing here, how long would *that* guilt and shame ride with him through his life? It did not bear considering. If nothing else, he had to tell Kyping what he thought.

But if he was going to do that, why not do the rest? Besides, it was his thought, and who was likely to carry it through better than he would? Besides that, if he were being fully honest with himself—a policy of doubtful worth but one he seemed unable to break as often as he would like—his curiosity would not be satisfied by leaving the attempt to someone else.

At camp he told the others as little as need be of how things were at Gosyn's and certainly not of Hal Medcote's offer, then went to Tisbe grazing along the edge of the woods. She acknowledged him by lifting her head and swinging it to bump against his chest and afterward stood willingly while he untangled and combed her forelock with his fingers and checked her feet to be sure her hoofs were clean and uncracked, her shoes still firmly nailed. He had done as much yesterday in readiness for the leaving today that hadn't happened; it assuredly didn't need doing again today, and Tisbe's patience ran out with her last hoof. When he let it go, she set it down with an impatient stamp and moved away from him, flicking her tail to be sure he understood her displeasure.

He did and slapped her rump apologetically, knowing he had been wasting her time as well as his, delaying what he meant to do next, doubting he should do it and knowing that his doubt wouldn't stop him. She drifted away in pursuit of better grass. Seeing Basset strolling toward him, he stayed where he was, and Basset, joining him, nodded toward Tisbe as if saying something about her while saying instead, "What are you thinking to do?"

"Do?" Joliffe echoed, trying for innocence.

Even as he said it, he heard he had over-played the innocence. Basset, as tuned as he was to subtleties of voice, said firmly at him, "Yes. Do."

So Joliffe told him, with voice low and their backs to the others, and when he finished, Basset gave him a doubting look and asked, "You think you have to do this thing, rather than just tell Kyping and let him set someone else to do it?"

"Yes."

Basset answered that with a long look before finally he said, "Best get on with it then," and went away, back to the others.

Joliffe, as if necessity called, went the other way, into the trees. There, out of sight of everyone, he sat down beside the stream and took off his shoes and hosen, fastened his shoes together by their straps and buckles and hung them and his hosen around his neck. He could only hope his doublet was short enough to stay dry because he was not minded to strip down to his shirt in the afternoon's damp chill with its returned threat of rain. Not that he was going to be very dry anyway, he supposed as he waded into the stream. The water flowed cold around his bare legs and he stood for a moment, considering, before turning upstream. Only later and if need be would he go downstream, toward Gosyn's manor.

* * *

It was later than he wished when he came to Gosyn's orchard, with twilight already thick among the trees under the overcast of clouds hiding what would soon be sunset. He would be going back to camp in the dark but at least he had found out what he wanted to know. And a little more besides.

From the shadows among the trees above him on the streambank someone said, "So. Was it worth it?"

Joliffe caught back his almost-lost balance before he glared up at Kyping and complained, "You might have coughed or something, rather than nearly frightening me off my feet."

"I did think of moaning like Gosyn's ghost," Kyping returned, holding down a hand to help him up the bank. "I spared you that."

"My thanks for it." Joliffe sat down on the trampled grass and began to dry his legs with one end of one of his hosen. "And, yes, it was worth it."

Kyping sat down on his heels, facing him. "You found the murderer came and went by way of the stream?"

"You had that same thought, too?"

"I did. You've saved me or someone else the wet walk. He did come that way then?"

"I'd swear someone came that way lately. There are broken branches a few places where there need not be except if someone grabbed them as they waded past, and two places at least where someone has been up and down the bank where there wasn't a crossing place." Joliffe began to pull on his hosen. His still-damp legs did not make it easy, but it was better than being chilled. "It could have been a poacher or someone else with reason to be going wading, but I doubt it. You know where this stream runs? Besides past where we're camped?"

"Yes," Kyping said.

"I followed it upstream before I followed it down. It's easy going the whole way. Mostly shallow, with none of the deep pools so deep they can't be waded, and alder and willow thick-growing almost everywhere along its banks. There's breaks for cattle to water and fords for wagons to cross, but with a little care to make certain no one was around, those could be passed well enough unseen."

"By someone coming here from upstream while it was still light yesterday," Kyping said. "Harder to see his way going back after Gosyn was killed and dark was coming down."

Now standing to tie his hosen to the points under his doublet, Joliffe said, "But still possible, and he wouldn't have had to stay in the stream all the way, once dark was come. Keeping close to the trees most places would have been enough, I'd guess. And when he was far enough away he could take to any streamside path there was."

"Likely true," Kyping granted. "The trouble is that we've only proved we're good at guessing and that someone *could* have come that way, not that anyone did or that if they did, that it was the murderer."

"There's one thing." Joliffe went on tying his hosen, waiting for Kyping to ask, "What?" Kyping did not. Joliffe finished tying his hosen, pulled down his doublet, looked at the bailiff, and said, "I found some of his clothing."

Kyping's interest quickened. "You did? Where? How do you know it's his?"

"It's somebody's, anyway, and there can't be too many people who lately troubled to hide a pair of bloodied under-braies under a bit of pulled-down bank along this stream."

"A man's under-braies?"

"With blood on them. I think they were shoved into a hollow bit of bank behind tree roots, but with the rain overnight more of the bank slid away. Another good rain and the tree will be down. As it is, there was white enough of the braies showing to catch my eye."

Kyping's eyes were shifting back and forth with the quickness of his thoughts as he caught up to where Joliffe already was. "He came down the stream naked except for his braies. That way there'd be no explanation of wet clothes needed afterward. But the braies were too bloodied to wash clean, so he left them."

"And even if they would wash clean, he couldn't wear them home soaking wet under his other clothes."

"Yes. So he left them. Sometime some servant will be upbraided for losing or stealing them, but that won't matter to him. Where are these braies?"

"I left them where they were."

Kyping nodded sharp approval. "They aren't sufficient proof, but they're something."

"A question. Do you think both these murders were done by the same man?"

Kyping blinked with surprise. "I do, yes. Don't you?"

"Oh, most assuredly I do. I likewise think he enjoyed the killing. Both deaths could have been done cleanly. Neither of them was."

"As if he wanted to feel his victim dying under him. Yes," Kyping said, looking as if he had bitten down on something rotten and could not spit it out.

Joliffe agreed with that rottenness. To murder someone was ugly enough. To take deliberate pleasure in the killing was far worse. But he kept his voice even as he said, "I think we likewise share certainty who it is."

"Yes," Kyping said again, his face hard. "I think we do. So. What do we do now?"

Chapter 22

The next day was a long one, with not much to be done and nowhere for any of the players to go after Piers went on one errand with a message at Joliffe's asking and returned. Joliffe spent some of the time currying Tisbe, and much of the time sitting alone beside the stream.

He had told Basset what he was going to do because that was as necessary as Basset's answer to it was expected.

"Joliffe, this isn't yours to do. Leave it to Kyping and the crowner."

"They won't be able to prove it without this."

"Let them set someone else to it, then. It doesn't have to be you."

"It has to be someone who can make him believe it." Joliffe had smiled and spread his arms, acting a bold assurance he wished he felt. "Who better than a player for that? And who better than me?"

Basset, probably believing neither the boldness nor the assurance, had looked at him for a long moment before finally saying, "Just mind you keep yourself alive. I've in

mind a play on Sir Gawain the Gallant I want you to write
for us. You'll do better at it if you're not dead."

"Write a play or be dead," Joliffe had said consideringly.
"You set a hard choice, Master Basset."

Basset had humphed at him and gone away, and whatever he told the others, it was probably not altogether the
truth but sufficient that they neither troubled Joliffe's soli-
tude during the day nor questioned where he was going
when he left them about an hour before what would pass for
sunset in the overcast afternoon's end.

Only Rose followed him a little ways toward the gateway to say, laying a hand briefly on his arm, "Whatever
you're about, be careful, yes?"

Not bothering with the lie a smile would be, Joliffe
looked down at her and said as quietly as she had, "Yes,"
and went heart-warmed on his way. He might have only a
very, very small corner of the world where he belonged and
only a very few people to whom it mattered much whether
he was alive or dead, but it was a corner of his choosing and
they were his own people and he did not mean to die and
lose them.

Despite that, he knew he was on his way to do one of
the stupidest things he had ever done, nor was he such a
fool as not to be afraid of what he meant to do. But afraid
was what he must not seem to be, and that was why he took
care to be early to where John Medcote had died, to be
leaning easily against a tree, one foot braced back against
it, his arms crossed on his chest, softly whistling, when Hal
Medcote came from among the trees along the stream.

From yesterday Joliffe knew of the slight path that ran
there. It was not secret or, by daylight, a particularly hidden
way to come from the Medcote manor. But then—today at
least—Hal wasn't in need of hiding or a secret way to go.

Joliffe straightened from the tree and stood waiting as
Hal came toward him. They neither of them gave the other

any greeting. Joliffe was careful to keep his hand away from his belt-hung dagger, but Hal's hand was resting on the hilt of his own as he stopped a few feet away and said with a hard wariness, "You can't have had your way with Claire yet. What's this for?"

Meeting his roughness with roughness, Joliffe said, "It's for talk about these murders you've done."

He was watching Hal's eyes. They momentarily widened, then narrowed as Hal answered harshly, "That's an ill thing to accuse a man of."

"They're ill things to have done," Joliffe answered back. "Especially when you're so poor at hiding your guilt."

"None so poor. No one but you has looked at me for being guilty."

"They've looked," Joliffe returned. "But they keep missing the needed piece." He pointed at the stream purling quietly to itself a few yards away.

Hal flicked a glance that way, but his gaze was fixed on Joliffe again as he said, making a challenge of it, "That means something?"

"It means you maybe came by way of the path when you came to kill your father, but when you went to kill Gosyn, you went along the stream from here. That's why no one saw you on any road or anywhere."

"That," said Hal with slow and deliberate insult, "is stupid past imagining."

"Stupid perhaps, but not past imagining," Joliffe returned. "I've imagined it, haven't I?"

"You're a fool of a player and no one will believe you."

"Did you know you still smelled faintly of tansy-herb yesterday when you were at Gosyn's with your 'sympathy' and 'pity'? You'd rubbed yourself with it the day before, to keep the midges and all off you when you went naked along the stream, didn't you? Or not quite naked."

Keeping his gaze as much on Hal as Hal's was fixed on him, he turned enough to take the wadded cloth from the fork of the tree he had kept carefully hidden behind him until then, and with careless scorn tossed the under-braies to the ground at Hal's feet. "Yours, I'll warrant."

Hal stared down at the small, dirty bundle for a silent moment. When he raised his head, his face was tight with anger and so was his voice as he said, "Whatever it is, it isn't mine. Even if it was, it proves nothing."

"It proves something." If nothing else, it proved how little Hal liked being shown he was less well-witted than he thought he was. "It proves the crowner will have to take a closer look at you, and when he does, I warrant he'll see more than you want seen."

Hal was staring at him in much the way Joliffe had seen a man stare at a cow when trying to decide whether to sell or butcher it. Needing more from Hal than that, he said, deliberately scoffing, "But these two aren't your only murders, are they? You killed your uncle, too, didn't you?"

Blank surprise at that sudden accusation momentarily swept calculation from Hal's face before, all unexpectedly, he laughed aloud, then declared delightedly, "Wrong! I only helped."

"Helped?" Joliffe jeered. "Helped your father, I suppose."

With warm, mocking approval Hal said, "There you're right."

"It wasn't Nicholas who killed him at all, was it?"

"Nicholas? No, but it's been good sport goading him with it all these years. Old Francis was bettering from the scratch the little idiot had given him. My mother had even had the physician in from Faringdon just as if there was a point to keeping him alive. I don't know what the brew was the man left, but it had to be thinned with water or wine or ale or cider before giving it or it would be strong enough to kill. So one day when almost all the household was gone to church, I watched my father pour a full draught of it, and when he took it in to Francis, I followed him." Hal was smiling at the memory. "Francis didn't want it. He said it wasn't time to have another draught. But he took it, started to drink it, knew it was wrong, and tried to put the cup aside. My father grabbed his hands and shoved him back against the pillows and forced the cup to his mouth. Francis was weak from the blood he'd lost but not so weak he couldn't struggle. My father saw me in the doorway and yelled for me to help hold him down. I wasn't so well-grown to be much use, but I threw myself over Francis' legs so they couldn't thrash, and that let Father straddle him on the bed, pinning his arms so Father had both hands free to force the drink into him, then hold his mouth shut so he couldn't spew or yell for help. Whatever the drink was, it worked fast. He gave over trying to kick free, and began to twist with the pain instead. When he was past crying out, with his eyes rolled back in his head and all, Father got off him, and stood there watching while he shuddered and spasmed and twitched and finally"—Hal smiled at the warm memory—"died. I've never forgotten how it felt to have him die under me like that."

His throat was so tight with sickened anger that Joliffe had to work to say evenly, "You stayed across his legs while you watched him die."

"Watched and felt," Hal corrected, still with warm pleasure. "There's no feeling of power like feeling a man die because you've killed him. Killing in the hunt doesn't touch it."

"That's why you killed your father the way you did. And Gosyn." Joliffe's loathing made his words thick. "So you could feel them die."

"Yes." Still smiling, Hal took a step toward Joliffe. "But

now that I've admitted all that, I have to assume you want money from me to keep your mouth shut?"

Holding where he was against the urge to draw back as from filth or a plague-carrier, Joliffe said with wholly false ease, "Money would serve well that way, yes."

"So will this," Hal answered.

And despite Joliffe had kept steady watch on his eyes, there was still too little warning as Hal had his dagger from its sheath and drove it in under Joliffe's lower ribs.

Or would have, except the dagger struck and slid sideways on Master Ashewell's steel breastplate under Joliffe's doublet. And then Joliffe had hold on Hal's wrist with one hand and with his other had his own dagger out and its point under Hal's chin, pressing in where neck met jaw, freezing Hal where he was.

Then Kyping was there, crashing from hiding, swearing at Hal, himself, and Joliffe. Neither Joliffe nor Hal moved, staring into each other's eyes for any flicker of intent until Kyping grabbed Hal's dagger away and threw it on the ground. Only when he had jerked Hal's hands behind him, to begin tying them with a readied piece of rope, did Joliffe take a step back, his gaze still locked with Hal's and his dagger still ready but no longer at Hal's throat.

"Damn you," Hal said at him.

"You first," Joliffe returned and was not jesting. Nonetheless he was diverted, in a side corner of his mind, by their angers at each other—his own at Hal for having so coldly tried to kill him; Hal's at him for not being dead.

Thus were men's desires so often contrary to one another's, Joliffe silently granted with mock regret.

Past Hal's shoulder, Kyping said, "You'd be the damned one if we'd not thought to ask that breastplate of Master Ashewell."

"True," Joliffe agreed. He fingered the slice in his doublet and the shirt under it. For several reasons Rose was going to be displeased with him about those. But not as displeased as she would have been if he'd lacked the breastplate.

Kyping gave a final hard jerk on the rope that drove Hal into an answering jerk of pain, breaking his eyes' hold on Joliffe even before Kyping shoved him to his knees, saying to Joliffe, "Keep him there. I'll get my horse."

He went away among the trees, leaving Joliffe and Hal looking at each other again; and very quietly to Hal's glare Joliffe said, "That thrust you made was meant to kill me, but not quickly. You were going to watch me die the way you watched the others."

Hal's smile was ugly with anger and maybe the pain of his arms bound uncomfortably high across his back. Between clenched teeth he hissed, "Yes."

Surprised to find his legs were not so steady as he would have liked them to be, Joliffe wished there were somewhere he could sit, but he kept his voice even as he asked, "How would you have explained killing me? Or did you think to go uncaught for yet another murder?"

"Oh, no, I meant to admit to this one freely enough. After all, you sent me word you knew something about my father's murder and wanted to talk to me. I meant to claim you tried to extort money from me for what you claimed you knew and that I saw suddenly it was you who'd killed my father, and when I said so, you attacked me and I killed you because I had to."

"Then people would suppose I killed Gosyn, too, for who knows what reason, and there'd be an end to it."

"Yes," Hal snarled, openly angry that he was thwarted, probably equally angry that Joliffe was alive when he should be dead.

Joliffe found his own anger was gone into a cold quease in his stomach. No one had ever so deliberately wanted him dead before this and he did not like the feeling of it.

Nor did he like his own urge just then to hurt Hal with his own hands. Hurt him badly. Hurt him not because there was need of it but for the pleasure of making him hurt.

And very carefully, Joliffe sheathed his dagger and folded his arms in front of him to put the temptation out of ready reach.

Chapter 23

With one thing and another, it was well past dark when Joliffe rejoined the other players. He had paused to tell them all was well when he and Kyping passed with Hal as prisoner, but there had been time for little else and he was not surprised to find the fire still burning and everyone around it, waiting for him—except Piers asleep with his head on his grandfather's lap. With a grateful sigh to be done with walking for a while, Joliffe sat down in the place left for him in their fire-lit circle, held his hands out to the fire's warmth because the night was cool, and said, "That's done then. We've leave to go tomorrow."

Ellis gave a satisfied exclamation and Basset nodded, pleased. It was Rose who said, "Tell us what happened."

He did. At one point Gil reached out and rapped knuckles on his chest and asked, "So where's the breastplate now?"

"Given back to Master Ashewell with thanks."

"Nothing like the thanks he owes you," Rose said. "That they all owe you."

"Except for Hal," Gil said. "He's not thanking you."

"Did he ever say why he'd killed his father and Walter Gosyn?" Rose asked.

Kyping and the crowner had both asked Hal that at different times. Watching the fire at play—light and liveliness against the tired heaviness of his thoughts—Joliffe answered, "By what Hal said, it came down to no more than that they were in the way of what he wanted."

"The saints defend we all take to killing for that reason," Basset muttered.

What Joliffe kept to himself was his own thought of Hal's deeper reason—or unreason—for the murders: that he had killed not so much to have his father and Gosyn out of his way but because he *could* kill them.

Some time, for Hal Medcote, the heavy line between *could* and *should* had broken and never mended.

Silence sat for a while then among the players, whatever each of them was thinking, until Basset asked, "Did you ever learn what Medcote was using against Master Ashewell, to force the marriage?"

"Kyping asked Hal that." And Hal had laughed. In truth, through everything, including the crowner's questioning, Hal—when he was not being angry at being bound and being questioned by men he would rather have scorned and ignored—had laughed over-much for a man faced with hanging. He had seemed barely able to believe these fools were daring to meddle with him, and if Joliffe had not thought it before, he would have known then that something was not linked altogether right in Hal's head. But at least Hal's ready tongue made answering Basset's question easy. "It seems that somewhat many years ago Ashewell made too free with Gosyn's sister. Hal made it sound like it was rape, but there's no way to tell the truth by anything he says. However it was, it seems no one knew about it save the two of them, and she took her disgrace away with her."

"*Her* disgrace? Only *her* disgrace?" Rose said dangerously.

Joliffe held up his hands in sign of peace. "It's what Hal Medcote said, not me."

"He would," Ellis growled.

"Whatever it was between them," Joliffe went quickly on. "Ashewell was married and she was not and she left without anyone but Ashewell knowing why and it seems not even he knew where she'd gone. She left home supposedly to visit a cousin in Faringdon but never went there or anywhere else her family ever heard of. Then, a few years ago, John Medcote chanced on her in Gloucester, not leading a very good life. From what Hal said, she was bitterly ready to tell her story in return for money. And afterward Medcote kept it to himself until he was ready to use it against Ashewell, who thought it was better to sell Nicholas into a Medcote marriage than risk whatever Gosyn's wrath might be if the truth came out."

Rose said bitterly, "If men ever learned to control their loins, what a simpler place the world would be."

"Their loins and their greed," Joliffe said. "But after all there's no saying how much at fault Gosyn's sister was in it."

"However much at fault she was, she's the one who's gone on paying the price, while Ashewell lost nothing," Rose returned.

"It nearly cost him his son," Basset said.

"Nicholas would have paid more for his father's sin than his father ever paid," Rose said, giving no ground. "Always everyone but Ashewell paid. And now again, with the Medcotes finished, he still doesn't pay."

"He will if someone doesn't keep their mouth shut and his wife hears about Gosyn's sister," Ellis said grimly. Then quickly, before Rose might answer that, he added, "At least the boy is spared. There's that much to the good." He warily made to slip an arm around Rose's waist, almost asking pardon for doing so.

For a moment Rose looked as if she might refuse him. Then her face softened and she said, "There's that, yes," and shifted a little sideways, leaning against him and into his arm's curve.

Basset poked a stick at the fire. "So. Nicholas Ashewell will likely marry Claire Gosyn as both their fathers wanted. The manors will prosper, the nuns will have their profits peacefully, and Lady Lovell will be pleased with us. What of the Medcotes? Do you think there's hope of Kyping's interest in Eleanor Medcote coming to anything?"

Joliffe shrugged. "Who knows? Given how little liking I ever saw among the Medcotes, I doubt she'll hold Hal's arrest against him. She might even marry Kyping to spite both Hal and her father, never mind who's alive and who's dead."

"Or to spite Kyping," Ellis said. "I doubt she's a comfortable woman."

"She's a landed woman anyway," Basset said. "There are men who'll put up with a great lot of spite for the sake of that."

Or maybe, without her father and brother to goad her, she might be as different as she had sometimes seemed to be, Joliffe thought. But that was Kyping's look-out, and unless they sometime came back this way, the players would never know how it went between them.

That was one disadvantage his curiosity suffered. In their wandering the players saw bits of other people's lives—a few moments out of lifetimes, that was all—and he could only wonder what came to them afterward. Supposing he wondered about them at all. After all, how much of anyone's life was worth anyone else's knowing? Rarely much at all. It was enough for someone to live and leave others to do the same, giving help when help could be given and not giving pain where pain need not be.

At least he hoped that was enough, but as he looked across the fire at Ellis and Rose, her head now resting on his shoulder, his cheek resting against her head, both of them for the moment content and at peace, he had to think, too, that if love could be added to the business of simply being alive, it was to the good.

Under a sky of thinning clouds that promised fair-weathered travel for the day at least, they were on their way in the morning as soon as there was light enough to see the lane. By the time the sun showed a golden rim above the horizon behind them, they were a satisfying few miles beyond Ashewell parish. But when Joliffe looked back, the White Horse was still to be seen in its endless gallop high on its hillside. Mankind fumbled onward, but there the Horse was, ages old and always young, with more beauty in its being than most lives ever had, and Joliffe raised his hand to it in both greeting and farewell, then turned ahead and did not look back again.

Author's Note

The White Horse of Uffington and White Horse Vale are of course real. On the other hand, Ashewell village and parish, while both realistic to that time and place, are imaginary, bearing no intended relationship to anywhere to be found today in the Vale where I've placed them. St. Mary's Abbey—sometimes known as Nunnaminster—in Winchester did hold lands in the Vale, though not where I've placed Ashewell parish.

It's no longer believed that the White Horse and the hillfort above it were made by the Saxons a mere eight hundred years or so before this story. By the time the Saxons saw it, the Horse was already more than a thousand years old, the work of Bronze Age or Iron Age people long before the Saxons or even the Romans were ever in Britain. Made by the digging of trenches that were then infilled with blocks of white chalk, the White Horse would be lost under spreading soil and grass in very few years if left untended, which means that for something like three thousand years the people of the Vale have kept the Horse cleared. At various times this was accompanied by a "Pastime," as detailed in Thomas Hughes' book *The Scouring of the White Horse* about one such occasion in the 1800s, from which I have extrapolated backward. For the archaeology, there is *Uffington White Horse and Its Landscape* by G. Lock et al., and for a novel imagining the Horse's making, there is *Sun Horse, Moon Horse* by Rosemary Sutcliff.

But best of all is to see the White Horse itself and walk the hillslope there, to visit it and the hillfort and the even older monuments near it.

One thing: older guidebooks will have the White Horse in Berkshire. Due to a shift in county boundaries, more recent books will have it in Oxfordshire.

Master Ashewell's career as villein, free man, soldier, and finally prospering landowner in his own right is no stretch of imagination on my part. By the late Middle Ages, buying out of villeinage was common and making your fortune in the French war very possible. The feudal system still existed but no longer had the stranglehold on society that it had had even two hundred years before. Times do change. Think how different the lives we lead now are from those of two hundred years before our present time, and how different those times were from two hundred years before then. The Middle Ages were not a monolith that clunked down upon Europe with the fall of Rome and lasted like a solid, witless lump until the Renaissance arrived to Make Everything Better. There was change and growth, experiments in government and thought and religion that made the Renaissance possible.

But of course there were villains as well as villeins. Medcote's cheating of Jack Hammond over his inheritance is derived from an example given in E. B. Fryde's *Peasants and Landlords in Later Medieval England*, a richly detailed, balanced study of rural medieval life, showing the good as well as the bad and the powerful societal shift going on at the time.